Critics and re

THE COLORS OF FRIENDSHIP

Finalist for the *Foreword Reviews'*
2013 Book of the Year Awards
2014 National Indie Excellence Awards Finalist
The Reader's Crown® Finalist

"Entertaining with suspense, romance, and a good dose of life lessons. Time is well spent enjoying these friends."

– USA Today

"*The Colors of Friendship* is a complex and deftly written novel showcasing the impressive storytelling literary talent of author K. R. Raye. A highly recommended and entertaining read."

– Midwest Book Review

"I thoroughly enjoyed this book. It's well-written with very realistic, strong characters. The storyline, with both suspense and romance, keeps you intrigued and you're left wanting more in the end. It touches on some very sensitive issues that we see in real life, especially in the college environment. The friendship the three share is heart-warming and one worth reading about."

– Author Alliance Book Review Team

"The characters were well-developed and had me frustrated at times… This was a good start to the series and has me anticipating the next book. I recommend *The Colors of Friendship* to others."

– A&RBC Reviews

"I loved *The Colors of Friendship*. K. R. Raye told a story about a friendship that lasted… The story line flowed well and I could really feel the love between Imani, Melody, and Lance."

– OOSA Online Book Club

"Mrs. Raye did an excellent job of pulling readers in and keeping their attention from beginning to end. This is definitely a book that I recommend you read."

– Olivia Evans Books

"*The Colors of Friendship* by K. R. Raye is a fun-filled story about three college friends, Imani, Melody and Lance. It is entertaining and the conflicts between the characters have been developed well. As a first in the series it will be interesting to see where the plot follows on from here."

– Christoph Fischer, Author of *The Luck of The Weissensteiners* and *Sebastian*

"This first installment of a new adult trilogy follows three college friends as they grapple with romance, jealousy, and threats. A compelling series opener about friendship that will make readers want to devour the sequel."

– Kirkus

Critics and readers praise the suspenseful sequel!

THE COLORS OF LOVE

AMB Ovation (The Angie) Awards Finalist - New Adult category

"This story is rich with unexpected twists and turns that keep you reading to the end. Once again friendships are tested to the max and detours are taken that heighten anticipation of the third book in the series. Raye has a knack for creating interesting, flawed characters. She is expertly developing them and testing them to their limits

– USA Today

"*The Colors of Love* was an entertaining book to read...the characters were more developed, the twists in the story were unsuspected as well as the ending. I look forward to book three in this series."

– A&RBC Reviews

Critics and readers praise the thrilling finale!

TRUE COLORS

**Steamy Romance Books – New Adult Featured
Book**

"Raye brings her characters alive and off the pages
with solid realism. K.R. Raye definitely captured the
flavor of the New Adult genre and has solidly planted
her worthy contribution in the field."

– USA Today

"The book is an engaging and entertaining read which
will keep readers glued to the plot. Life is the essence
of the main theme and it has been conveyed very well.
The theme revolves beautifully around Lance Dunn,
Melody Wilkins and Imani Cabrette in this story of
lasting friendship and love."

- Readers' Favorite

THE COLORS OF

FRIENDSHIP

BY

K. R. RAYE

J-pad Publishing

THE COLORS OF FRIENDSHIP
Copyright © 2013 by K. R. Raye
All rights reserved. Printed in the United States of America. No part of this book may be used or reproduced in any manner whatsoever without written permission except in the case of brief quotations embodied in critical articles and reviews. For information contact J-pad Publishing, www.JpadPublishing.com.

J-pad Publishing books may be purchased for educational, business, or sales promotional use. For information about special discounts for bulk purchases, please contact J-pad Publishing Sales at sales@JpadPublishing.com.

J-pad Publishing can bring authors to your live event. For more information or to book an event, please contact J-pad Publishing Events at events@JpadPublishing.com.

First Edition, August 2013
Hardcover Edition, March 2022
Cover Design by Nicole Hower

ISBN: 978-1-940361-00-0 (paperback)
ISBN: 978-1-940361-08-6 (hardcover)
ISBN: 978-1-940361-01-7 (e-book)

10 9 8 7 6 5 4 3 2 1
Printed in the U.S.A.

This is dedicated to Thomas Watson.
May the fish always bite and the jazz never end.

Acknowledgments

First let me give thanks to God for gifting me with the writing bug that I just couldn't kick.

To my exquisite husband, Jacques, your encouragement, support, and crazy edits mean the world to me and it wouldn't be as fun without you. I love you dearly.

Thanks to my mother, Alyce, for instilling my persistent, independent, creative drive. Rest assured, you did an outstanding job raising me! Cheerleaders, TiMom and TiPop provided the perfect place to write (and eat). For my sons, thanks for keeping me on my toes, your stories are next.

There are so many friends who helped me on this journey. I owe the biggest thanks to my lovely, loyal special readers who slogged through early drafts. Jess(al) Savarese, your bath and wine exclamations still ring in my ears. Lauren Dervish, my hilarious Scottish lass, you made sure I kept it real. Kat Davis, the Brazilian bombshell, I owe the title all to you. Kelly Russell, through the kids, work, and everything else, your insight proved invaluable and the lunches were a blast. Dr. Sabrina Watts provided lots of sisterly laughs, angst over a character's name, and links to other authors and publishers. Soror LaTanja Moody appealed to my Christian sensibilities. Dr. Michael Broom, no adverb is safe around you, thanks for the advice and character feedback. Terri Mallet is a talented singer who asks the deep questions. Heather Fischer, your passion and insight truly touched me, funny how Communications works. Kate Sutton, your excitement is contagious; I'm thrilled diversity brought us together. Nadia Krook, here's to relaxing by the lake; I loved our cool conversations. And to my Spanish sister, Cecilia Gomez, I hope that you like our girl more now!

Years of professional advice and support came from long-time friends Tony and Yvonne Rose.

Writers complain about loneliness, but I'm blessed with fellow sojourners to keep me inspired and up-to-date. The gems from Bay to Ocean: Justine Cowan, Judy Reveal, Sandra Bowman, Austin Camacho, Mindie Burgoyne, Ramona Long, and Melanie Rigney, impart wonderful words of wisdom. BWG of MD provides camaraderie and encouragement. And lots of love to Deidre Berry, TaNisha Webb, Rick R. Reed, Cherrie Woods, K. L. Brady, Angela Render, Allyson Machate, Dee Lawrence, Chicki Brown, Curtis Bunn, Omar Tyree, Kimberla Lawson Roby, Susan Fales-Hill, DeVon Franklin, Karen E. Quinones Miller, Sadeqa Johnson, Sonia Jackson Myles, Stephen King, Tom Clancy, and Pat Branch.

From the professional side, I'd like to thank: my editor Christy Payne for your incredible insight; Mary at Allen Design for creating beautiful covers that are an extension of me; my family at J-pad Publishing; Carla Walton, the phenomenal Soror with the life-changing phone calls; Justina Pollard, WBAL-TV 11; Stephen McDonald, ESPN; ΔΣΘ Sorority, Inc.; Unity Through Words, my new book club; Marla Svoboda at Rose Brooks and Elaine Bellinger at Renewal House, for helping abused women and keeping my work authentic; Violas Dyas, please stay In the Margins;

Oprah and Tyler Perry for shining brilliant beacons of hope; and Sara Camilli, the agent I wish I had.

If music soothes the savage beast, then the following lyrical geniuses helped me strike pen to paper: Jill Scott, Jamiroquai, Mary J. Blige, Dwele, Conya Doss, Robin Thicke, Al B. Sure!, SWV, Justin Timberlake, Earth, Wind & Fire, Stevie, Luther, Kirk Franklin, Toni Braxton, Faith Evans, Musiq Soulchild, Vivian Green, Mike Phillips, Will Downing, Jon B., 112, and Sade.

To the fans, you are incredible, thank you for spending your time with me!!!

I would like to thank anyone I may have inadvertently missed who provided advice, support, and love during this long, crazy roller-coaster ride. Thank you and big hugs!

PROLOGUE

Cold. Hard. Steel. Pressed against her forehead. Melody closed her eyes and willed the situation away. But when she reopened them, the gun remained lodged between her eyes.

The setting sun painted a crimson swath across the budding landscape. Crimson red…blood red. Oh God, how did it all lead to this she wondered as the ice cold barrel ironically seemed to sear her skin, like a poker fresh from a stoked fire. Her blood ran cold through her veins and her body began to shake.

Why? The faster her mind raced, the more she trembled.

Her friends had warned her, but she didn't want to believe them. If only she had listened to Imani or stayed with Lance, things might have ended differently. But then again, what if her friends were wrong? Imani and Lance always meddled in her business. They were too overbearing and judgmental. Really, they had no one to blame but themselves. In fact if they weren't here butting in now, making the situation worse…

The gun dug further into her forehead, threatening to break skin. Melody realized as cold dread soaked her skin, it didn't matter whose fault it was; all three of them were going to die here tonight.

THE ALPHA PARTY – JANUARY 2000

"Whew, we made it," Melody Wilkins said with a laugh as she, Lance Dunn, and Imani Jordan escaped the throng of fraternity partygoers.

Imani brushed past Melody, eager to enjoy the relative oasis of the makeshift bar. She pulled up a stool and swallowed her disappointment. During their mad, congested dash from the front door to the back bar, she scanned the two hundred plus, hard-dancing students looking for Trevor, but to no avail.

She pasted on a smile to prevent Melody or Lance from misinterpreting things. Hell, even she didn't know what to expect from the Trevor situation. All she knew was that she liked hanging out with him in and out of class. Imani checked her expression in the nick of time before Lance caught her eye.

Lance winked and arranged his muscular, 6'2" frame into a *GQ* stance while he stroked his goatee, a pose that he assumed oozed sexy charm. Please, like he didn't already generate enough attention when they entered the fraternity house, working the room like a campaigning politician or the ridiculous jock he was.

Imani tried to choke back a guffaw as Melody watched her in amusement. But much to Imani's awe and chagrin, Lance's ridiculous antics started working. Four attractive girls honed in on Lance's horny, homing beacon, their mouths almost salivating.

What the hell? Imani frowned as two of the girls shot her and Melody jealous daggers. All of this unwarranted attention just because Lance played football the last two games of the season and played well?

Imani sucked her teeth and turned to the bar. "Damn, I'm ready to get my swerve on!"

"Well, you deserve a drink," Melody replied as she hopped her petite, frame onto a stool to Imani's left. Melody's thick, blond curls bounced about like springs. "Heck, after our intense studying all week and your physics exam today; you deserve to unwind."

Right on cue the attractive fraternity brother acting as the bartender meandered over. "What can I get you, Sugar?"

"Two amaretto sours," she said gesturing to Melody and herself, "and one vodka tonic for him," she said nodding towards Lance.

"Sure thing, Sugar," he replied with a wink.

After the flirty bartender departed, she elbowed Lance in his side. "You're awful quiet."

"I'm sure he's thinking what I'm thinking," Melody said, swiveling her stool around to face them. "Looking at all these beautiful faces and wondering which person is *the one*, that magical one, true love."

"Oh Lord, here we go!" Imani moaned and leaned back against the bar.

"Ah, let me handle this, Imani." Lance clapped Melody's back. "Dear, deluded Melody," he said, then he stroked his mustache and goatee. "In actuality, I was looking at all of these beautiful women and wondering which *one* is going to end up in my bed. However, it seems I need to school you." He cleared his throat and his deep voice took on a preacher-like quality.

"Love is highly overrated. It's this fantasyland you read about in those Harlequin rags you devour. A vicious lie parents tell their little girls." He shook his head and shrugged. "That's why the divorce rate is so high. Unreasonable expectations."

"Thoughts, Imani?" Melody smiled knowing she could get a rise out of her. Melody's gray-green eyes twinkled in anticipation against her golden-tanned skin.

"Lance is kinda right." Imani's nose scrunched up, hating to agree with Lance. "You're one of these women that fosters unrealistic fantasies about the fairytale wedding and living happily ever after. That shit don't happen." Imani threw Lance a scathing look. "But love does exist and it ain't overrated."

Lance laughed and shrugged. "To-ma-toe, to-ma-toh."

"Well, when is it going to happen?" Melody asked. "I mean we're already halfway through our freshman year of college—"

"Oh, Girl, please!" Imani wanted to pop her upside the head. "One, it's the year 2000. College is no longer a freaking hunting ground for husbands. Two, you don't need a man, you need an education. Pay your own damn way. Three, we're only freshmen, so what the hell's your rush?"

"Amen," Lance replied, clapping both their backs. In a flash, he stood up straight. "Well, as pleasant as this conversation has been—"

A sweet, shy-looking cutie with cinnamon-colored skin and an asymmetrical bob gathered up enough courage to approach Lance. "Would you like to dance?"

Lance took her hand without a word and twirled her towards the dance floor. The two melted into the mass of writhing dancers, leaving Imani and Melody shaking their heads.

"Well, that's a new record, he didn't even get his drink first," muttered Melody.

Right on time, the bartender set their drinks down and left with a wink.

Grateful, Imani took a big gulp of the amaretto sour and let its sweetness smooth out her rough edges.

"I wish I could get a guy that easily." Melody released a wistful sigh.

Satisfied for the moment, Imani pushed her drink away. "No, you don't want Lance's shallow, short-term sluts. You want to be swept away by your one, true love."

"You insinuating there's something wrong with that? My parents met as sophomores and they had the perfect, fairytale relationship."

'And you're not your damn parents,' she wanted to say, but she held her tongue. "No, just telling you why you won't find anyone here tonight." Imani swallowed more amaretto sour.

"Not acceptable. I'm finding someone now." Melody chugged her drink, hopped off the stool, and approached the nearest cute guy. "Would you like to dance?"

The cute brunette eyed Melody, decided he liked what he saw, and escorted her onto the dance floor.

"And that just leaves me." Imani sighed, emptied her cup, and picked up Lance's. Wondering why she even bothered to come, she crunched on an ice cube until it shattered.

"This seat taken?" asked a man as he sat down uninvited on Melody's barstool.

"Yes, it is taken," she snarled, eyes closed, willing herself not to go off on the intruder.

"Damn, Imani. The physics test wasn't so bad that you dis' your friends like that," a familiar voice complained.

Imani opened her eyes to find her homeboy from the Bronx, Trevor Mathis.

"Oh my God, I'm so sorry, Trev," she replied, giving her tall, lanky, dark chocolate friend a relieved hug. "Guess I'm too tired tonight to deal with the whole party scene." She smiled and poked his side. "Besides you know I'd never dis' my boy like that."

"That's a relief," he said pretending to wipe his forehead. Trev laughed then hesitated and Imani could tell that he toyed with what to say next. "Hey, do you want to dance or just chill?"

Knowing she'd reached her alcohol limit, Imani tapped her toes. Trev put most video dancers to shame with his moves and it elevated her game whenever she partnered with him. "After you."

Trev shot her his big, toothy grin, took her hand, and led her onto the dance floor. Soon enough he had her feeling as comfortable as they did when they studied together for hours. The easy way they knew each other's moves and thoughts.

As the beat invaded Imani's body, she surrendered to the music and her tension melted away like cotton candy on the tongue. Maybe parties weren't so bad after all...

Then someone pinched her ass.

FORTUITOUS BUMPS

Melody flinched as Imani wheeled around fast, her right arm cocked and ready to fight. Her breath caught in her throat as they both stared at each other in surprise. Then the giggles hit and Melody burst out laughing. Unable to stop, she doubled over clutching her stomach.

"You're so wrong," Imani said as she landed a big, booty bump on Melody's hip that almost knocked her over. Imani wagged her finger in a mock threat and then resumed dancing with Trevor as he cracked up and bopped along.

Still giggling, Melody straightened up and rubbed her hip as she tried to refocus on her cute dance partner. However, her hip wasn't the only thing aching. Each step she took made her wince as her shoes pinched her toes like angry crabs.

Crap, she exhaled through gritted teeth, Imani warned her not to wear the sexy stilettos, but she wanted to look perfect tonight and they went so well with her long-sleeved, little, black jersey knit dress. Ready to rest her sore feet, she yanked her partner's sleeve. "I've got to sit down for a while," she yelled over the music.

Not missing a single beat, he shrugged, spun around, and danced with a group of girls behind him, leaving her gaping at his back.

"I guess you don't want to join me at the bar for stimulating conversation," she murmured to herself. Pivoting on her heel, she headed towards the bar before noticing the crowd. Great, it would take at least twenty minutes to get the bartender's attention! Sighing and unsure of her next steps, she surveyed the dance floor.

Imani and Trevor were just revving up. And with Imani's stressful week, it was probably best to let her finally cut loose. She kept looking, but she couldn't locate Lance anywhere.

Humph, knowing him, he was already getting personal attention from yet another pretty girl he just met. Melody frowned. Why did women constantly throw themselves at Lance? Granted he was handsome, possessed a drool-worthy body, and now there were mumbles about NFL potential after just his first couple of games playing, but really! Women needed to demand more respect than a meaningless one-night stand.

Frustrated and tired, she fanned herself, but she began to feel claustrophobic and faint. All at once the hot, crowded room turned oppressive and the rank air suffocated. The deafening music cloyed. As she struggled to squeeze through the mass of bodies to escape, her body tensed and her heart hammered in her ears. Pain radiated through her feet. Every breath hitched in ragged spurts as clammy perspiration coated her skin. In a last ditch effort she retrieved her coat and shot through the doors, not even waiting to pull on the double-breasted, wool trench coat.

The cold, January night made it difficult to catch her

breath. As she scrambled away from the frat house towards her dorm room, she wrestled into her coat and buttoned it up, snuggling in its warmth. Maybe attending college in frigid, upstate New York wasn't the smartest move, she thought as a bout of shivers wracked her body. Snuggling in deeper, she tucked her head down and began barreling against the cold until she slammed into someone.

Books and bodies flew to the ground.

"I'm so sorry," Melody stammered trying to regain her footing while gathering two books. She looked at the face that stared back amused. Steel blue eyes sparkled from beneath a crop of spiky, blond hair. Large, firm hands brushed over hers as they collected the textbooks.

Full, rosy lips let out a sonorous voice that vibrated under her coat. "Not a problem, I wasn't quite paying attention to where I was going either." The good-looking guy easily helped her up with one arm while cradling his books in the other. "Are you okay?"

Embarrassed but fine, she managed to nod. He stood about six feet tall and his jacket clung to the muscular body beneath. Her mouth went dry and her breathing slowed as his beautiful, blue eyes captivated her.

"Haven't I seen you in Calculus class?" he asked. "What's your name?"

"Um…" She licked her lips and swallowed hard, trying to generate any modicum of saliva in her parched mouth. "I think I've seen you around. I, uh, took Calc, um, last semester." His insistent, teasing stare made her hot and nervous. She fidgeted. "My name is, uh…Melody, yeah Melody." She dropped her head knowing he could see her red-hot cheeks ablaze.

Adjusting the books, he reached out to shake hands. "Well, Melody, nice to run into you, literally! I'm Kevin. Where were you headed?"

His hand calmed her down and she looked up without dropping her head in shyness. "I just came from a party and wanted to get out of these shoes," she said gesturing down. "My feet are killing me."

"Well, in that case," he replied, floating a heart-stopping grin her direction, "we'd better get you someplace where you can kick those puppies off, huh?"

Melody smiled and followed beside Kevin after he motioned towards the nearby Student Union. Once they entered the building he declined to go downstairs by the food court where the majority of students would congregate on a Friday night. Instead Kevin ventured upstairs to the more intimate conversational areas on the top floor.

He pulled out one of the four overstuffed chairs surrounding a small table for her, deposited his books in another, and sat in the chair opposite hers.

Melody glanced across the small table. What in the world was she doing? Why had she followed Kevin here instead of excusing herself after he recovered all his books? Normally she believed in good, old-fashioned chivalry, waited for the guy to pursue her. Although…she smiled, the amaretto sour, in combination with her desire to prove Imani's pessimistic outlooks on love wrong, drove her to abandon, or at least loosen, her normal inhibitions enough that she asked a guy to dance earlier!

"Would you like a mint?" Kevin asked offering her a peppermint candy.

"Sure," she replied accepting the cellophane-covered treat.

"You feeling better?"

"Hmmm?"

"Your feet?" Kevin laughed. "Are they feeling better now?"

Embarrassed again, but feeling more comfortable, she giggled. "Yes, they feel much better. In fact..." Melody kicked off both her heels and wiggled her toes.

"I'd offer to massage them, but I think I better get to know you first," teased Kevin.

"Yeah, I think, that would be best," she replied with a hint of flirtation. Wow, she couldn't believe her adventurous, less than lady-like behavior, but this felt exhilarating.

Melody checked her watch and then she did a sharp double-take. How had four hours slipped past so quickly? She couldn't believe how fast she and Kevin had broken the ice. They connected at once and talked, really talked, about everything: classes, parents, friends, dreams, and fears. She felt a twinge of anxiety at the thought of their easy, refreshing evening coming to an end. However, with the lateness of the hour she knew Imani would be worried. "Oh my God, I need to get home before my roommate summons a search party."

Kevin glanced at his watch. "It's 2:20? Wow, I can't believe you seduced me like that!"

"Yeah, right, you were definitely the one seducing me, making me lose track of time." She placed one hand over her chest and held the other by her head pretending to faint. With her best Southern drawl she pronounced, "I was totally enraptured by your charm and captivated by your charisma, kind Sir."

"Oh brother!" Kevin laughed. "Could you have been any further over the top?" He stood, assisted Melody with her shoes and coat, threw on his jacket, and grabbed his books. "Well, seeing as I'm such a gentleman, I have no choice but to walk you home, Little Lady."

"Thank you, fine Sir." Melody accepted Kevin's hand and he helped her downstairs.

They strolled out of the Union arm in arm into the cool, crisp night. Neither talked, but instead smiled at each other from time to time. The bright moon guided their steps along the path and Melody swore the stars winked down on them. They arrived at her dorm room far too soon. Reluctantly she released Kevin's arm to wish him a good night.

Before she could say a word, he swooped in close. Their noses almost touched and she could feel his breath tickle the fine little hairs above her lip. He leaned down so their foreheads touched and he placed a protective arm around her shoulders. "I know I'm being too forward, but I've told you more about myself tonight, than any ten friends know combined. You sparked something in me when you knocked me down. And I would be a little annoyed if you didn't share these intense feelings—the ones consuming me now."

Transfixed, Melody stood motionless at a loss for

words. Never before had she kissed a guy she just met, but she felt it inevitable. Her heart leapt in her chest and the anticipation killed.

Kevin took her silence as acquiescence and teased her anxious lips with his soft kisses. She couldn't believe how magical the moment felt. Her tongue willingly probed and parted his lips and then did a hesitant, searching dance with his minty tongue. Her heart couldn't stand much more and she pushed back, shocked that her lips were reluctant to follow. She glanced at Kevin for a fleeting moment and rushed inside, closing the door behind her, not slowing until she had raced up the two flights to her room. Only then, did she trust herself enough to stop.

Kevin probably thought she was a fool for running off leaving him standing there. But sudden urges had overtaken her when they kissed and she wasn't sure she could have stopped herself if she hadn't left then and there. What on earth was wrong with her? This felt wonderful yet scary. A guy had never affected her like this. Deep inside, she couldn't wait for more. "Oh my, God, you're such a harlot," she mumbled to herself. Taking a deep breath she unlocked the door and prayed Imani was asleep.

FUN WITH KRYSTAL

Lance flopped onto his back across the bed, utterly pleased and exhausted as Krystal crashed onto his chest in all her glistening afterglow glory. He ran his fingers through her cute, little funky bob, enjoying the silky feel of her hair and the tropical coconut fused smell of her hair products.

She slid her hand across his chest and flicked his nipple.

"Mm, I thought we were done," he said wondering if he needed to prepare for round three. Although he was tired, he definitely wouldn't mind.

Krystal giggled, a soft, sweet sound, and then squeezed him tight. "No, I swear I can't go another time as tempting as that sounds. I won't be able to walk right for a long while. You wore me out."

Lance chuckled at the thought of her walking funny to class. Sounded like a nice challenge. He stroked her back, letting his fingers trace down from her shoulder blades, along her spine, to the small of her back and then returning up again. She moaned and snuggled against him, making him…surprisingly sleepy. He stifled a yawn.

"You comfortable?" she asked snagging the covers and pulling them up over their bodies before her hand returned to his chest.

"Mm-hmm," he said so relaxed that he almost snored. *Whoa! What is she doing to me?* He tried to wake up enough to leave. He never spent the night with anyone; it set false expectations of more than just one night of fun.

Krystal's breathing slowed, lulling his body closer to slumber.

Lance considered making one last attempt at leaving, but then he surrendered to her siren song of sleep. *Maybe he could get used to this, settle down with Krystal. They could make appointments at the Infirmary; make sure she received a clean STD bill of health.*

He yawned and his breathing slowed. *Maybe, he'd introduce her to Melody and Imani; they were always on his case to settle down. And since Krystal wasn't like his normal conquests, they'd probably approve of her. And if Melody and Imani, the only two people who looked out for his best interests without wanting anything in return, trusted Krystal, then he could, too.*

Hmm, it would be a first…but not that unpleasant a thought. He smiled as he held her tight and drifted off into possibility-filled dreams…maybe, just maybe…

HOME LATE

"Nice of you to call me, so I wouldn't be sitting up worrying about your little ass!" Imani greeted Melody as soon as she opened their dorm room door.

"So much for hoping you'd be asleep," moaned Melody as she closed the door. Avoiding Imani's expectant stare, she hung up her coat, kicked off her shoes, and wondered how much to tell her friend.

"I'm waiting!"

"Oh, don't get all worked up, Imani," Melody said as she stretched out across her bed.

Imani got up from her desk—where it looked and smelled like she'd just removed her fingernail polish—and sat down next to Melody.

"I met someone."

"Obviously!"

"You were right about the shoes. My feet were killing me." Melody wiggled her toes for effect. "You were too busy dancing with Trevor and I couldn't find Lance. So, I took off to come home. That's when I bumped into this cute, Paul Newman-looking hunk named Kevin. He has adorable, spiky, blonde hair and beautiful, blue eyes that you want to swim in." She shot Imani a mischievous look. "And a body that would make even you drool."

"Keep talking."

"I don't know what happened. We went to the top of the Union and talked and talked and talked, I mean about every single thing." Tingling feelings coursed through her body, so Melody hugged herself and lay down to contain them. "Kevin's wonderful! My God, I never felt like that. It was so magical. I kissed him, Girl. Can you believe it?" She popped up again. "And I would have done more, too. I was just so enchanted."

"You? Miss I-Need-to-Get-to-Know-Someone-for-Years-Before-I-Consider-Kissing-Them?" Imani asked, surprise written across her flawless, walnut-skinned features. "This guy must really be something special. Tell me more!"

"That's really all there is to tell. I met him, we talked, and we kissed at the door."

"Well, when are you seeing him again?" Imani snorted. "Hell, when am I meeting his ass?"

"Whoa, slow down." Melody chuckled. "I don't want to scare him off." Her voice dropped to a whisper and she felt her cheeks burn again, "although we talked about catching a movie tomorrow after chapel."

"Chapel?"

"I told you we talked about everything. We're both Catholic and we're attending Mass tomorrow, second service."

"Get the hell outta here!"

"Watch the language, please," she replied, giggling. "So after Mass, we might grab a bite to eat and catch one of the dramas or the sci-fi comedy. I promise to come home right after that."

"Shit. You're grown. You can come in whenever you want. But thanks for the itinerary. If he's actually a serial killer, I can give the cops the clues."

She smacked Imani's shoulder. "Ooh, that is so wrong!"

Imani pretended to rub her shoulder.

With a sideways glance, Melody switched the subject. "So, um, how's Trevor?"

"Oh, puh-leeze! Tonight was not like that at all." Imani dismissed her insinuations with a wave. "Trev is just a friend. You know I don't think of him like that."

"Well, maybe you should." Melody sat up straight, smile gone. "He's been following behind you all year like a puppy dog. It's pretty obvious to everyone the boy likes you."

"That's too weird." Imani shuddered. "He's like a brother. That's like dating Lance."

"No, Lance is too much of a Ho to be considered dating. You'd never get past the second date if you didn't give him any. Hell, you wouldn't get past a second date even if you did!"

They both cracked up laughing.

"Anyhow, nice try turning the tables, but this wasn't about me, it was about your ass sneaking in here at 2:30!" Imani stopped scolding Melody long enough to look deep into her eyes. "Be careful, okay? Take this slow. You know you're too damn romantic for your own good. Especially since you insist on comparing your love life to your parents, with their supposedly-perfect marriage, and those awful Harlequin rags you read."

"I know, but I've waited so long to feel like this. Everything about us just clicked and it felt amazing!

Honestly, I could see myself spending every hour with Kevin and never getting tired or bored." Her friend's concerned gaze made her pause. "Okay, okay! I'll take it slow."

CHECK-IN CALL

Lance closed his dorm room door and dropped his keys on his desk. Hmm, no sign of his roommate. He glanced at his watch, **9:40 am**. The guy was probably hunkered down in the library already.

Feeling quite rested from his unexpected night at Krystal's he grinned and wondered how well the girls fared last night. The last time he saw Imani, she looked quite comfortable dancing with Trevor. Maybe they'd finally hooked up. Plus he hadn't seen Melody and her obsession with finding a man worried him. He decided to call.

Imani answered on the first ring. "Oh, you're awake? I figured you'd still be asleep after probably hanging out until the wee hours with the little librarian you were dancing with all night long."

"I just left her place now. How about you? Did Trevor finally get some action?"

"What the hell's wrong with you and Melody? She had the nerve to tell me I should get with him, too!"

"Oh-kay. I'll take that as a no. Any other action?"

"Hell, yeah! Your girl who plays all innocent and sweet went out, pretended to run into a cutie, and then *talked* to him for hours before coming home and tonguing him down—"

Scratchy, rustling sounds came over the line as

Melody snatched the phone from Imani. "Don't listen to this crazy woman, Lance. She makes everything sound dirty and sordid!"

"Well, you better clean it up because strange images are dancing through my head."

"Actually, I don't have time to set the record straight right now. I'm meeting Kevin for Mass and then we might check out that twisted, Jude Law, Gwyneth Paltrow movie; the football flick; or the sci-fi comedy everyone's talking about. I have to go, but please understand she's exaggerating."

"Church and either *The Talented Mr. Ripley*, *Any Given Sunday*, or *Galaxy Quest*. You know my vote's for the football movie, but I don't see how Imani's exaggerating. That's pretty intense for a first or is this considered the second date?"

"Oh, whatever. I'll enlighten you two later! Bye." The phone rustled again and he heard a muted exchange and a door slam before Imani returned to the line.

"See what I mean, Lance?"

"Yeah, that's crazy fast. You know the guy?"

"No! And she better introduce him soon, cuz' at this rate they'll be married by week's end!"

Lance almost choked laughing. "Melody mentioned a couple of times before that her folks met sophomore year. Guess she's trying to beat their record."

"Humph! I'm not buying it. Shit don't happen that damn fast. Love takes time and effort. None of that love at first sight nonsense. But if she's happy, I'll try to be happy."

KEVIN AND CHURCH

Mass dismissed at 11:30 on the dot according to Melody's watch. A smattering of locals, students, and a few teachers strolled out of the small, hundred-year old chapel, some stopping to greet the gregarious priest. Kevin linked arms with her and joined the line to exchange pleasantries with the priest before they headed towards the Union.

Walking along, Melody inhaled the scent of wood-burning fireplaces that wafted through the air. The sky sparkled a clear, deep blue and the air blew fresh with a playful bite. All of the colors gleamed brighter, sharper. Her senses seemed alive for the first time. Falling fast into a magical fantasyland, she clasped Kevin's arm to ensure he was real.

Kevin smiled and patted her hand. "Say, since we already graced the Union with our presence last night, do you want to venture someplace new?"

She couldn't care less where they went. "Anywhere you want to go is fine."

His smile brightened like a glorious ray of sunshine as he winked. "Hmm, want to take the campus bus into town? We could get something by the movie theater."

"Sounds perfect." Emotions bubbled within and Melody fought to catch her breath as her stomach filled with butterflies.

"Anything wrong?"

Kevin's concern warmed her entire body until she blushed. "No. Well, actually, my roommate, Imani, told me to take it slow. But you keep doing something to me."

"Moí?"

"Yes, you!" She gave his arm a light pinch. "You have me acting like a silly schoolgirl and I feel totally ridiculous."

"The only ridiculous thing would be if I didn't kiss you right now." Kevin stopped smack dab in the middle of the path. Gathering her in his arms, he kissed her slow and sweet, right in the middle of everyone walking past. Afterwards, he grinned, hooked her arm, and resumed walking. "I think we're *both* doing something to each other."

Melody continued too shocked to respond. Her feet moved of their own volition because she couldn't feel her limbs. Just her lips, still warm from the kiss. She had no idea how they made it to the bus stop.

Soon one of the many campus buses arrived with its bright navy and gold stripes, and they boarded it taking a seat in the middle.

Moments later she felt Kevin running his fingers through her hair. "You know you are so amazingly beautiful." His hot, minty-fresh breath so close to her ear, sent soft, sexy shivers down her spine. "I can't believe I was lucky enough to bump into you."

"The luck was all mine," she replied, her voice no louder than a whisper. Her head nestled on Kevin's shoulder while he stroked her hair.

The bus traveled its way ten minutes into downtown, stopping here and there to deposit and gather students. At the mall stop, Kevin led her off the bus. They wandered into the food court where she expected them to grab a burger or a slice of pizza. But Kevin surprised her and headed to the two restaurants at the end of the concourse.

"This one sound appealing to you?" he asked pointing to Chili's.

"Sounds lovely, although I wasn't expecting all of this."

"Only the best for you, my dear," he said leading her inside.

The hostess seated them in a cozy corner.

"What looks good to you?" Kevin asked a minute later as they perused the menus.

"Hmm, the Chicken Salad, Shrimp Alfredo, or the Country-Fried Steak. What about you?"

The waitress appeared. "Are you ready to order?"

"If the lady doesn't mind, I'd like to order for both of us now."

That took Melody aback. Never had anyone ordered for her before. She had always dreamed how romantic it would be for a guy to know her well enough to select her dish. "That sounds great," she said with a grateful smile, watching chivalry in action.

"Wonderful!" Kevin returned her smile then addressed the waitress, "I'll have the Country-Fried Steak and she will have the Shrimp Alfredo, please."

The waitress scribbled down their order, "and for drinks?"

"A Coca-Cola for me and an iced tea for her."

"Great, thanks. I'll put your order in now." The waitress took their menus and left.

"Wow, this is so exciting!" Melody beamed, straining to contain her overflowing emotions. First, church, then the public kiss, the romantic bus ride, this surprise nice meal, and now Kevin ordering her meal. What other surprises did Kevin have in store?

NEW FRIENDS

Imani slurped her spaghetti and watched as Lance came over to their table in the Union accompanied by three girls. She recalled one of the three as the cute little chick with the sporty bob that Lance got *acquainted* with last night at the Alpha party.

Lance gestured for the three to take a seat at their table and Imani almost choked on her spaghetti. What the…? Her eyebrow arched. Lance never introduced his conquests to his friends, much less invited them to sit down at their table.

John, Joe, and Big Tony, Lance's defensive teammates, stopped their conversation mid-chew as the trio of females waited for introductions.

Trevor gave Imani a funny look but continued to eat his burger.

"Hey everyone," Lance said getting their already-rapt attention. "This is Krystal," he said gesturing towards the cutie with the bob. He motioned towards her striking, dark-skinned and chestnut-colored, bohemian girlfriends. "And these are her friends Karen and Erycah."

"Hey there," said Big Tony.

"Hi," Trev said adding in a head nod.

Lance continued the introductions of those seated around the table. "The sole female holding down the house here is Imani."

"Pleased to meet you." She smiled and nodded. "I normally have extra estrogen in the form of our girlfriend, Melody—"

"And Melody has more than enough romanticized estrogen for all of us," Big Tony said provoking chuckles from the table regulars.

Lance shook his head and continued. "The intelligent, cool cat next to her is Trevor and these three knuckleheads are my football teammates. The first smooth operator here is John, the Free Safety. At Middle Linebacker is Joe. And this Defensive Tackling beast is Big Tony," he said pointing to Big Tony. "You have to watch out for this last one here."

Big Tony grunted. "Please, Lance is the one you need to watch out for."

"So, we've heard. And not just from Krystal," the bolder, brassy Karen said, giving Lance a suggestive glance.

"Karen!" Krystal whispered in protest as she elbowed Karen hard in the side.

Trev kicked Imani under the table and she tried hard not to laugh out loud in appreciation of the girl's honesty.

"Oh, my," Big Tony mouthed to Joe and John while Lance covered his head with his hands.

"Please excuse Karen. Sometimes her mouth is too big for her own good." Erycah gave her friend the evil eye.

"Whatever!" Karen continued on undeterred and turned to Imani. "So, Imani, how did you get stuck amongst all this ridiculous testosterone?"

Imani snorted and put down her fork. Okay, she could definitely hang out with this crazy, tell-it-like-it-is, mad-blunt-ass girl. "It's my charitable donation. No other self-respecting person felt bad enough to hang out with a bunch of dumb jocks. What's your excuse?"

"Ah, thanks," said Joe and John in unison.

Karen smiled and leaned back in her chair. "I'm just helping out my dating-challenged girlfriend here try to snag a certain football player." Karen pointed to Krystal who blushed beet red beneath her cinnamon-burnished skin. Erycah rolled her eyes and Lance's eyebrow rocketed off his forehead.

"I'll have you know I'm a chemical engineer like Imani, so you can't lump me in with these guys," Trev said finishing his burger.

"What?" Big Tony looked at Lance, Joe, and John then sniffed his massive underarms. "Do we smell now or something because I swore I showered this morning?"

"Wow, I didn't know you two were engineers," Erycah said almost gushing. "I'm a mechanical engineer."

Imani frowned; she swore she knew all of the black engineers at school as there weren't many of them at their predominantly white college. "I've never seen you at any of the NSBE meetings."

"Nehs-bee?"

"Oh, good Lord," Imani replied and gave Trevor an incredulous look. "The National Society of Black Engineers. If you're serious about engineering, you gotta come to our next meeting. Trev and I can give you the details."

"Sounds great," Erycah replied with enthusiasm.

"Sounds boring," Big Tony said pretending to stifle a yawn.

"And that's why Imani called you a bunch of dumb jocks," Karen muttered.

"Ooooohhhhh," Joe and John howled, doubling over in laughter.

"Yep, y'all can stay," Imani said with a slow smile. "Welcome to the gang."

MOVIE TIME

"That movie was creepy, especially Matt Damon," Melody told Kevin. "But Jude Law wasn't too bad on the eyes."

"Oh! So you're planning on trading me in for Jude Law, are you?"

Melody jumped on Kevin's back for a piggyback ride, hugging him tight around the neck. "No way, Jose. You can't get rid of me that quickly."

"Oh, yeah?"

"Yeah!"

Kevin bolted towards the mall fountain, carrying her captive on his back.

"What are you doing?" Melody squealed. "Stop, Kevin, stop! You wouldn't dare?"

"I wouldn't, would I?" Kevin teetered right at the fountain's edge, threatening to fall in or worse, deposit her in butt first.

"Okay, I'll do anything if you don't throw me in," she pleaded.

"Anything, eh? I like that." He set her down, safe from the ledge. "I think I need another kiss for my bruised ego."

This time her lips met Kevin's without a hint of hesitation. Giving in to the moment, the waves rushed over, engulfing her. They kissed for what felt like hours, mouths coupled together in a desperate attempt to explore every inch of each other.

"Eh-hem!" a familiar voice interjected. "Get a damn room… and not ours, either!"

Melody pulled away from Kevin and saw her roommate looking pleased to have caught them in the act.

***

Imani extended her hand. "You must be Kevin."

Kevin shook her hand with a firm grip and smiled. However, something about his initial look made her feel like he didn't seem pleased by her interruption. "And you must be the roommate I've heard so much about. Nice to meet you, Imani."

Imani felt the need to suppress a shudder, but she kept smiling. "Well, I'll let you lovebirds get back to making out in the middle of the mall. Nice to meet you, Kevin," she said excusing herself as fast as possible.

Not able to put her finger on it, Imani realized there was something about Kevin she disliked. Her mother always told her to follow her first instincts. But what was it? Melody was correct; Kevin did resemble a young Paul Newman. She had watched AMC, the classic movie channel, with her parents one weekend and saw *Cat on a Hot Tin Roof.* Paul Newman should have been nicknamed the "Hot Cat" because it marked one of the rare occasions where she drooled over a white guy. Kevin looked cute, but he was no Paul Newman because, dammit, she wasn't drooling. What was it about him? He acted nice—maybe that was it—

it seemed like an act. No, she chided herself; he probably just hated the interruption.

Determined not to make a big deal out of nothing, Imani shrugged it off and window-shopped.

MOVING ON

Lance flicked his wrist and checked his watch. Yes, 5:00 p.m. on the dot. With a smile he knocked on the girls' dorm room door ready to tackle their English study session. Even though they each pursued different majors: Melody, Communications; Imani, Chemical Engineering; and he studied Business; they all made a vow at orientation to align their core Freshmen classes and liberal arts electives whenever possible.

He heard movement behind the door as one of the girls checked through the peephole and then Imani threw open the door.

Lance smiled and landed a peck on her cheek before he strolled inside.

The phone rang and Imani shoved him towards it. "Could you get that? It's my mom," she said heading towards the bathroom she shared with Melody and the two girls in the connecting room.

"Are you expecting her call?" he asked as he walked over to the ringing phone.

"No, but I know it's her, I can feel it," she replied waving her right hand around her head. She stopped inside the bathroom doorway and peeked her head around the opening. "She doesn't want anything, so let her know we're about to go study," Imani replied before she shut the bathroom door.

True to Imani's weird sixth sense, he noticed the Jordan's name and their 718 Bronx home number. He grabbed the phone on the third ring, right before the answering machine picked up. "Hello, Imani and Melody's room."

"Hi, Lance," Mrs. Jordan replied, not in the least surprised to hear him answering her daughter's dorm room phone. "How are you doing?"

Like mother, like daughter, he mused. "I'm fine, Mrs. Jordan," he replied. "Imani's predisposed at the moment, but she wanted me to tell you that we're about to go study."

Mrs. Jordan chuckled. "Well, when Imani gets out of the bathroom, let her know it's not urgent. I just wanted to bother her. Tell her to call me when you're done studying."

Lance scratched his head with his free hand. Wow, they really did share some weird extrasensory connection. "Will do. Please tell Mr. Jordan I said hello."

"I will. Talk to you later, Lance," she said before disconnecting.

Lance heard Imani flush and he shook his head as he hung up the phone. The sink water turned off and Imani reemerged from the bathroom. "You were right," he said as she whizzed past with a big grin. "Call your mother when we're finished later."

He glanced around the room and it took him a second to realize that they were alone. "By the way, where's Melody?" he asked dropping his backpack on the floor and plopping down on Imani's bed.

"I'll give you one guess," Imani muttered as she sat at her desk chair.

"With Kevin." He shook his head. "Well did she at least call and confirm our study session this time or do you think she's going to ditch us without a trace like she did last week?" Lance felt his back stiffen and he frowned, not good. He needed to be loose to focus on his studies. Stretching his arms towards the ceiling, he kept reaching until his shoulder and back muscles lengthened and popped.

"She made sure to call today after I cussed her out real good for not showing up last time." Imani studied him for a moment. "Are you okay because that didn't sound good?"

Bingo! Lance cracked a grin. "Well, since you asked," he replied already envisioning Imani giving him one of her fantastic massages.

Imani rolled her eyes. "I walked right into that one."

"Yes, you did," he said patting the bed before he turned over and lay on his stomach. "Might as well get a massage while we're waiting for Miss Melody to show up."

Straddling his back, Imani flexed her fingers and went to work. "You know, I really should charge you for this."

"I would gladly pay." Lance stopping speaking and moaned as her fingers unlocked the kinks in his shoulders. He didn't know what kind of magic her fingers employed, but he truly appreciated it. "Seriously, if I somehow make it into the NFL, I swear I'll bring you to every game. I'll even add you to the payroll just so I can have my own personal masseuse."

"Please, if you made it to the pros, I'd pay *you* just so I could see each game!"

Lance chuckled then moaned more as she worked her way down his back.

"Doesn't matter though, I'm sure that whatever hoochie you marry won't approve." She laughed. "Unless, you're putting a ring on Krystal's finger. Now she seems pretty cool and low-key unlike all your other conquests."

"Oh, here we go!" He chuckled. "I wondered how long it would take until you started lecturing me over my love life or lack thereof. Sorry to disappoint but one, I'm not getting hitched anytime soon and two, Krystal is last week's news."

Imani slapped his back. "But she was just sitting at our table in the Union yesterday. What did you do?"

Lance shifted underneath Imani and chuckled again. "Like you said, Krystal's cool; so she's still at the table. But just as a friend. Hey, at least it lasted an entire week. That's way longer than my usual one nighters."

"Oh Lord, I hope Krystal's okay?"

"Why wouldn't she be?"

"Are you serious?" Imani slapped his back again. "I swear guys can be so dense!" She poked his shoulder. "Be careful. Women develop feelings easily and Krystal wants you."

"Please, she's fine. Every woman knows what she's agreeing to when she hops into bed with me. I'm honest upfront. Plus, with all the other pretty, young ladies waiting to ride the Lance train, I couldn't stay confined in one station for too long."

Before Imani could deliver a caustic response, Lance heard Melody unlocking the door.

"Well, time's up," Imani said finishing off the massage way too soon for his liking.

In two seconds flat, Melody rushed inside and screeched to a halt by Imani's bed. "Sorry I'm late."

Imani kicked her leg over Lance, jumped up, and hugged Melody. "We were beginning to worry that we'd have to start studying without you."

Melody gave them a coy smile. "Let's just say you should be happy that I came at all."

Imani shot him an incredulous look. "Did she just lose her mind?"

"Sounds like it," he replied as he stroked his mustache and goatee, all the while gauging the best angle of attack.

Wisely Melody threw her hands up in surrender trying her best to ward them off. "You're right, momentary lapse in reasoning," she said steadily backpedaling and easing her way towards the door. "I'm so sorry, please don't tickle me."

Imani cut her eyes towards Lance and he nodded. They grabbed their backpacks and gave chase after a squealing Melody.

TROUBLE! - FEBRUARY 2000

Hearing Kevin's key in the lock, Melody closed her English textbook and sat up on his bed, smiling in anticipation.

During the past three weeks she had spent a lot of time over here at his place. Almost every waking hour, when they weren't in classes, sleeping, or meeting their study groups, they spent together. Once again, she thanked God that Kevin occupied one of the treasured single dormitory rooms located on campus. Because of the solitude the single afforded, things had progressed between them fast and fantastic, much to Imani's chagrin.

The tumblers clicked unlocked and she saw the door handle turn.

Imani...God her annoying roommate kept harping to take it slow and it worked her one last nerve. Kevin was a sweetheart—respectful, kind, loving—at times he attended to her needs before she even realized they existed. They had talked so much that Melody felt they knew everything about one another, and she wished Imani could see that, too.

"Oh good, you're here," Kevin said when he entered the room with his head down. His back was to her as he locked the door and took off his backpack.

"Yes, Professor Charles dismissed class early, so I

came right over." She patted the bed, eager for him to plant a loving kiss on her lips. It had been oh so hard to wait, but now she felt primed to take it to the next level this weekend.

Melody smiled again, Kevin—ever patient—had never pushed her to have sex, never even mentioned sex in that context. In fact, he embodied the perfect gentleman and she wanted to reward him for that. Yes, it had only been four weeks since they met, but it seemed like forever; and more than enough people would have succumbed much sooner. Hell, look at Lance, she held in a snicker, he always got some on the first night! It was time; she was ready.

Kevin pulled his folders out of his backpack. With his head down and intent expression, she couldn't see his gorgeous blue eyes. He fumbled for a paper in his folder and thrust it at her. Surprised she reached out for it.

"Would you mind telling me what the grade on the paper says?" Kevin's voice sounded funny, strained.

She glanced at Kevin, wondering why this was more important than their usual greeting, the sweet kiss.

He repeated himself with more intensity. "What is the grade on the paper, Melody?"

Startled by his tone, she focused on the paper, still trying to process what the big deal was. "There's a C on the paper." Looking up, she noticed his stormy eyes glaring, his nostrils fuming.

Kevin's shout shook her. "Yes, it's a C! Have you ever known me to get anything other than an A or a B?"

She stammered. Why was he so mad? He would just have to study more for this class; she'd heard it was hard. "No, I haven't. Kevin, what's wrong?"

Her head snapped around from his hard slap before her ears could process the loud "smack." A weak yelp escaped her lips, her cheek stung, and her eyes watered.

"I told you I needed to study more Tuesday night, but you insisted I had it mastered and that we should make out! I will not let you ruin my academic career, Melody! Do you understand?"

Nodding her head in short, frantic bursts; she scrambled against the safety of the wall.

Kevin sat down, trapping her on the bed. He affixed her with his gaze of steel until she dropped her head to avoid his piercing glare. Kevin reached out, and sensing him, she shirked back. His hand dropped to his lap and she heard a muffled sound.

Cautious, she dared a glance. Kevin's head hung down, shoulders drooped and heaving. Was he…crying? "Kevin?"

"Melody, I'm so sorry, Baby." His cheeks glistened with fresh tears.

His pitiful look broke her heart. Kevin was so sad and remorseful. Oh God, she knew he hadn't meant it. He would never hurt her for any reason. It was just a big mistake; he loved her. He had told her that Tuesday night after they finished studying. She rushed to comfort him. Her arms couldn't embrace him tight enough to convey how much she loved him.

Kevin enveloped her and wouldn't let go, kissing her cheeks, lips, neck, eyes. He whispered soft and sweet over and over, "I'm so sorry, Melody. I'm so sorry. I would never hurt you. I love you more than the world."

She didn't know what had happened, but it was over. Everything was fine again.

HOME EARLY

"You're home early," Imani greeted Melody when she entered their room.

"You renting out my half when I'm not here or something?" Melody walked across the room and deposited her backpack onto her desk.

"Actually that's an excellent idea. You're never here anymore, so you wouldn't even notice." Imani rose from her desk for a hug. "Seriously though, I miss you, Girl. We never hang out anymore."

"Well, that's what happens when you get a man." Cautious, she half-hugged Imani, but her hair moved out of place. As they separated, Melody flipped her head so that her hair hid her red left cheek but not fast enough to escape Imani's eagle eyes.

"What is that?" Imani brushed Melody's cheek.

"Ah, dang, is it starting to show?"

"Yes, now how'd you get it?" Imani repeated, concern mounting across her features.

"It was stupid. I was walking across the quad minding my own business, when 'WHACK,' a football smacked me upside the head. The idiot jocks out tossing balls around, tried real hard not to laugh at me, too. Jerks!"

"Were they fellows from the football team? Lance will jack 'em up for you. Being the new, up and coming star wide receiver and an all-round playa has its advantages you know."

Turning away from Imani, she shuffled her books and folders over her desk and pretended to sort them. "No, it wasn't the football players; I think it was one of the stupid White fraternities." God, she disliked liars, and being a pitiful liar, she needed to change topics now, especially considering Imani's nose for ferreting out deceptions.

"Alright, well do you want some ice?"

"No, I'll be fine. I just need to get some studying in tonight."

"Well, okay." Imani walked halfway towards her desk and stopped. "Are you sure that's all, Melody? You're acting a little funny."

Crap, she spun around, not out of the woods yet. "What? Nothing's wrong, Imani. I'm just embarrassed, alright?"

"Okay, okay. I'm sorry." Imani backed off. "I just haven't seen or talked to you and then you show up with a bruised cheek. I'm kinda concerned, that's all."

"I'm fine." Melody concentrated on the clutter of papers. God she hated lying, but Imani would blow everything out of proportion if she knew that Kevin slapped her. Regardless, she missed Imani's generally sage advice and talks, especially when the topics were love and sex.

Squirming in her seat and unable to care about the scattered papers any longer, she decided to confess her big plans. "Okay, don't get all crazy...but I am keeping a secret."

Imani flew across the room in two giant leaps.

"Girl, you better spill the beans. I knew you were holding back!"

Sticking tight as glue, Imani accompanied Melody from her chair to her bed and almost sat on top her, she remained so close. Imani waited, ready to catch every word and expression.

"I think Saturday will be Kevin's lucky night," she said then held her breath.

"Aaaahhhh," Imani screamed. "Oh my God, this is a huge, gargantuan, humungous step for you. Are you sure, Girl?"

"He told me he loved me Tuesday night," she whispered.

"Whaatt? Get the hell outta here. Wait did you say it first and trap the man into saying it?"

"No!" she exclaimed, popping Imani's arm. "But I sure said it back to him with dividends!"

They shrieked together for a minute.

"Wow! I can't believe how sprung you two are." Imani swept Melody's hair back from her uninjured cheek, stroked it, and then planted a gentle kiss there. "Oh my, God, my little girl is growing up right before my eyes."

"You are so melodramatic," she replied rolling her eyes.

"Seriously, now," Imani said, "you talked about protection, right? And you have condoms, which he promises to wear?"

"Yes, Mom!"

"And you're not just doing this because he said he loved you, right? Because you know a guy will sink so low as to say that just to get a piece—"

"No, it's not like that," she replied then paused. "I considered this even before he said it, Imani. It just feels right."

"Yo, I'm shocked your hapless romantic ass didn't wait another week for Valentine's Day."

Melody's eyes grew with excitement, "I know, I considered it, too! But I really couldn't wait that long."

A loud knock sounded at the door, scaring them both. Imani regained her composure first and checked her watch as she walked to the door. "Oh, my God! I forgot about Lance." Imani peeked through the peephole, "yep, it's him, right on time," she said while opening the door.

"Hey, hey, hey," Lance said entering the room. As Melody raced over to greet him, he spied her. "Oh, ho! Lookie here, it's our incredible, vanishing friend!" He gathered her in a big bear hug, swung her around three times, and set her down. "You break up with the old man or is the tarnish finally starting to show through enough that you decided to spend some time with your old friends?"

Melody punched Lance's shoulder as he gave Imani a quick hello peck on the cheek. "It's not even like that," she said, bracing to run. "Plus, Kevin had to meet his computer lab group, so I figured I could slum it here with you two!"

Imani and Lance exchanged looks. "Oh, no she didn't," scoffed Imani. They chased Melody, tackled her onto her bed, and tickled her without mercy.

"I give, I give," she said snorting between fits of laughter.

Lance ceased tickling her and looked at Imani.

"Should we forgive her?"

Imani glanced back and forth between Melody and Lance. "Eh, I don't know, Lance. I don't think she recognizes the irreparable damage she's caused by leaving the two of us alone to argue without her silly banter as referee."

"Oh, so very true. It's been agony dealing with you these last few weeks. Maybe we should tickle her more?"

"Or better yet, raspberries!" Imani's eyes lit up.

"Oh, please no! I can't take anymore. I promise I'll make it up to you. Just no more tickles or raspberries, I'm about to pee my pants." Giving them her most pathetic face, she braced for another tickle attack, just in case.

"Oh, look at how pitiful she looks, Imani. I couldn't possibly tickle her again now."

"Please, I could." Imani attacked and tickled her for five seconds before relenting. "Alright, I suppose she's had enough." Imani moved to her desk chair and Melody struggled to sit up and get some air. "You know, Lance, you came right in time. Melody was just telling me some juicy ass news."

"Imani!" Melody gasped and frowned at Imani, appalled that she would bring it up.

"What? You know you would have told him sooner or later. Plus you need a man's perspective on this, Melody."

"Would somebody clue me in, please?"

Imani replied first, "She wants to give Kevin some this Saturday."

"Whoa!" Lance lurched back. "You've only *been*

with one guy, your high school sweetheart. And from what you told us, that was only after you dated for two years, *and* deemed the boy to be husband material." Lance appraised her. "You really ready to do this?"

"Yes, Lance, I really am. I love Kevin and he loves me. It all feels so perfect."

Lance raised an eyebrow. "What did I warn you about that fairytale stuff?"

"I know, I know," she said nodding. "It's not perfect, but it's a close second. This feels better than I ever imagined, Lance." She squeezed his arm, "I'm deadly serious."

"Well, in that case...go on with your bad self!" Lance smiled and hugged her before reconsidering. "Although, you tend to over-romanticize life, see everything a little too cheerily."

"Yeah, too damn optimistic! Even her bright, make-you-grin-back smiles say daffodils blooming and sunshine streaming," Imani said.

"What?" she replied trying to kick Imani's leg, but it lay just out of reach.

"Well, c'mon think about it. When you smile, sometimes I swear a bunch of animated birds and mice are about to come out of the woods and start singing while placing a floral wreath on top of your head!"

Melody gasped while Lance roared with laughter.

"Freaking makes you think of brilliant daffodils blooming through the cold, hard earth while warm, energizing sunshine streams down from the heavens!"

Aghast, yet somewhat delighted by Imani's crazy description, Melody just shook her head.

Lance slapped his leg and laughed some more.

"Hmm, daffodils and sunshine. Very apropos description for our bright, cheery Little Melody."

"Yeah, yeah, but what's your impression about Kevin?" Imani asked much to Melody's growing discomfort. "I still think the hussy's moving too fast, but I'm reserving judgment until I get to know the boy better."

"Hmm, well Kevin seemed cool the few times I met him," Lance said. "So, if Melody feels good about Kevin, then I do, too."

"I do." Melody rubbed Lance's back to reassure him.

"Alrighty then," Imani replied although she still appeared skeptical.

"Group hug, share the love," Lance said saving her from Imani's further scrutiny.

Luckily, Imani acquiesced and jumped on the bed, hugging them.

Melody beamed, life couldn't get much better.

THE ROSE

"Whew, I'm beat." Imani blew air through her teeth as they got up from the kitchen table.

"Well, after two hours of studying, I feel much smarter," Lance said.

"Yeah, like that really helped."

Lance bumped her hip, knocking her into the kitchen wall.

"Stop playing, Boy, I gotta pee bad!" Imani hit Lance and wished this once that their dormitory had a closer, floor bathroom setup like Lance's versus the bathroom she and Melody shared with their two suitemates, all the way down at the end of the hallway.

Lance threw his arm around Melody's shoulders. "So, can we expect your continued presence at our study sessions or are we relegated to the back burner once Kevin returns?"

"Damn, speak of the devil!" Imani pointed down the hallway.

Melody and Lance glanced up to see Kevin knocking on the girls' door.

"Ba-bieee!" Melody bounded from under Lance's arm and down the hall.

Kevin saw Melody and smiled. When Melody jumped on Kevin, he caught her with ease in his right hand and kept his left behind his back. Without delay the lovers' lips interlocked.

"Guess that answers my question," Lance whispered out of the corner of his mouth as they approached the amorous couple.

Kevin put Melody down to greet them with a huge grin. "Hello, Imani." Kevin kissed her cheek then welcomed Lance with the latest Black handshake.

"Alright, now," Lance said nodding, "I didn't know you could get down like that." Lance swung his arm over Imani's shoulders. "Imani and I were lamenting that we never get to hang out with Melody anymore."

Kevin gazed at Melody so intently that Imani almost felt uncomfortable. "Yeah, I like keeping her all to myself. In fact…" he brought his left arm from behind his back and presented Melody with a beautiful red rose. "This is because I missed you so much during study group."

"Oh, my God, Kevin. It's so beautiful!" Melody's eyes brimmed with tears as she inhaled the picture-perfect flower.

It took everything in Imani's power not to roll her eyes.

"Keep doing that and you'll mess things up for the rest of us players," Lance said.

Imani put a hand on her hip and scowled at Lance. "Please, when was the last time you gave a woman flowers?"

"For your information," Lance replied, batting his eyes, "I've given three campus cuties flowers."

"Yeah, but when was the last time it *wasn't* to get into their panties?"

Lance laughed. "Ah, see now you're getting

particular! I'll have you know I gave my high school girlfriend flowers for Valentine's Day, her birthday, at prom, and twice just because." He ended by raising a seductive eyebrow.

"Oh, please!" Imani shook her head and turned to Kevin. "Anyway, you were saying something Kevin?"

"Well, I guess it's not fair to keep Melody away from her friends, no matter how much I like staying locked up together. We should hang out sometime."

"That would be nice," Melody said grinning from ear-to-ear. "I know, how about this Saturday at the College Chill-Out?"

"Hmm, lots of games, food, and a carnival? We're so there. It's like the winter version of Homecoming, just without the big football game." Imani nudged Lance in his side. "Right, Superstar?"

Lance bumped her back. "Most definitely."

"Don't forget about the concert and the all-night party." Melody smiled.

"Plus it's fun meeting as many new people as you can," Lance said to Kevin.

"Yeah, but it's to break down boundaries and make new friends, not to increase your bed-hopping prospects," Imani replied, shaking her head.

"Regardless," Melody said, "it should be a blast."

Kevin hugged Melody but looked at Lance and Imani. "Guess we'll hook up there."

"Sounds like a plan." Lance glanced at his watch. "Hey, I need to split."

"Hot date tonight?" Imani shot Lance a disapproving glare as he kissed her cheek.

"And you know it." Lance laughed and shook

hands with Kevin. But the second Lance hugged Melody and kissed her cheek, Imani swore that Kevin gave Lance a look of absolute rage. It passed so fast, she wasn't quite sure she'd really seen it. When Lance disappeared, a sweet-as-pecan-pie smile graced Kevin's lips.

"Well, I'll let you lovebirds talk in private." Imani unlocked the door with haste.

SATURDAY MORNING

Melody's perfect plans for Saturday morning began Friday afternoon. Without Kevin's knowledge, she entered his room before their date, using the key he gave her after their first week of dating. She stocked his mini-fridge with a box of prepared omelets, a package of microwavable bacon, some croissants, strawberries, whipped cream, and orange juice. In his closet she hid a vase with three long-stemmed red roses, a plate, bowl, silverware, glasses, an in-bed serving tray, and a card that described in detail how much she loved him.

Then came their date, all his idea. First, they caught a comedy act on campus and laughed until they cried. Second, they dropped by the Union for hot fudge sundaes, and finally, they walked off campus two miles to The Pointe.

Inaccessible by car, they hiked up the winding pathway to The Pointe, a former private garden retreat of some dead, rich guy. They strolled along the Lover's Lane's evergreen-lined paths, past the dormant flowering trees and rose bushes—glorious and fragrant in the springtime, and sat on one of the park benches to enjoy the wondrous views of the campus and city below.

They looked out at the Union, holding court right in

the midst of campus then over to the four high-rise residential towers nicknamed "the Quad" that stood guard, marking the campus boundaries. South of the Union, the library loomed large, dwarfing the chapel beside it. Other various disciplined buildings were scattered about and off campus on a hill to the north sat the sports complex with its domed stadium, auditorium, and hockey rink.

While stargazing, they witnessed a shooting star and then Kevin read the original poetry that he had written about Melody. It took every fiber of her being not to let his enchanting words of love, devotion, and fate make her lose it right then and there, but Melody stayed strong. Instead they kissed and talked until 2:00 a.m. before they returned to his room and fell asleep wrapped in each other's arms.

Now his alarm clock read 9:00 a.m., so Melody untangled herself while Kevin slept peacefully, and snuck off to the bathroom that he shared with his suitemate. Once inside she took a super-speedy but thorough shower, freshening up her special parts. Next, she brushed her teeth, dressed, and combed her hair, finishing in eleven minutes flat. Pleased with the results, she opened the door to Kevin's inquisitive stare.

"Going somewhere without me?" he asked with soft concern.

"Absolutely not!" Grinning, she kissed his cheek, "but could you brush your teeth and shower for me? I've got a surprise for you before we meet Lance and Imani."

Kevin's gaze softened while his finger traced her

lips, sending tingles up her jaw. "Hmm, I love surprises. Be with you in fifteen minutes, will that work?"

"Perfect," she whispered trying not to drag him back to bed. Something about his touch set her ablaze. "Now, get going," she said slapping his ass as he let her pass.

Kevin winked and blew her a kiss before he shut the bathroom door.

In a daze, Melody stared at the door until she heard the shower start. Time to set the big plan in motion! After grabbing the plate and bowl from their hiding spot, she ran to the mini-fridge, placed the omelets and bacon artistically on the plate, and microwaved them. Next, she skipped back to the closet, retrieved the tray, and arranged the card and vase on it. Then she added the croissants and bowl of whipped cream-topped strawberries.

When the microwave beeped, she heard Kevin emerge from the shower singing. Music! God, she'd almost forgotten the CD she burned with their favorite songs. Running to his stereo, she cued the CD. Noticing the tray sitting out in plain view, she hid it from sight. Perfect, everything was going according to plan!

"Ready or not, here I come!" Kevin sang out as he opened the door. "Mm," he said sniffing around, "what smells so good?"

Melody hit the play button on the CD player and Jamiroquai started singing *Falling*.

"What have we here?"

Melody guided him to the bed. "This is in

appreciation for what a wonderful guy you've been." She made Kevin sit and straddled him, swimming in his clear blue eyes. "These last few weeks surpassed anything I imagined. Our courtship, this love, or dare I say the word, soulmates?" Swallowing hard, she continued. "After breakfast, read the card and follow the instructions inside. Okay?"

Kevin gazed deep into her soul and nodded. "Anything you want, Baby."

Melody rose up far enough to position Kevin with his back against the headboard. Then she grabbed the tray from its hiding spot and placed it on his lap with a flourish.

Kevin's eyes widened in amazement. "Is all this for me?"

"Well, actually I was hoping you would share," she replied blushing.

He patted a free spot beside him. "Only if you let me feed you."

Feeling like she could burst from extreme happiness, Melody sat where Kevin requested and opened her mouth.

Kevin forked some of the cheesy omelet and pretending the fork was an airplane, he flew it around towards her waiting mouth. When he landed the omelet in her mouth, he followed it with a peck on the lips. Breakfast flew by in much the same manner with as many kisses rewarded as food devoured.

"Now for the last bite," said Kevin placing whipped cream on the tip of her nose. She squealed with delight as he tossed the tray aside and licked off the cream.

"The card, the card," she screamed before he got too

carried away.

"Promise you'll stay right there?"

She nodded and lay as still as the sexual tension coursing through her limbs would allow.

Kevin leaned back and grabbed the card off the tray. He ripped it open and stared stupefied as he read the front. Gaping at her, he opened the card. Two condoms dropped out and he studied them in disbelief before reading the inside. When he finished, he stood the card on his nightstand. "Are you sure, Sweetheart?" he asked so tender she melted.

"I want to with all of my heart," she said unbuttoning her blouse.

Kevin stopped Melody's hand and laid her down comfortably, making sure the pillow supported her head. "Don't move, okay?" He placed the condoms on the nightstand and stared at her for the longest time, his face filled with longing and anticipation. At last, he lowered himself on top of her being careful not to crush her petite body underneath his muscular one.

Soft and slow he kissed her lips before his gentle mouth progressed down to her chin, which he nibbled. Giggling and giddy, she tried her best to remain still and not squirm. Kevin continued kissing his way up her right jaw, to her cheek, and over to her ear lobe. As he sucked the lobe, she melted feeling like he'd liquefied her body.

Kevin whispered in her ear as he moved past to her temple, next her eyebrow, down to her eyelid, and then he brushed his lip across her eyelashes.

Oh God! She couldn't take anymore and wanted to scream for Kevin to stop, but at the same time she never wanted this blissful feeling to end. Much to her pleasure and discomfort, he repeated his movements on the left side of her face.

"Baby, I want this to be everything you ever imagined."

Melody could barely hear Kevin speak through what seemed like a tunnel of water.

He stroked her cheeks and lips. "If I do anything you dislike, just tell me okay, Melody?"

Unable to respond, she lay there like putty in his hands.

Kevin didn't wait for an answer. Instead he finished unbuttoning her shirt, kissing each new piece of exposed skin. His hands slid around her waist, under her now unbuttoned shirt, and up her body, enjoying each and every curve. Upon reaching her shoulders, he raised her into a sitting position.

With her body so weak, it was difficult to remain upright. "Oh God," a whisper escaped her lips. She was definitely not in control. Kevin could do whatever he pleased; she just didn't care. Never had she felt so alive. Nerve endings tingled with an incessant fire wherever his lips met her skin.

As Kevin slid off her shirt, he tickled her spine then eased her back down. His tongue traced a line from her chin, over her neck, between her breasts, to her belly button. Kevin's hands found new homes on her breasts, squeezing them whole, then tracing around the swells and teasing the nipples. She writhed and squirmed from the tremendous sensations.

Next he lifted her thighs and buttocks enough to remove her jeans and underwear. Tossing aside the last of her clothes, Kevin spread her legs and kissed and licked from her right big toe to her ankle to the back of the knee to her inner thigh.

"Pleassseee," she pleaded to no avail as he simply ignored her and retraced his steps on her left leg.

When finished he popped his head up from between her thighs. "So, you say no one has ever *tasted* your sweet secret?" he asked in a husky voice.

"No one, Kevin," she replied breathless.

"Interesting. So, if I'm the first to taste your nectar that kind of makes me your first, huh?"

"Yes!" She couldn't take it. Kevin whispered each question right above her clitoris and she felt it pulse, straining for him to taste or touch it. He obliged by kissing her vaginal lips before she could prepare herself. Her right arm slapped the bed repeatedly as her left hand clapped over her mouth to restrain the scream of ecstasy. As her back arched, she realized she was grinding on his face. He didn't seem to mind and she couldn't stop if she wanted.

Kevin finished his lower exploration with a kiss. Pleased with his work—with good reason, she thought—he grinned while he stripped off his shirt, jeans, and underwear.

He looked ready to burst and she gasped at the sight of him bare. Although, she had touched it in a moment of passion, she tried not to bother him for fear of giving him blue balls or putting him in an uncomfortable predicament. Now, with him on display, she was drawn to touch him. God, he felt hard and much bigger than her previous boyfriend. It felt smooth to the touch but pulsed under her stroke. Moved by instinct, she attempted to kiss the tip.

Kevin shook his head and stopped her. "Not yet. I'll explode." Gentle and loving, he laid her back down. "Are you sure you're ready for this?" he asked stroking her cheek.

"Yes, please," she answered looking deep into his eyes.

He snagged a condom from the nightstand, tore it open, and discarded the wrapper.

"May I help?" she asked half-sitting.

Her genuine offer seemed to strike a chord as he paused and gazed at her before he nodded in approval. Working together they unrolled the condom over his pulsating penis.

As she lay back down, he questioned her again with a final glance. With a smile she helped guide him to the promised land. Although soaking wet, it had been almost two years since she'd last made love, and Kevin was well endowed—her muscles strained to accommodate him.

Kevin recognized her tenseness and halted, still half out. He accompanied each soft kiss with a gentle thrust until he eased inside. "Are you okay?"

It had hurt at first, but Kevin's tenderness allowed her to comfortably expand. "Thank you," she said nodding as the tears crested.

He kissed her eyes and moved in and out tender and slow.

Melody followed his rhythm and moved in time, working them from a gentle rocking to a more feverish pitch. Hungry for him she gripped his butt, willing him further inside. His response came hard and she felt something surge inside him. It clicked with something deep within as a tidal wave crashed down over her body and subsided in gradual stages.

Kevin let out a long, low moan, exploding until his body wracked in tremors. Spent, he collapsed in an exhausted, drained pile.

SECOND THOUGHTS

Melody remained in bed with Kevin for a half hour. They laughed, talked, and twice she shed a few tears of joy. Finally, she suggested they freshen up before meeting Lance and Imani at the College Chill-Out.

Once Kevin guided her into the shower, the harsh fluorescents illuminated them in a different light. This time Kevin discovered her body anew but with a bar of Irish Spring and a washcloth. Afterwards her grateful hands accepted the washcloth and they caressed and slid over every inch of his delectable body.

Although she wanted to make love again, her tender body said no. Hell, when they first got up it took her legs ten minutes to gain a consistency more solid than rubber. By the time they dried and lotioned, her body felt like it did after a great workout, tight and alive, muscles fatigued but stronger and happier. As Melody finished dressing, she snuck a peak at Kevin.

Kevin sat motionless on the bed, chest glistening with lotion. Although his jeans were on, he didn't attempt to don his shirt or socks. Meeting her stare, he smiled. "You look absolutely gorgeous, Melody."

Kevin's words sounded to Melody like an express invitation to bound over and jump on his lap. "You look damn hot yourself, Handsome!"

"I always want to make you this happy." Kevin

held her face in his hands and gazed deep into her eyes. "You need to know that I always want to make you as happy as you make me. I never want you to leave me," his voice sounded deep and husky.

Melting under his intense gaze and warm hands, tears welled in her eyes. "You make me the happiest woman in the world. I could never leave you, Kevin."

"I love you more than life itself. Do you understand?" His voice felt so earnest and loving.

"God, yes, I love you, too," she said snuggling her head in the crook of his neck.

Kevin enfolded her in his strong grasp and kissed the top of her head.

Leaning back she caught a glimpse of his clock. "Oh no, it's 11:10! We need to meet Imani and Lance," she said half-rising, but Kevin grabbed her arms.

"I don't feel like going anymore. These feelings, I don't want them to end. Plus, I want you all to myself."

"I know I feel that way, too, but we promised," she said settling on his lap.

"Maybe later," he replied lying back on the bed. Still holding her wrists he guided her hands up his chest, starting at his rippling abs, over his ribcage, around his pecs, stopping at the nipples.

Her fingers tweaked them of their own accord and it sent a chill through his body. Oh man, she loved the way he trembled beneath her fingertips. Mm, she felt inexplicable joy and power from bringing him pleasure with simply one touch.

Damn, but she wanted to share these emotions with Imani. Just one look and her roommate would know that she altered her earlier plans of a Saturday night tryst to this morning's escapades. Imani would beg for all the juicy details and Melody couldn't wait to blab.

Smiling, she removed her hands from Kevin's addictive chest and winked. "Come on, Kevin. It will be fun to go and let your room air out a bit. Plus, I'm getting hungry again; I think we worked off all the calories from breakfast."

"You shouldn't have teased my nipples like that." Kevin pulled her down and sucked her bottom lip.

A loud ring broke the mood and they searched for the intrusive sound's origin. "Oh! My cell phone." Melody blushed and jumped to answer it.

Kevin caught her wrists. "Just ignore it, Baby."

"But it'll be Imani and Lance wondering where we are."

"Yeah and they'll figure out that we're busy." He tried to make her reassume her previous position.

She resisted. "Well, at least let me tell them that we'll catch up later."

Kevin won the slight tug of war and got her lips within inches of his. Nice and slow, his lips rubbed across hers until her heart raced. The phone stopped ringing and she succumbed to his playful lips.

"Briii-rinngg," Kevin's dorm phone startled them both.

Melody moaned. "That's probably Imani and Lance. They know we're here."

"You've got to be freaking kidding!"

"I'm sorry. My friends are persistent. I can get it right quick," she said, but that last kiss cracked her resolve. All she wanted now were his lips enveloping hers.

Kevin must have sensed the change in her mood because he leaped on the opportunity to extend their incredible morning. Mere seconds later, they became consumed with passion, oblivious to Lance's message.

Hours later Melody realized the warmth and security she swooned in emanated from the duvet wrapped around her like a cottony cocoon. Light tapping alerted her to the fact that Kevin wasn't in bed but typing at his computer desk. She rolled and stretched languorous as a fat cat. "Hey Handsome, what time is it?"

The clicking ended and Kevin grinned. "About time you woke up, Sleepyhead. It's going on 8:00."

Melody bolted upright. "What? Eight at night? We never left the room all day or returned my friends' phone calls." She jumped up and started getting dressed. "We can still make the big concert if we leave now."

Kevin stood beside her calm and collected. "Why? We could have dinner delivered here."

"But I wanted to experience *some* of College Chill-Out. Plus, Imani and Lance must be worried wondering where we are. I mean, we did promise to meet them today."

"Yeah, well I don't really feel like it." Kevin halted her rushed movements by placing her arms by her sides and stroking them up and down. "I'd really like to finish off this perfect day like it started. Just the two of us, relishing in the essence of each other."

"Relishing in the essence, huh?" She slid her arms

up his shoulders and draped them around his neck. "I do like the sound of that. However, I don't know how much more I can take, if you catch my drift."

"I promise to be gentle…"

She pouted just a bit, bottom lip pooched out. "But I really want to go out, get some air, and catch the concert—"

"Hang out with Imani and Lance instead of me?"

Something about the way his body tensed beneath her arms or the sudden treble of his voice, made her refrain from pushing him further. She wanted to assure him that it wasn't a matter of them over him. Hell, she wanted all three of them together right now, but she refused to mar this wonderful day.

Giving him her most winning smile, she ran her fingers up the back of his neck. "Would you mind if I at least called Imani, so she doesn't worry?"

Kevin scrutinized her before releasing her arms, his heart-stopping smile returned. "That would be perfect, Baby." He kissed her cheek, "I knew you'd see it my way."

CONVERSATIONS AFTER THE CHILL-OUT

Imani felt she'd been run through a wringer she was so worn out from all of the partying. Crashing onto her bed, she splayed out in exhaustion and replayed the day's adventures. Lots of fantastic food from all the countries represented on campus, a few new friends made after the icebreaker games, and the concert and all-night party were outrageous. All in all, it equaled a lovely time.

Just one problem, no Melody. Sure the cow finally called after 8:00 but that was way too late and her excuses far too pathetic. Imani grunted, but she couldn't fault Melody for "wanting to spend quality time," as she put it, with her new man. Still, something bothered her though. Melody didn't sound quite right and Imani doubted it had anything to do with her getting some twice in one day.

The phone rang and she rolled over to answer it. "'Lo."

"Hey, Imani, Baby," rumbled Lance's deepest, most sultry voice over the line. "You alone or is Trevor keeping you company?"

Imani sucked her teeth before she responded. "I know your ignorant behind saw all of us go our separate ways after the concert."

Lance chuckled, happy to get a rise out of her.

"That could have been a ploy to keep up appearances." Lance bowled on without taking a breath to ensure she didn't interrupt him with a   caustic retort. "So, have you heard any more from our local lovebird?"

"Not since she called at eight with her sad excuses. Her Ho-ish ass ain't back yet either!"

"Now, now, you said you were happy for her. You're not suddenly growing jealous that she's finally getting some *and* spending less time with you?"

She rolled her eyes. "You're a complete ass, Lance. Have I told you that lately?"

He chuckled. "Not today at least. You're definitely slacking."

Imani laughed in spite of herself. "Yeah, yeah. Seriously though, I know this sounds suspect, but I don't get a cool vibe from Kevin."

"However you don't want to piss off your girl, so you haven't mentioned your freaky sixth sense. No need to fly off the handle until you have a concrete reason to, right?"

Imani squirmed. Sometimes Lance knew her a little too well, too. He wasn't always the sex-crazed, egotistical jock persona that he relished.

"Well?"

"I'm not sure if I'm reading the signals correctly." She stretched and sighed. "Maybe you're right. People have had the nerve to say that I'm a bit critical."

"Hmm, you think?"

Imani guffawed and then smirked. "See that's why I can't talk to you! You're a pain in the butt. I'll catch you later."

"And what a pleasant pain I am. Have a good

night," Lance rushed out his words so that he could disconnect before she retaliated.

"Good night, you ass," she muttered to the dial tone as her thoughts returned to Melody.

CHANGE IN PLANS - APRIL 2000

Melody could barely contain her happiness while she waited for Kevin to return to his room. She bounced on his bed, brimming with excitement to share the good news.

His keys jangled in the dorm room lock and she leapt up to greet him.

"Hey, Baby," she said bounding into his arms.

"Mm, hey yourself." He dropped his backpack and kicked the door closed while he encapsulated her in his strong arms and rewarded her with a warm kiss.

Melody turned to putty under his loving spell and she forced her feet to take two steps back to break his trance enough so that she could speak. Even with the space between them, she felt the air spark with electricity. It took a moment before she could catch her breath and compose her thoughts enough to utter coherent words.

Kevin waited with his expectant, amused eyes, blue and clear as the Caribbean. God, he was so adorable and cute…and sexy! Nothing would please her more than to just return back to his arms and let him have his way with her.

She shook her head to banish the thoughts, at least momentarily. "How was your day?" she asked trying to work her way up to a more serious conversation.

"Good, but it's even better now."

Oh God, she could feel her insides percolating and simmering from his loving gaze. She closed her eyes to concentrate on her words. Once she felt more in control she reopened them. "Well, my day's better, too."

"Really?" Kevin licked his gorgeous lips and Melody tried hard not to pant or gape.

With her insides liquefying more by the second, she decided to quit drawing out the suspense. "WNBC called me today. I got the television internship in New York City!" She squealed and bounced up and down in delight.

Kevin's jaw set in a concrete line and his beautiful, blue eyes hardened. Even his spiky, blond hair seemed to stiffen. "What?"

Melody's bounce deflated like air released from a balloon. Whoa, that wasn't the response she expected.

"Are you fucking kidding me? We already have everything settled! You're working for the local radio station right here. I'm interning nearby. We already worked with the Housing Department to stay in our dorm rooms for the summer. You were going to work normal business hours." He smacked the back of his right hand into the palm of his left hand so hard and loud that she jumped. "We made concrete, summertime plans and then like a fucking idiot you recklessly decide to disrupt everything?"

Oh God, she was an idiot! But it would be career suicide not to take this offer. Melody desperately wanted to hold Kevin and explain, but he literally steamed, so she wrung her hands in front of her. "I know we did and I'm so sorry, but this is like the Mecca of the media world. You know I'm a Communications major and my preference has always been television over radio. This is my dream job! I've always wanted to be the next Diane Sawyer or Barbara Walters."

She raised her hands to delay his protests. "Yes, the hours can be crazy, but think about the experience I'd receive and the contacts I could make. If I'm lucky, I could even meet Tom Brokaw or my idol, Katie Couric." Tears brimmed in her eyes, why did this have to be so difficult?

"I understand it's a great opportunity, Melody, that's not the freaking point," he said, poking her chest with his hard as iron index finger. "I'm angry that you made this radical decision without even consulting me!" He crossed his arms and glared at her with his steely blues. "If you do this, what else will you do without me? We're supposed to be a team," his voice softened and broke. "Hell, I thought you loved me."

Melody almost cried out in anguish at his statement. How could he believe that she didn't love him? Distraught, she ran to his arms, but he refused to hold her. "I do love you," she stammered. "This doesn't change that one bit." How could he not know that? Her heart ached to touch and hold him, but he wouldn't give one inch.

Not knowing what to do, she tried another tactic. "I thought you'd be happy for me."

"Are you stupid Melody? Why would I be happy when you're three hours away? I need you here beside me. I guess you lied when you promised me you'd never leave."

Her lip trembled as she attempted to hold back the watershed of tears. "I didn't lie, Kevin. I'm not leaving you. I would never leave you. This is just for the summer. It'll fly by in a split second before we even realize it."

Kevin's eyes darkened like storm clouds rolling over a mountain range. "Is that supposed to make me feel better?" He glared at her until her eyes dropped with shame and her cheeks burned. "I guess it's up to me to fix this?" He shoved her once until she looked back up at him as she struggled to regain her balance. His angry face loomed so close they were almost nose to nose. "That's what men do, right, Melody? They fix their woman's mistakes and solve their problems."

"I'm so sorry." God, how could she make him see this as a good thing instead of the breach of trust that he imagined. "You're right. I should have talked to you first."

"Damn it!" In a flash, Kevin spun around and slammed his fist into the wall inches beside her head. He let out a pained wail that had nothing to do with the impact.

Melody flinched, her eyes popped open wide. As Kevin dropped his arm, she saw his bloody knuckles and her eyes widened further then drooped as her heart broke. "Kevin!" She grabbed his hand and hurried him over to his bed. She pushed him down onto the bed then she retrieved a blue ice pack from his mini-fridge's freezer compartment.

When she looked up, he looked so contrite and broken that her heart shattered more. "I love you,

Kevin." She gently straightened out his hand and placed the ice pack on it. "Everything will be okay. You're right, we'll figure something out."

END OF THE YEAR WRAP - MAY 2000

Imani shifted right at the large, round, Union table to make room for Melody and Kevin as they sat down to her left with their trays of burgers and fries. The Union buzzed with more activity than she'd seen all year as students flitted about talking, studying, and saying good-byes. Maybe Kevin was saying good-bye, too, she chuckled under her breath. Intrigued by his appearance, she glanced at Kevin. Odd, he never joined them for lunch before.

"So where are you going this summer, Imani?" Big Tony asked between bites of pizza.

Imani looked at Big Tony and then pointed towards Trevor who sat to her right. "Same as Trev, we're both interning at Avon." She took a bite of her taco.

"As what, door-to-door saleswomen?" Big Tony almost choked on his pizza.

With her mouth full, Imani could only roll her eyes while Trev howled in disbelief.

Karen shook her head and wagged a finger at Big Tony. "Why do you insist on letting all of us see just how ignorant you are?"

"What?" Big Tony asked while Lance slapped him on the back in a sympathetic gesture.

"You know that cosmetics, lotions, and perfumes

require some kind of chemical formulations, right?" Trev asked while leaning his elbows on the table. "You don't just say, hmm, let me mix this strawberry essence I got from the guy on the streets in Harlem with some Vaseline and this red dye or better yet some red food coloring and call it lipstick."

"Now that would be a sight to see," Erycah said under her breath.

"Okay, fine, you're using your chemical engineering degrees and not going door-to-door. Are you heading back to NYC like this fellow?" Big Tony said elbowing Lance. "I don't know how he got on at Chase Manhattan."

"Don't hate me because my wonderful charm, handsome looks, and good grades open doors." Lance replied flexing his biceps.
"Oh, please! We don't know how he managed that either," Melody replied, sticking out her tongue at Lance. "Some of us have to work hard *and* without pay to get ahead."

"That's really not right how radio stations run you ragged yet refuse to pay you a dime. At least Albany boasts a low cost of living," Krystal said.

"Except she's not taking the job here," Kevin replied, his voice brimming with displeasure. "She decided to intern at a television station in NYC."

Imani felt her blood simmer at his audacity. "That's because the New York market ranks as one of the top in the world. Working at WNBC will open doors. Not meaning to bastardize Old Blue Eyes' quote, but if she makes it there, she can damn near write her ticket anywhere."

"Preach!" Lance said kicking his chair back to balance on its hind legs.

Imani threw him a dirty look while Trevor nodded and added, "Yep. That's why I love the Big Apple."

"Damn, you got on at WNBC?" John asked then whistled before he finished his hot dog.

"Yes, I did," Melody said with a huge, proud smile as she winked at Kevin. "Actually, Krystal, the costs won't be too much since I get to stay in Queens with my mom."

"And I'm not too far away in the Bronx," Kevin said as Melody wrapped him in a big hug.

Imani's eyes bulged. Now that was news to her. "I thought you were interning up here in Albany?"

"I changed my mind when Melody did. Decided I couldn't be that far away from my baby for an entire summer." Imani swore that Kevin sneered her way before he snuggled against Melody and returned her hug.

"Get a room!" Big Tony wrinkled his nose at their public display of affection.

"Speaking of rooms, Kevin," Imani continued not letting him off the hook. "Where are you staying in the Bronx because as we've said, living in the City's not cheap?"

Kevin gave her a steely, blue glare and she could tell that he wanted to snarl, 'it's none of your damn concern.' Instead his voice sounded surprisingly pleasant. "My friend, Ty's staying on campus to attend summer school. So he and his parents were nice enough to let me crash in his childhood room this summer for a small fee." Kevin snuggled against

Melody again. "I've been told that his home's not too far away from this pretty, little lady. Isn't that right, Baby?"

To Imani it sounded more like a threat than a question. Regardless, Melody lapped it up like a kitten at a bowl of warm milk.

"Yes, you can reach pretty much any destination in the City with a quick hop, skip, and a jump on the subways," Melody replied in seventh heaven.

"How convenient," Imani replied with a smirk, still not through with Kevin yet. "Although it sounds like you're losing money on the deal. If you're paying rent here on campus and there at Ty's, and if your last minute NYC internship pays less than your Albany internship—especially when you factor in the cost of living, well…"

Melody kicked her under the table and gave her a pleading "please, behave" look. All the while Imani felt Trev nervously drumming his left hand on her chair.

Kevin unhanded Melody and returned Imani's stare. "Both internships pay the same but thanks for your concern." Kevin flexed his hand and Imani wondered if he were subtly threatening her because she'd gladly give him a run for his money.

Lance studied Imani and Kevin and decided to defuse the tense stand-off. "So, Big Tony, sounds like you and Kevin's friend, Ty, are in the same boat."

Big Tony finished swallowing his mouthful of pizza, oblivious to the flickering friction. "Yep, some of us need a little more help than others with our classes. I'll miss my mom's cooking, but hey, you got to do what you go to do, right?"

"That's right," said John wiping his mouth with a napkin. "I figured out this year that I'll need to improve my skills if I plan on getting into the NFL, so I signed up for a football camp."

"I considered registering for the session that takes place right before we head back up here for training camp." Lance stroked his mustache and goatee. "But making money on Wall Street won out," Lance said dropping his chair on all fours.

John shook his head and Big Tony snorted out pizza to everyone's dismay.

"Summer camp sounds fun," Krystal said nudging John. "Erycah and I will be working at Proctor & Gamble in Ohio, not quite the same as summer camp."

John laughed. "Neither is football skills training camp but I might be able to sneak away from time to time and hook up with these guys for a little fun in NYC."

"We look forward to hanging out with you whenever," Melody replied with her patented smile.

Imani swore that Kevin scowled.

Going Home

"This isn't too bad, is it?" Kevin asked Melody as he offered her a peppermint candy.

Melody declined and nestled under his arm. "Not with you here," she said looking away from the Greyhound bus window as it rolled down the Albany highway towards New York City. She smiled up at Kevin's beautiful face. "But let's see what you think when we're at Port Authority trying to make our way to my home in Queens."

"Are you suggesting that you should have taken Lance up on his offer for a ride home?" Kevin's eye color swirled from aquamarine to sapphire as he adjusted his position to run his fingers through her hair although it felt like he inadvertently pulled it.

"Well, he cuts over to the 678 and passes my house on his way home to Cypress Hills in Brooklyn."

"Yes, but Ty's place is all the way over in the Bronx. He didn't offer to take me there."

"That's because you didn't ask." Melody readjusted her head so that his hand loosened its grip on her hair and she placed her hand on his chest. "He would have done it if he knew you needed a ride."

Kevin gave his head a slight shake. "No, I didn't want to be a bother and cause any hassle."

"Well, you could have asked Trevor. He lives in

the Bronx not too terribly far from Ty's. Plus, he was already taking Imani home since she lives just a few blocks away from him. They wouldn't have minded."

It almost felt like Kevin bristled, but when she looked up, he beamed down at her.

"No need to put him out like that. Plus, I wanted to spend some quality time with you." Kevin lifted her chin. "Remember, you and I can manage alone just fine without anyone else. There's nothing out there," he said gesturing at the world outside their window, "that can stand in our way."

Just hearing Kevin talk about the two of them conquering any obstacle together made her heart pitter-patter faster. She snuggled into Kevin more and he leaned down and kissed her lips so soft and tender. Nerve endings throughout her body awoke and simmered into a slow burn.

Kevin broke their tasty kiss just in time and Melody nestled against him wishing they could do more. Hmm, depending on when they arrived at her mommy's house…

Oh my God, you Harlot, she chided herself. Only once before had she dared to bring a guy home to meet her mommy and that was her high school sweetheart. Now she was considering sneaking Kevin inside to make love quickly before her mom returned home from work. She flushed with shame, her mommy raised her better!

"Question," Kevin said breaking free from Melody and breaking Melody free from her naughty thoughts. "What's up with Imani? Sometimes I get the feeling she doesn't like me very much, if at all."

"That's just Imani's way," she replied with a chuckle. "It normally takes her a minute to warm up to people as she's getting to know you. But you should feel honored."

"Really?" he asked, clearly skeptical.

"Yes, she trusts you enough to let you into her inner circle of friends and that's saying a lot. She generally keeps a wall up around people she doesn't know. A quick way you can tell if she likes you is by how she talks around you."

Kevin frowned, not understanding.

"See, if she doesn't know you, she sounds like a dictionary or like she just prepped for her SATs. It's similar to how she speaks in class and around people in authority. But when she's comfortable around you, she lets loose and talks like someone straight from the neighborhood."

"If anything that sounds sneaky to me."

Melody laughed. "I guess you could think of it that way, but she's not. Imani's smart as hell, extremely loyal, and very discerning."

Kevin pondered that a moment. "Well, what about Lance? What excuse do you have to explain his nasty behavior?"

Melody giggled again. "Well, unlike Imani and I, Lance didn't have two great role models for parents. His mom is a single parent who curses a lot and he mentioned once that his dad is mainly in rather than out of jail. So unfortunately he derived some of his behaviors towards women from that history. However, he didn't let his upbringing affect everything, he detests profanity. We usually censor our speech when we're around him."

"I guess that's something," Kevin said drawing Melody into his arms.

Feeling warm and loved, she nuzzled against his body and watched the landscape rush by for hours as Kevin nestled his nose in her hair.

"Are you sure you don't want me to carry anything else?" Melody asked as Kevin negotiated through the crowds of Port Authority carrying her large suitcase and rolling his carry-on bag behind him.

"No, I've got it," he said although he looked flustered. "You have your hands full with your duffle bag and purse." He adjusted her bag and powered on. "Although I'm definitely packing your suitcase for you next time. There's no reason you need a load of steamer trunks just for a summer at home."

"Hey, I'm a woman," she replied with an innocent smile. "I need my stuff."

"Trust me. You're beautiful without all this unnecessary crap."

"Ahhh, thanks." She glanced at him and blushed. When she looked up, she noticed they were finally close to the E train platform to Queens. "Hang in there, Baby. We're almost there and a train's coming."

Once they'd settled on the subway, bags securely located between their legs, Kevin threw his arm around her and she nestled in, inhaling his wondrous, spring clean scent. "How far is your home from the subway stop?" he asked, kissing her head.

Melody didn't want to talk. She just wanted to revel under Kevin's loving arms. "I'm three blocks away from the Jamaica/Van Wyck station."

Kevin glanced up at the MTA subway map and his eyes widened. "Isn't that almost the last stop on the line?"

"Yep, third from the end."

Kevin wiped his forehead and gave her an exasperated look. "We're nowhere near each other, Melody. Ty's place is all the way up in North Bronx. The Pelham Bay station is at the top of the number six train!"

Melody rubbed his worried brow until his gaze softened. "It's not that bad. We're in the same city; you could be three hours away in Albany." His eyes darkened so she kissed his cheek. "At least now we'll see each other after work since both of our jobs are located in midtown. Plus we can spend every weekend together. We'll be fine."

"Maybe you're right," he said sounding doubtful. "It's just that I worry when you're not with me. I need to know where you are and what you're doing to make sure you're safe." He gazed deep into her eyes, his fantastic blues swirling with concern. "But I guess we'll make it work. That's what we do." Satisfied, he drew her tight and stroked her hair.

Melody relished his hypnotic touch so much that she almost nodded off and missed her stop. Jumping up with a start, she motioned to Kevin. "We're here!"

As they made their way up to the street, she kept checking on Kevin to see how he fared in her predominantly African-American neighborhood. She and her mommy were used to the place and the neighbors were used to them. However, whenever she brought Caucasian friends home in the past, she couldn't help but notice their discomfort. Afterwards, in most cases, they wound up treating her differently, as if she was somehow less than. Melody frowned. Not that her African-American friends were much better either. Most times it felt as if they never quite trusted her or they couldn't get past the tanned white skin, blonde hair, and gray-green eyes.

Melody sighed and bit her lip. Why didn't she fit in neatly anywhere? She glanced at Kevin and couldn't help but smile. Kevin, Imani, and Lance loved her unconditionally despite her background.

Like a beacon of hope, memories of her mommy's strength and perseverance elicited a soul-stirring smile. If her Caucasian mother could raise a mixed child in this neighborhood after her African-American husband died unexpectedly, Melody could continue to find the positive in every situation.

In fact, she always felt motivated to help others overcome their obstacles and find the silver lining in their perceived, dark clouds. And since Kevin, Imani, and Lance loved her unconditionally, she felt an obligation to help them uncover their true happiness. Melody checked on Kevin again and smiled.

Just as he assured her before, he didn't seem fazed in the least, well at least not with his surroundings. However, Kevin was doing his valiant best to maneuver their suitcases over the curbs and sidewalks.

A few passerbys gave them funny looks, but for the most part people ignored them in typical New York fashion. A couple of people that she recognized from over the years nodded or said, "Hi," as they rushed past.

When they reached her block, Mrs. Strickland, the neighbor lady from Atlanta, spied her and barreled over for a hug. "Ooo, Little Melody Sunshine," she said afterwards as she extended her arms to get a better look. "Your momma said you were coming home today. She's just so excited to have you back. And you look right lovely as ever." She released Melody and fixed her curious eyes on Kevin and waited for an introduction.

Kevin wore his most charming smile and Melody almost melted although she wasn't even the focus of his beautiful gaze. "Hi, I'm Kevin, Ma'am," he said extending his hand.

"Kevin, this is our adorable neighbor, Mrs. Strickland," Melody managed to introduce them in her dazed state.

Mrs. Strickland seemed just as dazzled as she shook Kevin's hand. "Pleased to meet you, Kevin." Mrs. Strickland winked at Melody. "Guess I'll let you two get settled in the house."

Kevin chuckled. "No, I'm just making sure Melody gets home safe, and then I'll be on my way. It was nice to meet you, Ma'am."

Melody almost gasped in dismay, but she kept her grin in place until after they waved good-bye to Mrs. Strickland. Once they were out of earshot and going up the steps of her mother's well-maintained, semi-detached row-home, she let her sorrow show. "I thought you'd stay for a while," she said as she unlocked the door. "My mommy should return home from work in another thirty minutes."

Kevin dropped her bags inside the door. "Oh, Baby, I'd love to." He pulled her into his arms and buried his head in her hair. She sensed him inhale her floral shampoo before he stroked her hair so soft and sweet.

Mm, she desperately wanted to take Kevin upstairs to her bedroom and let him stroke other parts of her body, too.

Kevin kissed the top of her head then he held her at arm's length. "I need to find Ty's house well before it gets dark. Plus, his parents were pretty adamant about what time I arrive. So, I have to leave now as this is cutting it pretty close."

"What if I call you a taxi?" she asked trying to figure out a way to refrain him longer.

"No, too much money and I'm pretty sure it would take even longer than the subway when you factor in traffic."

Melody pursed her lips into a pout as she stroked his arms. "Please, Kevin."

Kevin chuckled at her sad attempt to coerce him to stay. But he at least softened the blow by kissing her lips long enough for her to forget about everything else in the world. "I'll see you tomorrow."

Melody's breath was so far gone she could only nod in resignation.

FIRST WEEK OF WORK

Imani waited for Trev to leave Avon's headquarters so that they could catch the train home.

Trev exited the building and his face lit up as soon as he spotted her waving. "Thanks for waiting."

"Of course," Imani replied scrunching up her nose. "Why would I leave my ride to work for the rest of the summer? You know it's kind of a hike up to Suffern, NY."

"Oh, so you're being nice to me this week while we're training in the City? So that you can use me as a shuttle service to and from Suffern for the rest of the summer?" Trev asked as they walked to the subway station.

"Yep, it was my master plan from day one at school." Imani tried to keep a straight face but failed miserably.

"So you planned that we would meet after orientation, matriculate with the same major, decide to become labbies, and get almost identical internships? Not to mention that you demanded our parents live three blocks away from each other so that we could carpool?" Trev's goofy grin couldn't get any toothier or more incredulous if he tried.

"Exactly! And I have to say that I love it when a plan falls into place like clockwork."

Trev shook his head and laughed as they descended the subway stairs at 51st and Lexington. "You really need prayer, Imani."

Imani chuckled. "So, I've been told."

They swiped their metro cards and ran down the stairs to catch the 6 train. They rode it one station and switched to the 4 at 59th. Once they found seats on board, Imani grabbed her latest Stephen King paperback, but Trevor decided to continue their conversation.

"So, in all seriousness, now that we're almost done at Headquarters, how did you plan to get to our jobs up in Suffern?"

Imani set her book on her lap and sighed inwardly. Maybe she should have left Trev, so that she could enjoy her book and Walkman in peace for the next forty minutes on board the train. "Well, I've been saving up for a car for the past two years. My folks just didn't want me to get one until after I completed freshmen year. As if that was ever in doubt. Anyhow, I would have bought one this summer, probably at the police auction this weekend."

Trev nodded.

Imani rolled her eyes at his lack of response. "Anything else, Nosy?"

"Yes," he replied crossing his arms to get more comfortable. "What part of the job do you think you'll like the best?"

Imani suppressed a snort. "Well, seeing as it's only been a week and we were in orientation training, I can't really say for sure."

Trev elbowed her in the side. "Stop being a smart

ass and answer the question."

"Excuse you?" Imani leaned back getting ready to put her ghetto attitude on. Where did the shy, little Trev she know disappear to because this fool beside her was about to get a beat down.

"Look, since I don't feel like reading now and since I'm driving your behind to and from work for the next two and a half months, the least you can do is make some simple conversation with me today. Don't you think?"

Imani glared at Trev half in disbelief and half with respect as he had the audacity to sit back and stare at her like he hadn't just lost his ever-loving mind.

"Please?" he asked with his infectious, toothy grin.

"Only because you asked so nice," she replied with an indignant huff. "Wait, what was the question again?" she asked and they both cracked up.

"Fine, I'll go first," Trev said. "I'm hoping that we get to do some real product testing. You know I'm in the Fragrances group. It sounds like they cover everything from perfumes and colognes to candles. Which group are you working with?"

"The Eye Color group working in Product Development. I can't wait to work in the lab mixing compounds and analyzing formulations." Imani rubbed her hands together like a kid let loose in a candy store and her pace quickened just thinking about the opportunity.

"Now, that's the cool, happy Imani I love to see," Trev said as he leaned in close. Although his smile remained playful, she could see his eyes flickered with a serious intensity. And she definitely caught his slip of the "L" word even if he didn't directly say, "I love you."

The air between them sparked with electricity until Trev short-circuited it by flicking her nose. Frowning, she swatted his hand away.

Trevor laughed and his eyes twinkled with mischievous glee.

Imani crossed her arms and gave him the evil eye and Trev laughed even more.

"Hey," he said trying to straighten up. "Since we'll be spending so much time together, tell me this. What are you looking for in a guy?"

Imani's eyebrow leapt sky high. "Seriously? You're going to ask me something like that right here on the subway?"

Trev's voice dropped a notch as he became more serious. "Would you prefer I ask you when we're all alone in private?"

The thought of them alone flirting with this conversation changed Imani's mind in a jiffy. "No, well, I guess not. Safety in numbers, right?" she joked trying to play off her nervousness as nothing.

Trev's eyes still twinkled with a mischievous light, but Imani couldn't tell what he was thinking. "So what are you looking for in a guy, Imani?" Trevor leaned in closer so that their conversation remained as private as it could on a rush-hour packed subway train full of folks.

Imani swallowed a nervous gulp and then figured hell, why not play along. "Well, first off he has to be intelligent."

"Okay," Trevor replied real slow as if he were

checking that box off the list.

"Look, he needs to be able to debate intelligibly or hold a real conversation. Can't have any numbnuts dragging down the world population's IQ pool."

Trev shook his head. "You are too nuts. Hopefully, you don't consider me a drain on the world's IQ pool."

"No, quite the opposite," she replied before she caught herself. No use letting Trev think he had an in where no entry existed. "Anyhow, next on my list is humor. The brother needs to be funny because I'm serious enough for two people."

"I'd say at least three," he joked.

"See, I know you think you're funny but…"

"Please," Trev replied. "You're still sore because I kicked your butt playing the dozens. You know I slam down witty insults faster than lightening." He motioned like he was brushing off his shoulder. "I told you, you didn't want to play in the big leagues with me."

Imani shoved his shoulder. "Boy, whatever," she said unable to hide her grin. "Anyhow, last but definitely not least, the boy's gotta be cute." She held up her hand to stop his protests before they even began. It wasn't like she was totally going to nix Trev's chances because he didn't fit her mold of typical handsomeness. He was 6' 2", tall like she preferred but skinny as a beanpole whereas she agreed with Diana Ross when she sang, "I want muscles!" And just like his body, Trev's face was just a bit too long and slender for her liking.

Hell, she wasn't all that either. Although a lot of people told her how pretty she was, Imani knew in reality that when your skin color was the rich, walnut-color hers was, a lot of people lost interest real fast. Plus when you added in her love of short, ethnic hairstyles like twists, knots, braids, and baby dreads, well that was the straw that broke the camel's back. "I know that sounds shallow," she explained, "but sue me, I'm human after all. And yes, I do appreciate a little nice eye candy or at least a slamming body."

"Well, you know the ladies do like the tall, dark, handsome type," Trev said stroking his chin and preening like Lance.

"Oh good Lord you need to stop," Imani said busting out laughing. "Okay, I might give you the humor nod because your ass is hilarious as hell right now."

Trev laughed and held up his hands in surrender. "Fine, I'll leave you alone for now." He glanced out the window as they pulled into the next station to check where they were. Satisfied, he leaned back in his seat. "Anyhow, I'm really looking forward to working in the 'real world' this summer. It should be lots of fun."

"Me, too. Hopefully, it's not like the internship horror stories we've heard from some of the upper classmen who spent their summers delivering mail, making copies, and getting coffee." Imani shuddered at the thought.

"No, Avon doesn't seem like the kind of place that does that." Trev shrugged. "Now poor Melody on the other hand… The media and entertainment industries are renowned for making you work your way up from the proverbial mailroom."

Imani shook her head. "Yep, those places are

brutal. I hope she fares better than that. Which reminds me, I gotta call her and Lance. See what time we're hooking up for the party Saturday. Lance mentioned something about possibly meeting up at his house beforehand."

"Oh, we get to meet the infamous Mrs. Dunn. That definitely sounds like fun!"

First Date

"This is going to be so much fun," Melody cooed as she dissolved into Kevin's warm embrace. "I can't believe it's our first New York City date!"

"Looks like someone had a fun Friday at work," Kevin said before he gave her a long, lingering kiss as if they weren't standing in the middle of a crowded, bustling 30 Rockefeller Plaza. When he finally pulled back, leaving her giddy and breathless, he glanced around the area. "So this is the famous 30 Rock?"

Melody managed to nod and summon her legs to shuffle forward to give him an impromptu tour. "This building is the NBC Studios where they tape the news, Saturday Night Live, and various other shows. I could get you a tour whenever you like."

"That sounds nice," he said as he wrapped his arm around her waist.

Melody beamed and pointed across the street. "And that's where they tape the Today Show each morning."

"You run into Matt Lauer or Al Roker yet?"

"Not yet but I did see Al walk into the building one morning." Walking arm and arm, she directed them to the lush greenery that erupted like an oasis in the middle of the concrete jungle. "Now these are the Channel Gardens," she said as they meandered through the trees and flowers at a leisurely pace enjoying each blossom and bloom.

"And finally the pièce de résistance," she said gesturing to the golden statute and sunken plaza area. "This is where you'll find the Christmas tree and ice skating rink in the winter."

"Looks almost as captivating as you." Kevin pulled and twisted her into his arms until her back snuggled against his chest. "Maybe we'll make a trip back during Christmas break and go skating?"

"That sounds perfectly dreamy," she said basking in his cocoon of love.

Kevin nestled his nose in her hair. "Do you know how beautiful and sweet you smell? Like the world's most exotic and delicate flower."

Melody's heart skipped two beats. Seriously, did Kevin step straight from the pages of her Harlequin romance novels? Every word from this gorgeous Adonis sounded more melodic than the works of the great British Romantic poets like Keats, Shelley, and Lord Byron. Each touch electrifying, all actions tailored for her consideration.

"You know I keep thanking my lucky stars that you bumped into me." Kevin kissed the top of her head and turned her around in his arms until she faced him. "I've never been this happy in my life. And I always want to make you as happy as you make me."

"I don't think anyone could be happier than me." Melody blushed as she glanced at him through her eyelashes.

"That's debatable." Kevin paused and gave her a thoughtful look. "This may sound strange but...how would you feel about us having a special song?"

"Are you serious?" Melody's eyes almost popped out of her head. "That would be perfect."

"You really think so?" he asked as he gave her a skeptical look.

"Of course!" She bounced twice in glee. "Do you have a particular song in mind?"

"Actually, I do." Kevin frowned. "But it may be a little corny."

"Try me," she replied trying to contain her excitement.

"Well, this sounds strange and it's probably a turn-off, but Ty's parents like to dance to the oldies station after dinner. Normally I jet out of there as fast as possible, but yesterday I sat and watched them."

Melody nodded and smiled.

"A song came on the radio that stopped me in my tracks." Kevin paused and his beautiful blue eyes turned skeptical again. "Have you heard of the Bee Gees?"

Melody grinned so hard it felt like she sprained a cheek muscle. "Of course, they're one of my mom's favorite groups. I love them!"

Kevin looked dumbfounded but he continued. "Well, the song that came on reminded me of us. They were singing all the things I'd love to say. The song was called, "How Deep is Your Love." Have you heard of it?"

"Of course, I have," she replied before commenced singing it to him.

Kevin's lust-filled eyes watched her spellbound.

Feeling invigorated by his stare, she threw her head back and fixed him with her most sultry gaze, all the while singing low and private just for him. "We're living in a world of fools, breaking us down, when they all should let us be…"

When she finished, Kevin's hungry eyes looked like he could devour her at any second. He licked his lips. "Looks like we have a winner." His voice sounded deep and hoarse. "We should probably get going," he said sounding reluctant to break the spell swirling around them.

"That's probably best," she replied, surprised at how husky her voice sounded as well.

With them agreed on a course of action, Kevin steered her into a chic, Spanish café where they enjoyed boatloads of tapas and sangria. After dinner, he guided them to the movie theaters where they watched the 7:00 pm showing of *Gladiator* with Russell Crowe.

After the movie ended, they exited the cinema arm in arm.

"Despite whether you liked the ending or not, you know that movie's going to become an instant classic," Melody said squeezing his arm.

"Well if it were up to me, the movie would have been fifteen minutes long because I would have made it back home to you and our son in time." Kevin stopped in the middle of the sidewalk and held her face in between his strong, warm hands. "I'd never let anything happen to you." The beautiful blue currents he called eyes, swept her along on the waves of love and her legs felt unseaworthy as his lips captured hers and carried them along through surges and swells of emotions.

After what felt like an eternity, Kevin broke off their kiss and Melody wobbled beside him, safely anchored by his arm, as they made for the subway. Unable to speak, she sat beside him in silence with her head resting on his shoulder as he stroked her hair. To her dismay, the train ride back to Queens flew past in an instant.

Ever the gentleman, Kevin escorted Melody to her doorstep. She raced up the steps eager to invite him in to meet her mommy and maybe for a small nightcap. However when she unlocked the door, Kevin stood on the sidewalk checking his watch.

"Is everything okay?"

"Actually, I have to run," he replied looking quite cute and apologetic.

Melody couldn't help but pout. Where else did he need to be besides here? "But I thought you were coming in for a second. At least stay long enough to meet my mommy."

"I wish I could, Baby. But I need to get back to Ty's house." He bounded up the steps two at a time and planted a chaste kiss on her wanting lips. "I'll have to take a raincheck. Love you."

"I love you, too," she replied to his retreating back as he took off in a sprint for the subway. Crestfallen, she entered her house after Kevin disappeared from sight.

Melody hadn't realized that she'd dozed until she almost fell out of bed when her cell phone rang. Fumbling around on her nightstand for it like a blind man, her hand finally connected with the phone and she hit answer after seeing Kevin's number on the Caller ID.

"It's late, I was getting worried about you," Melody whispered into the phone, the sleepiness in her voice still lingering.

"Instead of worrying about me, you need to worry about Ty's crazy-ass parents!" Kevin's flat, strained tone jolted Melody completely awake.

"What's wrong?" she asked sitting upright on her bed.

"Everything," he hissed, making her want to hold and console him. "I never told you this because I thought they were kidding, but they're freaking serious."

"What?" she asked, her frantic heart fluttering in her throat.

"They have me on a strict curfew!"

"Curfew?" Melody wasn't sure she heard him correctly.

"Exactly! Although I can supposedly stay out as late as I want to on Fridays and Saturdays, they expect me to be home by 10:00 pm Sunday through Thursday nights. I'm not some fucking, little kid! They're acting crazy!"

Melody frowned as she tried to understand. "Did they give you a reason why?"

"Yes, and this shit takes the cake. They feel that because they were too lenient with Ty's stupid ass growing up, they need to throw down the law with me now, so I won't follow in his dumb ass's footsteps. They need to talk to him and leave me the hell alone. I'm not the one having to attend summer school because I jacked off all semester!"

Melody stifled a giggle; Kevin wouldn't appreciate hearing her laugh even if his description of Ty was too spot on and funny. "Well, did you try to explain that to them...maybe using less inflammatory word choices?"

"There's no reasoning with these stupid people! Their final decision was that I'm either here well before they go to bed at 10:30 or I find a new place to live. Damn it, Melody! I didn't sacrifice everything for us to be together just to have these two imbeciles try to tear us apart this summer."

Melody's hands flew to her lips. If they weren't together this summer, her world would fall apart. This week alone had been more magical than in her wildest dreams. And there was no way that Kevin could afford to stay in the city if he had to pay a "real" rent.

"So what did you say?" she asked afraid to hear his answer.

"Not what I wanted to, that's for damn sure." Kevin sighed and Melody ached to hold him. "There's nothing else I could do except agree to their idiotic terms for now."

Melody exhaled with relief. "Good, we can work with that." Her mind scrambled to find options that would work best for everyone.

"Are you fucking crazy, Melody? How the hell do you figure we can work with that?"

"I know you think this is an impossible situation, but it's okay. I have a plan," she cooed trying to calm him down. "See, let's just think about this. If you would have gone straight to Ty's instead of accompanying me home like the gentleman that you are, you would have easily made their curfew. Therefore it proves that we can still go out after work, at least when I'm working the afternoon or morning broadcasts. But now instead of you escorting me all the way out to Queens, we'll both go straight home. You're in before curfew, my Mom's happy that I'm not staying out too late, and we all get a good night's sleep each night so that we're ready for work, especially when I'm working mornings. This is a win-win-win."

"Plus, remember our new song," she said trying to show him how there were never any coincidences. "A major part of the chorus is, 'Living in a world of fools—'"

"Well they're trying to do a lot worse than break us down and I know what I'd like to tell them to do," he replied still sounding pissed and indignant.

"I know, but it'll be okay. Things will work out fine," she said with complete confidence.

"Wow, you're an incredible piece of work," he said sounding either shocked or surprised, Melody couldn't tell which. "But I still don't agree with letting you go home at night on your own."

"I know," she replied with pride. "That's because you're the perfect gentleman." Melody couldn't wipe the grin of love off her face. "But I swear it's okay. Remember, I grew up in this neighborhood. Everyone here looks out for my mommy and me," she explained trying to short-circuit his reservations.

Kevin took a moment to respond. "Well," he replied, finally sounding a little more appeased. "I don't like it because I'm not with you. You know I only want to protect you and keep you safe."

"I know," she replied wishing again that she could just hold and soothe him. Melody swore she could hear Kevin debate it in his head one last time before he finally sighed and relented.

"I swear, somehow you can make catching pneumonia sound like a good thing, Melody."

"Thanks, I think," she replied with a shy grin.

"I meant it as a compliment. Although I'm not going to lie, I truly don't understand how you can find the positive in every situation. I'd go crazy trying to remain so damn optimistic. But you do. I guess that's just one of the multitude of things I love about you."

Melody hugged her knees and rocked on her bed sporting a grin so big that her cheeks felt like they were about to crack open.

"However, I want you to know that I'm not settling for their verdict yet," Kevin said breaking her triumphant celebration. "This weekend I'm going to help them out with some odd jobs around the house and yard in an attempt to get them to change their minds."

"All weekend long?" she asked as her heart sank at the thought of not seeing him for such an extended period of time.

"Yes, I know it's not what we planned, but I hope it's okay," he replied, his voice sounded so soothing. "If this works, we can go out any time for however long we want."

Melody started to protest, but then she remembered they were supposed to meet Imani, Lance, and Trevor

Saturday. Problem was Imani and Kevin didn't always see eye to eye. And frankly, Melody didn't feel like acting as a mediator this weekend to ensure the two behaved and peace prevailed.

Hmm, maybe this was a blessing in disguise. Kevin could work on loosening up Ty's parents so that they could hang out whenever without worry. Meanwhile she could hang out with Imani and Lance like they used to before Kevin entered her wonderful world.

Loving her decision, she pasted on a cheery smile. "You know I'll miss you, but hopefully this will work to our advantage in the future."

Thankfully, Kevin didn't ask what she planned on doing. Knowing how overprotective he was, Melody knew he wouldn't appreciate her hanging out at a party without him and he'd tell her to stay home. However, the more she thought about going out with Trevor, Lance, and Imani Saturday, the more excited she became. For whatever reason, she couldn't wait to just let loose and dance.

Kevin sighed. "I wish we were back at school where I could control the situation."

And just like that, Melody melted inside. "I know, Baby," she replied wanting to snuggle against Kevin's chest. "But this will work out fine. I promise. Despite everything, we'll have a wonderful summer regardless."

"You know I love you." Melody could hear Kevin smile. "… and I love spending time with you, my beautiful Melody."

Melody's heart performed a joyous, perfect ten, gymnastic routine. "I love you, too, Kevin. Don't worry. We have all the time in the world."

Meeting Ms. Dunn

As quiet as a church mouse, Lance unlocked his mother's front door, snuck inside, and locked the door behind him. The smell of jasmine incense assaulted his nose.

"Bout time your ass came home from a long night of partyin'," his mother, Oleta Dunn, said clicking on the living room light.

Lance sighed and pocketed his keys. "You didn't have to wait up. I told you I'd be home before 1:00 am and here I am as promised."

"Don't get fucking smart with me as long as you're livin' under my roof." She crossed her arms and stomped over to her recliner. "Even if it is just for the summer."

"I'm sorry, Mother," he replied as contrite as he could muster with his blood starting to simmer. Thank God, it was only for the summer! Not that he could ever forget but now he recalled vividly why he couldn't wait to escape for college in the first place.

His mother seemed satisfied with his apology and she grunted. "Those were two fine, little girls you brought by earlier tonight." Her tone and expression suggested more. "I'd love to have one of them as my daughter-in-law someday."

"Eww, gross, Mother!' Lance rubbed his hands

over his head. This was not a conversation he ever wanted to engage in with his mother. "Imani and Melody are friends and only friends and that's how we plan to keep it." He frowned. "Plus, you're always telling me to watch out for gold-digging women, I thought you didn't want me to settle down."

"Of course, I want you to settle down and get married. But as you just pointed out they're good girls, friends, not dumb-ass, gold-digging bitches." She kicked open her recliner ottoman and used the remote to turn on the television. "I swear sometimes you're not that bright."

Lance felt his jaw clench and his nostrils flare. "Good night, Mother." He headed towards his bedroom, determined not to have a fight.

"Shit, don't get your panties all bunched in a bind, Boy. I'm just saying I wouldn't mind if you brought those Melody and Imani girls over here more often," she yelled at his retreating back. "You might want to make it fucking soon, too, because that Trevor boy's already sniffing around Imani like a dog in heat. I don't know why you'd bring the competition home, too."

Lance made sure not slam his bedroom door behind him as he escaped her ridiculous tirade. He figured the chances were zero to nil that he would ever subjugate the girls or Trevor to his crazy mother ever again in life.

SERIOUS CONVERSATION - JUNE 2000

"Coming," Imani yelled as she peered through the peephole of her parents' front door. Trev's long face appeared even more drawn and narrow through the peephole's distortion. She chuckled as she unlocked the door wanting to ask him, 'why the long face?' Instead she settled for, "what's up, Trev? You're early. We weren't planning on leaving to meet Lance and Melody at the movies for another hour."

He managed to look embarrassed as he shifted from foot to foot. "Sorry, I can come back later if you like."

Imani grabbed his arm and pulled him inside. "Of course not, Silly. I was just joking around with you."

A sheepish grin preceded, his full-on, toothy smile. "I know I just wanted you to invite me inside. You even went one step further and manhandled me, too. I think I liked it."

She faux punched his forearm. "I'll manhandle you alright, I can kick your butt right back out on the front porch. How would you like that?"

He held up his hands in surrender. "No need for threats." Then he stood up straight with a slightly cocky air. "Although I could take you. But you wouldn't dare."

Imani stopped and studied him, her arms crossed tight over her chest. "Oh, you think you know me now?" she asked a little gruffer than she meant for it to sound.

Like a popped balloon, Trevor deflated before her eyes and he shrugged. "Maybe not."

Feeling like a heel, Imani dropped her arms and tough girl act and squeezed Trev's arm. "Geez, I was just kidding."

Trev watched her carefully as if she'd told him to sleep with one eye open.

Imani softened her tone even more. "Look, I'm sorry, I know I can come off a little too intense sometimes. The fact of the matter is that I actually appreciate it when you call me on my shit. This new, more confident Trevor is pretty cool."

Trev's eyes burrowed into hers as he pondered her off-handed compliment. "Really?"

Imani rolled her eyes. "I suppose so, but don't let it go to your head."

Trevor smiled but didn't say a word although she could sense a little bit of his cockiness returning.

"Anyhow, the last thing I want is for you to ever feel uncomfortable around me. Okay?"

"Okay," he replied, back to normal or at least his new normal.

"Good," she tapped his arm and danced around trying to ensure the mood remained light and carefree. "So now that you know I trust you. You want to test our friendship out? I'll give you one free pass. You can joke around or tell me anything."

"Anything, hmm?" His eyes took on a mischievous glint.

"Yeah, anything," she replied with the same look,

up for a challenge.

"Well, in that case..." He crossed his arms and became deadly serious. "I didn't know how to tell you this, but I want to get another lab and study partner next semester. You're too high maintenance."

Imani's jaw dropped for a second before she regained her composure. Her feelings were hurt, but she'd never let him know. "Are you serious?" Her mind spun trying to figure out how to find another excellent, Black, engineering study partner as good as Trev.

Slow as molasses on a cold day, his toothy grin reemerged. "Of course not! How else am I going to keep up my 3.8 GPA?"

She punched him in the arm, harder this time. "You are so not funny, but I know your game now."

Trev burst out laughing while he rubbed his arm.

"Just for that, I should leave your ass stranded next semester. See what your GPA looks like then!" She laughed and turned to head back to her bedroom. "Hey, since you arrived early and interrupted my groove with all of your nonsense, do you mind if I finish up what I was doing?"

Trev looked uncertain. "Sure, do you want me to chill out here?" he asked pointing towards the living room couch.

"No, silly. I'm just burning some music to CD's. I'm almost done." She recommenced walking to her bedroom and Trev followed. "Now that I know you really do have an evil sense of humor, I'm going to have to watch you. In the meantime, I think we'll need to schedule round two of our dozens matchup."

Trev laughed. "Do you think you can hang? You've already experienced how raw I can get. I don't want to have to send you home crying."

Imani entered her bedroom and pointed for him to sit on her bed. "Oh, no, Buddy, you're the one who's going to be crying, begging me to stop." As Trev sat down, Imani went over to her computer and pulled up her desk chair.

"Good, maybe in between jokes we can console each other this summer." His voice took on a melancholy quality.

Imani pretended not to notice Trev's sudden change in demeanor. She still wasn't sure how to keep their growing flirtations rooted firmly on the side of friendship. Playing it off, she inserted the last CD into her computer and pulled up the correct playlist.

"Can I really talk to you about something serious?" Trev asked sounding earnest.

Imani tensed, *please don't ask me to be your girlfriend.* Cautious, her eyebrow arched as she hit record and burn. The CD drawer whirred to life and her answer came out more as a soft, drawl. "Sure, what is it?"

"I want you to know that you're the first person I'm sharing this news with. I haven't even told my mother yet."

Whoa! Okay, that definitely sounded more serious than what she expected. She caught herself exhaling quietly with relief before she refocused her attention on Trevor. She swiveled her desk chair around to face him and she kept her voice soft and concerned. "I'm listening."

"My dad called me today for the first time since I was ten."

Ten? Shit, that was damn near half his life! Imani leaned back in shock. Both her eyebrows rose to full tilt. "Wow, what did he want?"

"For me to come visit him in Jamaica. Finally get to know him."

Imani leaned forward in her desk chair. "And how do you feel about that?"

"Mom's raised me as a single parent since they divorced when I was seven. She never bad mouthed him, but she didn't really mention him either." Trevor bit his lip and shook his head. "I don't know what to think. And what's worse is I don't know how to tell my mom either."

"Well, the truth never hurts," Imani said then her tone softened. "Do you want to visit him? Think of it like this, at least it's a free trip to Jamaica. Hell, I always wanted to vacation there. The tropical climate, slamming food, crazy people, and reggae music."

"Yeah, that parts sounds fun," Trev replied with a laugh before he became serious again. "I think I'd like to know more about him, see what he's like. Figure out why he hasn't been around all this time."

Like a tornado, Imani's mom burst through Imani's bedroom door. The mocha-colored whirlwind in a navy blue suit and heels screeched to a halt by Imani. She opened her mouth to speak and then she noticed Trevor sitting on her daughter's bed and her mouth snapped shut.

Not until that instant did Imani realize how the situation appeared. She leapt up immediately, feelings of nervousness and guilt flushing her face. What was she thinking when she told Trevor to come up to her bedroom? This wasn't college; this was her parents' house, and they didn't play that. "It's not what you think, Mom."

"Oh, I know it better not be what I think." Her mom didn't look amused as her hand flew up to smooth a few stray hairs back into her bun.

Trev looked flustered. "I'm so sorry, Ma'am." He jumped up to shake her hand. "I'm Trevor Mathis, and yes my mother raised me better than to go up to a girl's bedroom without consent from her parents."

Mom cocked an eyebrow. "Where are you from, son?"

Trev smiled his natural toothy grin. "I live three blocks away. Please don't tell me you're going to report me to my mother?" he asked only half joking.

Mom frowned for a second and Imani swore she actually considered the option. "Did you say, Mathis?"

Oh, crap! Imani tensed and held her breath. This couldn't be good.

Trevor looked concerned, too, and he swallowed hard. "Yes, Ma'am," he replied sounding unsure.

"As in Sadie's son?"

Now Trev looked truly worried. "Yes, do you know her?"

Mom cracked a big smile. "Sadie and I work together at Bronx Science. She's the nurse and I'm the vice-principal." She watched Trev's jaw drop. "Yeah, you're right; your mom would kick your behind if she knew you were up here in my daughter's room unsupervised. I'm surprised Imani didn't say anything as it's her alma mater."

Imani blanched, she never put two and two together. Especially since Trev always bragged about attending Fordham. She knew he lived in the Bronx, but it wasn't until the day before he drove them home from school did they even realize that he lived practically right around the corner. Regardless, she would have never associated him with her school nurse. Especially since Trev looked nothing like his mom!

"Lucky for you, I know you're a good kid." Mom clapped Trevor's back. "What a small world. I guess Sadie and I never shared which colleges our kids were attending. Hmm, well let's get you back downstairs before I have to tattle on you."

"Yes, ma'am," Trev replied in relief.

Imani exhaled a sigh of relief, too. That was too close. The last thing she wanted was for her mother to go ballistic or think that Trevor was anything more than a friend.

BEST DATE EVER

The warm, June breeze lifted Melody's curls, ruffled the hem of her yellow, cotton sundress, and tickled her face as she entered Central Park. Even this early on a Saturday morning, the park bubbled with activity. Joggers puffing past to the music from their Walkmans, bicyclists whizzing along the path, mothers pushing baby strollers to the playground, dogs dragging their owners along.

Melody rounded the bend and spotted Kevin waiting in line at the Delacorte Theater. When he spied her, his beautiful smile lit up the morning even brighter as he waved her over.

Unable to resist his enchanting summons, Melody skipped over and bounded into his welcoming embrace.

"Hello, Beautiful," he said, his silky voice sending shivers down her spine. "You smell as divine as a bouquet of roses." Before she could reply his luscious lips locked with hers. As their tongues intertwined, he slipped the small remnant of a peppermint candy into her mouth. Melody crinkled her brows and nose in surprise. Odd, but kind of nice, she thought as Kevin broke off their kiss. She bit the candy, chewed the tiny fragments, and swallowed it.

Mentioning nothing about the candy exchange,

Kevin waved his hand towards the box office. "I wanted to surprise you by getting free tickets to Shakespeare in the Park. Tonight's performance is *The Winter's Tale*."

Melody clapped her hands together and jumped up and down. "I always wanted to do this, but we were never able to get tickets."

"That's why I asked you to join me here this morning. We have to camp out in line until this afternoon." He glanced down at the blanket and picnic basket by his feet. "I hope you don't mind waiting?"

"Are you kidding me?" Melody grabbed the blanket and spread it out behind the other people waiting in line. "Of course I don't mind spending time with you on a picnic in Central Park." She smiled as she sat down and patted the space beside her for Kevin to join her.

Due to their 7:30 a.m. arrival, they had a great place in line, about fifteen people back. Prepared and romantic as ever, Kevin opened the picnic basket filled with orange juice, breakfast pastries, fruits, water, and snacks. The morning and afternoon hours flew by as they feasted and fed each other stretched out on the blanket and from time-to-time joked around with the other patrons as the burgeoning line took on a party-like atmosphere.

After they got their tickets, Kevin packed the blanket in the picnic basket and they strolled around the park. They started at Belvedere Castle with its stunning views of the park, meandered across some of the bridges and across the lake to rent a gondola.

Feeling warm and thirsty after the boat ride, Kevin

read her mind and they walked hand in hand to the Bethesda Terrace and Fountain. They hung out on the blanket eating hot dogs and guzzling lemonade while they watched the tourists frolic.

Ready to reconvene the adventure, Kevin took her to the world-renown carousel. When their turn came to ride she jumped on board and rode the prettiest horse side saddle. Giddy as a school girl, Melody threw her head back and laughed as Kevin rode beside her on a stallion.

Dizzy and ecstatic, Melody stumbled from the carousel holding hands with Kevin. Evidently not through with their adventure they journeyed to the famous Central Park Zoo. Once inside, they explored every inch, from the smelly but cute, barking sea lions and funky birds to its Rain Forest house and all the creepy crawlies that Kevin threatened to put on her.

"Do you trust me?" he asked with a mischievous grin sprouting from ear to ear.

"Don't even pretend to put any of those icky things on me!"

Kevin's eyes flickered as he became more serious. "Do you trust me?"

Melody prepared to protest again, but then the world seemed to drop away until nothing remained except Kevin, his burning eyes and his hypnotic voice.

"Do you trust me?" he repeated beckoning like a calm island oasis.

"Yes." She replied feeling breathless.

Kevin smiled his approval. "Good," he said bridging the gap between them until he held her in his strong, loving arms. "How much do you trust me?"

Different scenarios crossed through her mind and they all began and ended with Kevin. "I trust you with my life."

Kevin's eyes danced and she felt them connect on a spiritual level. "Good, because as long as you trust me and stay with me, I swear I'll never let anything bad happen to you."

"I know," she replied, resting her head against his chest.

As the evening approached, they wandered back to the Delacorte. Settled under the stars in their great seats they watched an electrifying performance of *The Winter's Tale*.

After the show as they walked arm in arm towards the exit, Melody rested her head on Kevin's shoulder. "I'd love to come back in August to see *Julius Caesar* with Jeffrey Wright. That was amazing!"

"Did you enjoy the day?" he asked smiling down at her.

Melody looked incredulous. "Are you kidding? This day couldn't get any more perfect if you tried."

"Oh really?" asked Kevin, looking like he had one more trick up his sleeve.

Just then they emerged from Central Park and Kevin led her over to one of the horse and buggies waiting to traverse couples and tourists around the park. He stopped at the elaborate, Cinderella-themed buggy. "Your carriage awaits my Lady," he said with a wink and a bow.

Melody squealed and pecked Kevin on the cheek. "Can you get any more amazing?"

Home Away from Home – July 2000

"Welcome to my home away from home," Kevin said as he unlocked the door to Ty's parent's place and waved with a flourished bow for Melody to enter first.

"Are you sure this is okay?" Melody asked, nervous to cross the threshold.

"I told you, his parents are in Boston this weekend for his cousin's wedding. They left after work and they're staying at a hotel up there tonight and Saturday night," Kevin replied as he placed his hand in the delicious dip at the base of her spine right above her bottom. His searing hand gently guided her inside the house and he followed right on her heels.

Once inside, Kevin closed and locked the door. Still standing behind her, he wrapped his arms around her waist and pulled her back against his solid chest. "See, no one here except us."

Nestled against his chest, Melody leaned back and let Kevin nuzzle her neck. God, she never realized how much she missed making love with Kevin until now. Not that he invited her over for that reason. No, in fact, when they made plans for tonight, Kevin only mentioned making dinner. Struggling to maintain her composure at the thought of the two of them finally garnering some privacy for the first and probably only time all summer, she tried to keep her voice even. "Yes, it looks like we're all alone."

Ever the gentleman, Kevin chuckled, released her waist, and walked towards the kitchen. "Would you like anything to drink before I start cooking dinner?"

"Water's fine," she replied following him into the kitchen and leaning against the doorway. "I'm still shocked that you planned out an entire four-course dinner," she said watching his beautiful, built body snag two glasses from one of the cupboards and fill them with ice and water from the refrigerator dispenser. Even his spiky, blond hair and slight five o'clock shadow exuded smooth, suave sexiness.

Melody shook her head with an appreciative grin. All day long at inappropriate moments during work, her naughty mind reminded her of the last time they had relations right before leaving school for the summer. And standing here watching Kevin's easy movements, her traitorous body realized they were alone and unsupervised and it ached for Kevin. Mm, Kevin looked so scrumptious, too. Ever the gentleman, he hadn't alluded to anything besides dinner tonight and his desire for them to be all alone. Realistically she wasn't altogether sure how she felt about having sex at Ty's parent's house, but those urges kept calling.

She tried to pull herself together as he turned around with their glasses. "Having a man that cooks— honestly, how does one girl get so lucky?"

"The luck was all mine," Kevin replied as he handed her a glass. "Here's to luck," he said clinking their glasses together. "I know I'll need it to pull off dinner tonight." He smirked and swallowed some water as she laughed out loud at his joke.

"I'm positive that whatever you make will be perfect. You always seem to know just the right thing to do," she said with a little more sexiness and innuendo in her voice than she planned. Her cheeks rewarded her with a blazing blush and she glanced down, hoping he wouldn't think her too forward.

When she glanced back up, Kevin's eyes smoldered with promise. For whatever stupid reason, she belted out the first thing that crossed her short-circuiting mind. "So are you ready to meet my mommy?"

Kevin almost spit out his drink and he spluttered and coughed for a second while Melody patted his back. "You might want to wait for me to finish swallowing my drink next time you suggest something so unexpected and drastic."

"Drastic?" Melody slumped back against the doorway wearing a pout. Granted her timing lacked a lot, but his response stung. "I thought you wanted to meet my mommy?"

"Poor choice of words on my part. I meant 'drastic' change in topic from our prior conversation." Kevin reached out to take Melody's glass and the slight graze of his fingers sent electric tingles up her arm and down her spine. In an instant, he set both of their glasses down on the counter and turned to face her. His eyes twinkled and sparkled while his beautiful, full lips parted into a sensuous smile. Soft and gentle, his right hand caressed her face until she melted under his loving gaze. "If she's anything like you, I can't wait to meet her."

Okay, his response worked wonders on her completely recovered, formerly hurt feelings. Melody bit her lip in an effort to concentrate enough to speak. "I explained to my mommy how difficult it's been to find the time, considering our work schedules and your strict curfew. But the summer's two-thirds done and she's beginning to wonder if I'm just making you up as an excuse not to hang out at home with her."

"Not a chance," he replied slightly breathless, his eyes darkening with desire.

Liquid flowed through her limbs as his lustful look penetrated right through to her loins. Kevin embodied the roles of friend, confidant, and exquisite lover like a tailored suit. Melody's knees trembled. Wow, the way he could make her feel with just one loving look, one electric touch, or the simple, sexy sound of his voice.

Acting as if he knew the thoughts rolling through her mind, Kevin leaned in and blessed her mouth with his tender lips. As their kiss intensified, he placed his hands around her waist and lifted her up, quick and easy.

Melody's legs took on a mind of their own and wrapped around Kevin's waist, and Kevin moaned in her mouth which drove her even crazier.

Carrying her with ease, Kevin walked back into the living room and sat facing sideways on the end of the couch. Once they settled on the couch, his hands slid down from her waist to her bottom. His hands squeezed her bottom with pent-up desire and he adjusted her on his lap on top of his growing glory.

A surprised but satisfied gasp escaped her lips. "What about dinner?" she asked in jest.

"Suddenly, I'm ravenous for something else," Kevin replied reconvening their delicious kiss while his insatiable hands traversed her inviting body.

NEXT STOP, FOOTBALL CAMP

"Thanks for dinner, Mrs. Wilkins," Lance said as he, Imani, and Melody prepared to excuse themselves from the dining room table. "I really appreciate that you offered to host my 'Farewell for Training Camp' dinner." He suppressed a chuckle, knowing full well that he was nowhere near as accommodating when his own mother suggested the same idea earlier. It was one of her so called "generous" offers that he had absolutely no intention of taking her up on.

Pushing his mother from his thoughts, he threw on the charm. "The meatloaf, green beans, and mashed potatoes were absolutely delicious." He patted his full stomach.

"You're quite welcome. It was truly my pleasure to hang out more with my sweet, little Melody and her two best friends," Margaret Wilkins replied as she jumped up and began quickly clearing the dishes from the table.

It amazed Lance to see the bubbly, petite, blonde whirling dervish in action. Like mother, like daughter, he guessed. He glanced at Melody and saw her somehow blushing with pride as she beamed at her mother. Imani looked like she was busy suppressing a belch. He waited a second for her to finish and then she nodded that they should get up and assist.

Before they even rose from their chairs, Mrs. Wilkins had finished gathering all their plates and silverware. "Why don't you make yourselves comfortable in the living room while I clean up here?"

"Are you sure we can't help you with anything?" Imani asked.

"No thank you, Dear, I'm fine. These are going in the dishwasher and then I'm retiring to my room. Go enjoy yourselves," she said before she whisked into the kitchen leaving them looking at each other.

"Well, what are you two waiting for," Melody asked with a smile. She gestured them past the wall of family photos and into the cozy living room with its matching couch and loveseat.

Similar to his mother's place, the furniture wasn't expensive, but it felt like home. Although the fragrant smells of garlic and meatloaf lingered in the air here versus the cloying incense his mother tended to burn. Lance followed Imani's lead and took a seat on the inviting couch upholstered in a plush, chocolate brown floral print. Somehow it managed to look homey and comfortable without appearing too feminine.

Melody walked past them and the wicker trunk coffee table over to the massive wicker entertainment center. She powered on the radio and tuned into Hot 97 before joining them on the couch.

Imani slapped her thighs. "Oh, man, I forgot to ask your mom if she ever met Kevin or is he continuing to play Mr. Elusive? Maybe he's scared that mother knows best and she'll forbid him from dating you."

Lance shook his head and stifled a chuckle; let the craziness begin.

Melody elbowed Imani and narrowed her eyes. "You are so ridiculously wrong! I'll have you know that Kevin was not evading my mommy in any way, shape, or form." She crossed her arms tight over her chest and Lance couldn't help but laugh. "I told you both that Ty's parents implemented a curfew that prevented him from making the long trip out here most nights."

"I thought you said that the weekends were curfew-free?" Imani asked, not giving poor Melody an inch.

"They were, but as you recall, we've all been pretty busy going out." Melody shot Lance a look. "And it's typically not been with our parents."

"Oh, Lord," Lance said rubbing his hands over his head. The last thing he wanted to recall was when he exercised poor judgment and decided that it would somehow be a good idea to have them meet his mother. Never again!

"Stop deflecting onto Lance and answer the question." Imani raised her hand to signal stop. "Actually before you answer that one, I have another question for you. Have you ever talked to Kevin's parents? Honestly, I don't recall you ever mentioning anything relevant about his past."

"Damn, you're nosy tonight," Melody replied with a huff. "Look, he's really sensitive about his upbringing, so that's why I never mention it. And you have to promise not to either."

Imani nodded and Lance tilted his chin up in acknowledgement.

Melody took a deep breath and continued. "Let's just say, it wasn't the best; drunk mother, absentee father, no other real family to speak of besides his maternal grandmother. So he cut all ties to home as soon as he departed for college, although it sounds as if his grandmother is the only one left alive and they're not close."

"And that doesn't bother you?" Imani asked with true concern wrinkling her brow.

Melody shrugged and shook her head.

Lance remained silent. This was one of the times he sided with Melody. You couldn't hold a person's upbringing against them. Although his mother wasn't a drunk, the woman wouldn't win any Mother of the Year awards either. And Kevin's father situation mirrored his own a little too close for comfort.

"Sounds intense and it definitely explains some things about the boy." Imani pondered that nugget of information for a moment. "Sorry, I brought it up. Hey, guess I need to lighten the mood and go back to my original, much more important question." Wearing a bright smile, Imani clapped her hands together and sat up straight. "So tell me, did Kevin ever meet your mom? Because if you don't answer me, you know I'll march right back into the kitchen or up into her bedroom and ask." Imani's eyebrow arched sky high to emphasize her point.

"Not that it's any of your concern," Melody replied, trying to snap back but failing in her sweet, innocent way. "But yes, they did! I'll have you know that Kevin was his naturally charming self and my mommy absolutely loved him."

"Now see that's what I find hard to believe," Imani replied while gesturing with her hands. "Kevin is about as charming as a slug. Now if you would have said Lance," she said pointing her thumb Lance's way, "was charming—"

Lance sat up straight and stroked his goatee.

Imani punched his arm and continued without missing a beat. "Well, then I might have believed you, regardless of how delusional Lance is in reality. But at least that would have made some small semblance of sense."

Melody shook her head and sighed.

"So what you're really telling me is that not only do you get your looks from your mom—by the way, y'all almost look like twins. She's just a little older looking and even daintier, if that's possible—but from what you're saying, she's just as naïve and romantic." Imani snorted. "Well, she'd have to be if she thinks that Kevin is charming and lovable."

"Oh, my God, I'm so through with you, Imani!" Melody slapped Imani's leg then looked his direction. "Lance can you please intervene or talk some sense into her?"

He howled and slapped his own leg. "Now that's a funny joke. I know you don't think I can talk sense to Imani."

"That's because you don't have any sense to begin with," Imani said before she sucked her teeth and glared at him. "You need sense to talk sense, and you're about as nonsensical, egotistical, and backwards chauvinistic as they come."

"Yet, you can't get enough of me and my charm," he replied while turning on his megawatt smile.

Imani busted out laughing. "See that's why we

keep you around. Laughter is the best medicine and you're so ridiculous, you usually have me in stitches."

Lance smirked and elbowed Imani in the side for her troubles.

"Well, we definitely know where he gets it from," Melody said already laughing. "His mother, because she was hilarious as hell."

"I'll have you both know, you think it's funny now, but my mother's been begging me all summer to bring you back around. There's no way that's ever happening again."

"Now why not?" Imani asked cracking up. "You afraid she's gonna let the cat out of the bag and spill all your secrets?"

"The only secret is guessing which embarrassing thing she'll say next." Lance shook his head. "So far she's assured me you're not gold-diggers."

"Well, I can understand her surprise." Imani rolled her eyes. "I doubt she's ever seen you hanging around two intelligent females who have absolutely no desire to chase after your warped behind."

"Actually, I still don't understand why you settle for all those sleazy, one night stands." Melody wrinkled her nose in distaste.

"As if you don't know this already." Lance leaned back and stretched his legs out in front of him. "Unlike you, I'm not searching for my soulmate or my one true love nonsense. For now I'm just having fun."

"It's all supposedly fun and games until you come home with an STD or a baby." Imani smirked.

"I told you no glove, no love. So that's not a problem. But that's what I love about you two. You always keep me in line." Lance shrugged. "And even when you don't agree with me or approve of my actions, you still have my back."

"We're just trying to save you from yourself," Imani said sucking her teeth.

"Or at least trying to impart a little love into your life," said Melody sounding romantic. "Just like in the vows, we'll be there for you through thick and thin, for richer or poorer, in sickness and in health, yadda, yadda, and all that jazz."

Although she was half joking, for some reason her words touched him deep inside. It took him a second then it dawned on him. Melody's words and sentiment were real and sincere. Thanks, Mother, he scoffed inside. Due to his mother's constant brainwashing, he realized now just how much he didn't trust people, especially women.

Lance snuck a glance at Melody and Imani as they relaxed in comfortable silence broken only by the sounds from the radio. That innate distrust changed the minute he met them at freshman orientation when they muddled through the newness together. Right from the start he felt at ease. They were the first people in his life to not want anything from him. With them there were no hidden agendas. Ever since he started playing Pop Warner football at seven, people paid attention and they seemed to think even back then that he might somehow be their ticket out. But when he was with Imani and Melody he could truly be himself and that was the most freeing feeling imaginable.

He leaned forward and rested his elbows on his knees, wondering if he should push his introspective luck. After years of suppressing his feelings, he didn't quite feel comfortable sharing. Men didn't "talk" and they definitely didn't expose their weaknesses or insecurities. With a resigned sigh, he decided to hedge his bets.

"I wonder sometimes," he said voicing one of his few concerns. "Will it always be like this?"

Melody put her elbow on the back of the couch. "What do you mean?" she asked, propping her head on her hand and slipping her legs underneath her on the sofa.

"Will we still get together and hangout and talk like this? Especially if I do make it into the NFL. I mean, what if we wind up living on different sides of the country? You know they say that fame and fortune changes everything."

"I don't see anything changing," replied Melody. "We're like the Three Musketeers." Melody placed her left hand on his knee. "All for one and one for all."

Lance couldn't stifle his laugh.

Imani rolled her eyes. "Boy, please! If anything, you'll get a big old, gassed head and try to act like you don't know us anymore. Trust me; we'll be there to remind you that we knew you when…as a crazy ass freshman who we took pity on during orientation."

Lance leaned back and dropped his jaw in feigned surprise. "Pity?"

"Yeah, Boy. We didn't bit more know or care about you playing football. We were just trying to save you from your silly self even back then."

"Gee, thanks," he replied unable to contain his smile.

"See, when Imani agrees that you're not getting rid of us, you're definitely not getting rid of us." Melody leaned back and winked at him. "And when you make it into the NFL, we won't suddenly expect any presents or start asking you for any loans."

"I know you two won't, but will you promise to fend off the other crazy chicken-heads and gold-diggers my mother constantly warns me about?" he asked semi-serious.

Imani twisted her lips into a frown. "I'm with your mom on this one, that's on you to be a bit more discerning in your choice of bed partners."

"Gee, thanks again for siding with my mother of all people."

Imani held her hand up to signify more forthcoming 'advice' that only she could deliver. "But as your friends we will warn you when you've lost your ever-loving mind. And if you still demand on getting serious with a gold-digging chicken-head, we'll at least force them to sign a pre-nup."

"Although if he follows my rules for finding his one, true soulmate, a prenuptial agreement will become a moot point."

Both Lance and Imani gave Melody an incredulous look.

Melody shrugged. "What?"

Lance glanced at his watch. "Wow, look at the time. You know I should probably be getting home. I have a long drive back up to campus tomorrow and I need to get rested before training camp begins."

"Yeah, right!" Imani punched his arm. "Give Joe, John and Big Tony our best. But you're not leaving me here alone with Miss Fantasy-Dwelling Uber Romantic."

Melody crossed her arms but smiled. "That's fine. I know you're both just jealous. Don't worry, you'll come around. And when you do, your first love advice session is on the house!"

SUMMER'S END - AUGUST 2000

Savoring the sweet, fizzy taste of Coca-Cola on her tongue, Imani tried to tune in to Melody's hyperactive conversation.

"The summer's flown past so fast," Melody said as she drummed their table top at Katz's Delicatessen, the place made more famous by Meg Ryan's fake orgasm scene in *When Harry Met Sally*. "Can you believe it? June, gone in the blink of an eye. July zipped past like a cheetah, and now August is here."

"Yep, and school starts in two weeks," Imani replied with a sigh of regret. She stifled a belch of delicious pastrami and pushed away her empty plate.

"But what a wonderful summer it's been." Melody almost bounced in excitement in her seat. "And to think that we experienced so much of it with minimal cash outlay. When Kevin found the *Freetime* paper, I never realized how much New York offered for free or next to nothing."

And here it comes; Imani sighed again and braced herself for Melody's upcoming deluge of romantic prattling. God, she should have told Melody about that paper and tons of other things just to stop the relentless Kevin love fest!

"Central Park is now one of my favorite places on earth," Melody said in her breathy, sing-song way.

"Do you realize how many concerts we attended at the Summer Stage alone?"

No, Imani wanted to say, I didn't keep a love scrapbook like you did.

Melody counted off on her dainty fingers. "We saw all manner of musical genres and artists from the Indigo Girls to Nile Rodgers and Chic, Common to Randy Newman, Roy Avers, DJ Jazzy Jeff and Jody Watley to Joan Jett."

Imani rolled her eyes and held her tongue. Trying to be less sarcastic was killing her. She had promised Melody that she would be on her best behavior whenever they were out with Kevin. So, Imani was trying to extend that good behavior to other aspects of her life, but damn it was hard. And Melody's unnecessary recollection of their summer itinerary bugged her to no end because Melody, Kevin, Lance, Trevor, and Imani were damn near attached at the hip most of the summer, so she already knew it firsthand!

"Then dancing under the stars to the live bands during the Lincoln Center's Midsummer Night Swing." Melody stopped cooing long enough to smile at Imani and ruffle her hair. "You know it got to the point where we basically had a different spot each night."

Imani's eyebrow arched as she tried to follow Melody's latest tangent.

"Well, think about it, Imani," Melody continued as she settled back into her uber romantic mode. "Tuesday nights in July meant Washington Square Park's free music festival. Wednesdays were the free Verdi opera performances by the New York Grand

Opera back in Central Park. Friday and Saturday evenings, when we weren't out clubbing or at the movies, were spent listening to concerts in the Museum of Modern Art's Sculpture Garden."

"Yep, I know," Imani interrupted, growing tired of the summer litany. For one of the first times ever she wondered what was taking Kevin so long in the bathroom. She needed an auditory reprieve, and with Lance already on campus in training camp and Trev at a family function, Imani was on her own. She took another sip of Coke and wished she could add some rum.

"In between time, we watched the classic movies at Bryant Park." Melody bounced in her chair again. "Some of my most cherished memories of the summer were made there on that beautiful patch of grass in between the midtown skyscrapers."

Imani did her best not to gag and yell for Kevin to hurry back. What the hell? Was he taking a dump in the bathroom? One, that was nasty and two, she didn't want to relive the one fool time she made the mistake of accompanying them to Bryant Park. She probably resided on the exact opposite end of the spectrum from Big Tony when it came to public displays of affection. But hell, even she felt extremely uncomfortable with Melody and Kevin making out on the picnic blanket she shared with them!

Melody continued reminiscing. "Remember watching greats like *His Girl Friday*, *The Maltese Falcon*, and my personal favorite, *Pillow Talk*?"

Thank heaven! Imani waved Kevin over as soon as he reemerged from the bathroom area.

Kevin frowned and looked around to see if Imani were gesturing for someone else.

Imani contained her reciprocate frown as she lowered her hand. Guess Kevin still didn't buy this new side of her either. She didn't blame him. She didn't trust him as far as she could spit and it probably still showed on her face despite her best efforts.

Melody stopped reminiscing and kissed Kevin when he joined them. "I missed you, Baby," she said almost cooing. "Let me run to the bathroom and then I'll be ready for us to go see the indie, romantic comedy playing in the theater in Tribeca."

Kevin smiled and nodded, but his attention turned to Imani as soon as Melody departed.

Determined not to repeat the uncomfortable Bryant Park experience, Imani vowed back then never to accompany them to another romantic movie. So when they were exploring the Soho shops and art galleries earlier, she had gladly declined their invitation. She really hoped they would see *What Lies Beneath*, the thriller with Harrison Ford and Michelle Pfeiffer, but Kevin probably felt it hit too close to home. Imani smiled at the thought. "You kids have fun all alone at the movies," she said joking around with Kevin.

"It's about time you left us alone," Kevin muttered under his breath as Imani busied herself with her drink.

His words caught her off guard and she set down her cup knowing she must have heard wrong. "Excuse me?" she asked making sure to keep the accusatory tone out of her voice.

"You heard me," Kevin replied looking her dead in the eye.

"I'm praying I heard wrong because I've been nothing but nice to you today." Imani's hand toyed with her cup.

"Please, I don't know what you're trying to pull, Imani, but it's not working." Kevin's voice sounded amazingly pleasant, but his flinty eyes burned with complete and utter seriousness. "I don't know why you dislike me so vehemently, but frankly, I don't care and I'm done trying. I shared Melody all summer long and now the summer's almost finished."

As her jaw clenched to prevent her from going off, Imani's back stiffened and her hand tightened around the cup.

"When we get back to campus, there's no more Mr. Nice Guy. I expect you to leave Melody and I alone in peace."

"Is that a threat?" Imani felt ready to knock his crazy block off!

"I'm just stating the facts. Feel free to take it whichever way you like."

Imani tried hard not pimp slap the cocky expression off Kevin's stupid face. "That's not your decision to make." Imani's voice sounded hard and cold even to her own ears. "Melody's my best friend and I plan to protect her."

Kevin broke into a sparkling smile and Imani could almost see how people might find the arrogant bastard partially charming...almost. "You're the one she needs protection from, Imani. You act like you're Melody's friend, but in reality you're a controlling, foul-mouthed liar."

Imani's blood boiled over, but before she could

react, Kevin stood up as he saw Melody emerge from the bathroom.

"If I were you, I'd think twice about continuing to disparage me. Because if you push this and try to make Melody choose between us, you'll lose. She's going to choose me." Kevin smirked and left to join Melody. The asshole had the audacity to turn, smile, and wave good-bye to her when Melody did.

Imani realized her fingers were about to shatter the cup in her hand. With a concerted effort, she relaxed them enough to set the cup on the table unharmed. Shit, what should she do? It bothered her deep down in her gut to think Kevin might be right. If she kept haggling Melody about Kevin and making it difficult for all three of them to hang out together, she might just push her friend straight into the fool's arms. Damn!

DECISIONS

"Hey, there you are," Imani said as she exited her parent's kitchen door and sat down on the back stoop steps next to Trevor. "My crazy family too much to deal with?"

He smiled his toothy grin. "No, they're fun and cool. But don't forget my mom's in there, too. Nothing says back-to-school party like hanging out with your parents."

Imani chuckled and Trev shook his head.

"I just needed to grab some fresh air and escape our moms for a while." He rested his elbows on his knees and cradled his head in his hands. "I can't believe that school starts up next week for our moms and for us. Here we are all packed up and ready to drive back to campus tomorrow. Seems like summer's over before it even started."

"Yep, it went pretty fast. But at least we had a lot of fun times." Imani leaned back on her elbows and stared up at the moon and the few visible stars.

"Indeed, we did." Trev gazed at her while she pretended not to notice.

She could feel the air between them thicken with hopeful anticipation. Would it be so wrong for her to succumb to Trev? He was such a nice guy. Fun and well-mannered with a good head on his shoulders.

What was she so worried about? Maybe they could make it work without ruining their lab partnership.

"What are you thinking about?" Trev asked leaning into her space.

For a minute she wrestled with which path she should take. His hand innocently rested on his knee. But it lingered in such close proximity to her hand that the fine hairs on her arm stood on end as though they were statically charged and attracted to him. If she really wanted to she could end all of their back and forth, will-they-or-won't-they posturing now. Respond by saying, "you," and then lean in and let him kiss her.

Meanwhile Trev looked so earnest and smitten...and determined? Each second that ticked past seemed to embolden him more. Imani could feel him easing in towards her and she panicked inside. Her palms turned sweaty as her pulse accelerated. Feeling cornered and trapped, forced into a decision she felt ill prepared to make, she made up her mind in that instant and reacted. To make a relationship work, you needed to spend time and effort on it, and she just didn't want to take that time away from her upcoming engineering studies, at least not now.

Instead of leaning in towards Trevor as he expected or hoped, Imani shifted her entire body to face him. The movement effectively reinstituted the space between them and then some. "Believe it or not, I was thinking about our lab partnership," she replied. Although her tone sounded friendly, she knew the abrupt change in her mannerisms killed the earlier simmering mood.

"Oh," Trev said with disappointment dripping from his pores. "You're already thinking about school work."

"Sophomore year's a big deal. We finish our compulsory prep courses and officially declare our majors. We'll need to continue knocking out the great grades and more."

"Well, I'm your man," he replied then frowned at his choice of words. "I mean, you can count on me to continue working my butt off. I like seeing my name on the Dean's List."

"Excellent!" Imani slapped Trev's leg then popped up and stood over him. "Well, Labbie, we should probably get back inside before our moms start searching for us." She extended her hand to help Trev stand up.

He smiled and accepted her hand.

Innocent Kisses

"We've been back in school for two weeks, Imani." Melody made sure to keep the burning curiosity out of her voice. Acting nonchalant, she gathered her textbooks from her desk and packed them in her bookbag. "How are things with Trevor?"

"So, what your nosy behind is really asking me is if I'm finally going to get with Trev?" Imani gave her the evil eye and sucked her teeth.

"Take it however you like," she replied playing coy. "I simply asked you how things were. If you prefer to disclose any additional feelings, well that's entirely up to you." Melody attempted to give Imani an innocent look. "But you know you should give him a chance. You don't have to choose between good grades and a love life; you deserve some happiness. Plus, Trevor adores you for some warped reason."

Before Imani could utter her normal caustic comeback, they heard a knock at the door.

"Aw shucks, saved by the bell." Melody batted her eyes at her roommate as she answered the door.

Right on time, Lance barreled inside. Immediately he scooped her up in his tight bearhug and swung her around three times, much to the tickled delight of her butterfly-filled belly.

As soon as Lance set her down she wavered two

steps and stopped, deciding it might be best to wait until she regained her balance.

Meanwhile Imani bustled past to greet Lance. However Imani and Lance's signals got crossed up and Melody watched in fascinated horror as the two played a weird game of chicken. While they attempted almost in slow motion to plant a kiss on the other's cheek, they kept simultaneously readjusting their faces and mirroring each other's actions. The distance continued to close between them. Before they could correct course they ran out of room...and accidentally connected lips.

"Whoops," Melody said with a laugh as Lance's eyebrow shot up and Imani stepped back with her hands covering her mouth.

"Eh, no big deal," Lance said recovering quickly and dismissing the misstep as nothing. "People kiss each other on the lips all the time as a friendly welcome."

"True," Imani agreed with a shrug. "It's normal in other cultures to kiss both cheeks like the trés romantic French," she said batting her eyes at Melody. "Or hell, in some places they kiss on the mouth all the time, even the guys."

"I'm not going that far," Lance said waving off Imani's ludicrous suggestion.

"Come to think of it," Imani said ignoring Lance's interjection. "My mom has kissed me on the lips on a few occasions."

"And your father?" Melody asked not buying it.

Imani frowned at her. "My dad's more of a hugger, like Lance," she said pointing her thumb towards

Lance, "is with you. Throughout his life, Dad's never been a big kisser," she replied acting indignant as if Melody should have known this random factoid.

"So you're fine with kissing guys on the lips?" Melody asked as crystal clear as possible trying to pressure Imani into realizing how ridiculous they sounded.

"Sure," Imani replied with a shrug. Then she checked with Lance. "Are you fine?"

"Again, I don't understand what the big deal is," Lance said. "I'm thinking we should start a new trend. If the spirit moves us, why not kiss our close friends on the lips?"

Melody stomped her foot in disbelief. "Um, hello! Maybe because a kiss on the lips implies something special. You should reserve it for your significant other and only them!"

Lance looked at her like he needed to explain the concept to a child. "We're just talking about a quick, innocent peck, Melody." He glanced at Imani to get back-up support. "We never said anything about tonguing people down. There's a big difference."

Imani nodded as if Lance just preached the most profound word she'd ever heard.

Melody released a loud, exasperated sigh. How could they be so dense? She used finger quotes to emphasize the obvious point they were missing. "*Innocent* peck or *not*, it's still way too personal a gesture."

"It's really not all that big of a deal," Imani restated in a more exasperated tone.

Melody refocused her efforts on Imani. Determined

to stop her friend from instituting such a ridiculous new habit, she smiled as she realized a new tactic she could use. "So, you're down to kiss any of our friends, female or male?"

"Sure, I don't see why not. But like Lance said only our close friends."

"Meaning, you'd kiss Krystal, Erycah, or Karen?"

Imani shrugged and nodded. "Yes, I'd just need to let them know first."

Lance interjected although Melody hadn't asked for his opinion. "You know I absolutely don't have a problem with that."

"What about John and Joe or Big Tony?" Melody asked building up to what Imani should have seen as the obvious next question.

Lance let loose a loud belly laugh. "Big Tony doesn't believe in public displays of affection, so I doubt you have to worry about him."

Imani joined in Lance's laughter. "Yeah, that one's not going to happen. But I doubt Joe or John would have a problem with it."

"I sincerely doubt it," Lance replied. "But like I stated earlier, you're on your own when it comes to our guy friends."

Melody couldn't wait to burst their jolly little bubble. "And Trevor?" she replied pursing her lips together into a tight, thin line.

Imani's face fell and the laughter ceased in a heartbeat.

"I didn't think so," Melody said answering her own question.

Lance ran his hand over his head. "Guess she got

you there, Buddy," he said to Imani.

"Well, Trev's different," Imani said trying to formulate an excuse. "I don't want to lead him on. For instance, in Lance's case, he understands there's definitely no chance of anything happening between us."

"Amen," Lance interjected.

"But in Trev's case that would be cruel and unusual punishment to lead him on. Why confuse any already convoluted situation."

"Exactly," Melody replied while making an exaggerated circle with her hands. "Why plant seeds of confusion in anyone's head, Trev, Lance, or Big Tony? Reserve your lips for your significant other only."

"You insinuating that you won't let Lance kiss you?" Imani asked tongue in cheek just to rile Melody up again.

"Ew, no!" Melody replied too far gone to care. After a second, she considered Lance's feelings. With a courteous but abrupt motion, she gave Lance an apologetic gesture. "Sorry, no offense intended."

Lance chuckled and cracked opened the door in a not so subtle hint for them to leave and go study. "No worries, none taken."

"No, I guess you're right, Melody," Imani said with a sly wink as she strolled over to her desk and grabbed her backpack. "I doubt that Kevin would appreciate Lance kissing you on the lips. He seems like the jealous type."

Now it was Melody's turn to blanch. Oh God, she never even considered Kevin's response. He would go ape-shit ballistic. Playing Imani's comment off, she grabbed her backpack and followed them out of the dorm room. However her mind wouldn't drop the subject. She could never imagine cheating on Kevin. The mere thought made her sick to her stomach.

GAME TIME - SEPTEMBER 2000

With the game so close, Lance suppressed a few nervous jitters. Taking a deep breath, he jogged onto the field focused on the play call. They were playing local rivals, SUNY-Albany, which should have been a piece of cake because SUNY-Albany's team was never any good.

Scoring continued hot and heavy throughout the game, but their team was down by three with only thirty seconds to go. For whatever reason neither defense could stop the other one's high-powered offenses today. Although it was very early in the season, that didn't bode well for his team's chances at compiling a winning season and making it to a bowl game.

Lance took his place at the line of scrimmage. All they needed was a field goal to tie and send it into overtime. Two problems; one, they were starting at their ten because of a stupid penalty and two, their kicker wasn't automatic unless it was forty yards or less. That meant they needed to cover about sixty yards in twenty-five seconds.

He glanced across the line to read the defensive coverage. Interesting. SUNY-Albany's coach decided to double-cover him again and he brought their fastest player over in the safety slot hoping to shut him down.

Guess they hadn't learned their lesson yet, Lance thought, because today he and Steve the QB were clicking on all cylinders like a Lamborghini. Anything Steve threw near him, Lance managed to haul it in and catch. Plus, when they double-covered him, it left the other wideouts and the tight end free for days.

Lance smiled, no worries, both he and the team were prepared for either option.

Waiting for the count snap, his muscles hummed in anticipation. Their offensive coach decided to go for broke and called a Hail Mary, a long, deep, last-ditch throw towards the end zone.

Lance honed in on his quarterback's voice, careful not to flinch as he tried to draw the defense offsides. No luck, the defense miraculously stayed put, so Steve called for the ball.

Once the center snapped the ball back, Lance took off down the left sideline. Within three steps, he'd blown past the poor cornerback. The guy huffed to stay near Lance. Like a race car, Lance shifted and threw it into fifth gear, pulling ahead of the defender by two yards with ease.

The internal countdown in his head, told him he'd need to turn and locate the ball soon. Knowing Steve, he'd unleashed the ball like a rocket and he'd need to muster every ounce of speed to make it to the overthrown missile. Meanwhile he sensed and heard the speedy free safety zeroing in on his position. He glanced to his right, yep, the guy now matched him stride-for-stride as he repositioned himself in hopes of an interception.

Time! Lance looked over his shoulder trying to

locate the incoming ball. Secondary senses heard the crowd almost draw one, loud collective breath, so he knew the ball loomed near.

There! He found the ball on its fiery trajectory. And as predicted it was coming in high. He felt the safety bite too soon, starting his jump too early. There was no way he could intercept the ball, but he could deflect it and mess up Lance's chances big time just by being in the way.

Lance made a subtle adjustment, sprang and reached, the ball just grazing his outstretched fingertips. In a millisecond, he hyper-extended his middle finger, deflecting the spiraling ball just enough that it turned end-over-end up in the air over his head as the safety sailed past out of bounds.

With one defender out of the picture, Lance could sense the slow cornerback finally catching up to the play. More than likely he had a huge smile on his face thinking he was about to blindside Lance and disrupt the play.

Lance grinned and lassoed the spinning ball out of the air. His momentum made it appear like he was heading forward and to the right and that's exactly where the cornerback lunged. Too bad for him that Lance stopped cold and pivoted back to his left, employing a deft spin move that left the cornerback on the ground with an armful of empty air and a facemask full of AstroTurf pellets.

Free and clear, Lance shifted into top gear and raced into the end zone.

Touchdown! He thought about showing off some dance moves, but coach had started cracking down on excessive celebrations. So, Lance acted like he was about to spike the ball. He stopped mid-arc just before he released the ball, psyching out the crowd, and then he spiked it for real and the crowd erupted.

Before the ball even bounced back up, the other two wide receivers jumped on his back congratulating him, "nice catch", "did you see that spin move, you left him in the dust."

Steve, the QB, came in for a chest bump. "I know, I know, it was a little high but that's what makes it more fun."

As they ran off the field to let special teams take care of the extra point. Steve bumped him and pointed to the scoreboard as they showed the replay. They put it in slow-motion when Lance spun and the inspired announcer flashed the words, "You got Dunn" on the bottom of the screen. Evidently the crowd loved it just as much because they started chanting "You got Dunn! You got Dunn! You got Dunn!"

On the sidelines, Joe and John ran up to him, preparing to take the field for the kick-off. "Niiiiiiiice!" Joe gave him a high five and John slapped his butt. Then came Big Tony, "you got Dunn, huh?"

"You just make sure Defense takes care of business," Lance shouted and Big Tony growled back in response as he ran onto the field.

Lance laughed and then took a second to soak in every minute detail, hoping to savor the feeling forever. The lights of the dome, the gold and blue. The smells of the artificial turf, salty concessions, funky athletes, and blood. The sounds of 70,000 screaming, fanatical people, the referee's whistles, and the clash of pads on pads. The feel of the thunderous crowd stomping in time with, "We will, we will, rock you," and the cleansing sweat that dripped down his face and back.

If they kept this up during their next few road games, they would be playing back here against Arizona State for Homecoming. Then possibly a bowl game?

He smiled and swept the thoughts from his mind. Take it one day at a time, he chided himself as he relished in the awe-inspiring moment. God, this was the life! He hoped it never ended.

HOMECOMING ACTIVITIES – OCTOBER 2000

Imani waved for Lance and Trevor to quiet down so she could hear Melody through her cell phone. "Where are you?" she asked taking a seat at one of the smaller, intimate tables on the top floor of the Union.

Trev sat back and quieted down however Lance scowled at her and placed his elbows on the tiny, round table.

"It's rude to take calls at the table," Lance said with a wink.

Imani shot him a look. "It's Melody, you ass! Informing me that Kevin has a," Imani used air quotes with her free left hand, "*headache*. Supposedly from cheering so hard during your wild, edge-of-your-seat, Homecoming game. I, of course, just think they're coming up with more lame-ass excuses to leave us high and dry as usual."

Unperturbed, Lance attempted one of his charming smiles. "In that case, tell her to give Kevin two Tylenol and rest for a few hours. They can miss the impromptu Homecoming festivities taking place right now on the Quad and downstairs in the Union, but they can't miss the Homecoming dance later tonight. After today's trouncing of Arizona State, it can't be missed!"

"Did you catch all that?" Imani asked Melody into

the phone that she'd placed on speaker.

"Yes," they heard Melody reply. "I already gave Kevin two aspirin and he's resting now, so we'll see you around eight o'clock tonight."

"See you then," Lance said.

"Catch you later," said Trev.

"I noticed you didn't promise," Imani said knowing what that meant.

"Fine, Imani," Melody said in a huff. "I promise we'll see you at eight pm tonight at the Homecoming dance in the gym. Is that specific enough for you?"

Imani smiled and laughed. "That will do! Bye, Roomie."

Melody chuckled. "Later!"

Imani disconnected and pocketed her phone. "So where do you guys want to go now? It looked like they were pushing back all of the tables downstairs so that people could dance and party."

"Or I heard some of the fraternities were setting up games on their lawns or in the Quad," replied Trevor.

"Which typically means lots of beer and eventually drunk kids stumbling around acting stupid," Lance replied. "Which isn't necessarily a bad thing." Lance smiled then checked his watch. "Actually, I need to catch up with the team. We're supposed to meet back at the locker room in fifteen minutes." Lance jumped up to leave. "We're trying to throw together a skit to unveil at tonight's festivities."

"That sounds hilarious," Trev said.

"Sounds like a mess waiting to happen," Imani replied with a chuckle. "Well, have fun. Should we meet you at the auditorium at eight or hook up before hand?"

Lance stroked his mustache and goatee. "Let's just meet there to be safe."

Imani and Trevor stood up to wish Lance good-bye.

"Later, Man," Lance said giving Trev a pound. Then he turned towards Imani and gave her a hug. "Take care," he said, but their signals got crossed up as he tried to give her a quick peck on the cheek and the kiss landed on the corner of her lips.

Since they were used to their more familiar greetings now, neither she nor Lance paid any attention to the mishap and Lance waved as he left. When Imani turned to look at Trev his eyebrow stood at attention and he wore a weird, I-know-that-didn't-just-happen look on his face.

Imani decided to play it off. "So, what do you want to do?"

Trevor let the incident slide without comment. "You know if I'm given an option, I'll always choose to dance." He placed his hand on her shoulder. Trevor didn't act like he meant anything by it, but his touch sent a slight tingle through Imani's arm. "That is if you're cool with dancing right now and then again at the party later tonight?"

"Dancing with you is a work-out in and of itself." Imani chuckled and Trev dropped his hand and mimicked lifting weights. "But there's no one I'd rather dance with." Even to her own ears, it sounded like she was channeling Melody and flirting with Trev.

"Ah, shucks," he said dropping his head and pretending to blush. "It's fun dancing with you, too. You're a great partner."

"It's only because I'm trying to hang with you," she said tapping his chest lightly with her index finger. "You're always elevating my game and keeping me on my toes."

"So, I guess it's settled," he replied looking proud and honored. "Shall we go?" At first it looked like he was reaching for her hand, but then he adjusted and hooked her arm with his.

For some reason, Imani felt disappointed as they walked arm in arm across the top floor of the Union to one of the stairways leading down to the main floor. She wanted to reach down and hold his hand, but she knew if she did, there would be no going back.

When they arrived at the top of the staircase, Trev unhooked his arm, so that they could maneuver the steps with both hands free. He caught sight of her sad expression. "Hey," he said lifting her chin with his finger to better see her. "Is everything okay?"

Trev's concerned eyes and tender touch pulled at her heartstrings more causing Imani to swallow hard. The last thing she wanted to do was explain to Trev why her feelings were a touch bent out of shape. So she averted her eyes and came up with the second biggest issue on her mind. "I'm fine," she said feeling more comfortable and in control of her fluctuating emotions. Composed again, she looked into Trev's large, chocolate brown eyes. "It's just that I worry about Melody a lot."

Trev nodded and dropped his finger. "I understand why. She spends a lot of time with Kevin. And even a blind man can see you don't think much of Kevin."

"Is it that obvious?" Imani asked knowing full well

that it was. Although she still attempted to act civil after their tiff in the City, she didn't know how much longer she could remain cordial.

"Of course it is!" Trevor laughed and shook his head. "But what isn't as obvious is why."

Imani sighed and decided not to reveal their beef at Katz's. "I know people just think I'm jealous of him spending so much time with Melody. In fact, Kevin had the bold-faced audacity to tell me once that I should get my own man to worry and leave him the hell alone." Imani snorted in contempt at the fool's ridiculous suggestion.

"Yeahhh, that might not have been the best tactic to use with you," Trev replied.

"And he wonders why I don't like him!" Imani shook her head and then calmed down again as she crossed her arms and gazed at Trevor. "Honestly, do you want to know why?"

Trevor nodded and it felt like during their exchange, they'd crossed a barrier. Somehow it seemed as if they'd grown even closer during the last few minutes.

"It's hard to explain." Imani paused and touched Trev's arm. "My mom always advised me to follow my first mind. And from the very first instant that I met Kevin in the mall, I just didn't get a good vibe off of him."

"They say first impressions mean everything," Trev said soft and slow and for some strange reason, Imani felt like he was about to reach out and stroke her cheek.

Trevor didn't move an inch and that unsettled Imani even more.

What in God's name was wrong with her? She half-smiled, half-snorted in an attempt to continue the conversation without Trev thinking she'd lost her ever loving mind. "Exactly, and Kevin's still trying to overcome my initial, bad impression of him." She sighed and wondered if maybe she'd misjudged Kevin. After all this time, no one else had any problems with him except for her. Maybe she was acting too pushy?

"It's just that I feel like he's a jealous, controlling ass, but no one else seems to notice." Imani looked up at Trevor and touched his forearm again. "Do you think I'm being too harsh on Kevin? Please be honest." She smiled and squeezed his arm before letting go. God, she needed to quit flirting with Trevor! "I promise I can take it."

Trev cracked a toothy grin. "Famous last words," he replied as he tapped her shoulder. "In all seriousness, though," he said standing up straight. "I think you're a pretty good judge of character. Go with your gut reaction."

"Thanks," she said feeling genuine relief. Her eyes searched his and she decided to end their confusion and go for it. Just as she was about to throw caution to the wind and lean in to kiss him, the music coming from the basement of the Union, two floors below, erupted into a building-shaking cacophony.

Imani jumped and then the music dropped back down to a normal background noise. "I guess they're saying let's get this party started." Imani smiled, taking the interruption as a sign to keep their friendship platonic. "Ready to dance?"

Trev smiled back. "Always."

STUDYING IN THE LIBRARY – NOVEMBER 2000

"Are you sure it's not checked out," Imani asked scanning the supposedly correct campus library bookshelf for the errant chemistry book. Giving up, she rocked back on her heels and crossed her arms about ready to catch a real attitude.

"This is not how I planned to spend my Friday night," she said uncrossing her arms and gesturing towards her cute little, black dress and sensible but sexy black pumps that made her calves pop out like Mary Hart's from *Entertainment Tonight*.

"Let's not forget it was your bright idea to stop in the library 'real quick' before we went to the Alpha party." Trevor gave her a pointed look as he motioned towards his not too shabby outfit of black jeans, a black dress shirt open at the neck, a gray and black checked vest, and chic, black club shoes. "I recall how certain you were that we could get a head start on our project. Since as you put it, no one else would be crazy enough to even think about checking out the books until Sunday."

"Yeah, whatever," she said cutting her eyes and sucking her teeth. "Just help me find this damn book." She turned her attention back to the bothersome bookshelf while Trevor walked over behind her.

"It's supposed to be right here," she said pointing to the spot on the next to the top shelf, just slightly above her eye level. "QD251.2 .R6 1977, right?"

Trev peered over her shoulder and scanned the area for about twenty seconds before he chuckled. "Whoever shelved it the last time made a slight mistake." He reached around her and guided her hand up to the top shelf. Imani craned her neck and head backwards a bit to see.

"They inadvertently shelved it under QD241 instead of QD251."

For whatever reason, Imani stopped paying attention to Trevor's words and focused on his motions. With Trev's arm practically resting along hers, their hands still slightly intertwined, her breath hitched. It felt like one of the moments in the movies where the guy is showing the girl how to shoot pool or swing a golf club and they become aware of how close their bodies are before the situation warps from innocent to intimate in a flash frozen instant.

Her heart raced at the thought of Trevor taking the situation further. In fact, she prayed that he would, their lab partnership be damned. In that moment, she wanted Trev more than an "A" in their engineering classes. Realistically, she'd led him on for far too long.

Imani could tell that Trev felt the sexual tension, too. She knew she only had a millisecond to react before Trevor retreated back a step to safer realms. If she left him to his own devices he would ruin everything by behaving like the considerate gentleman he'd become in recent months.

Utilizing subtle movements, Imani arched her back

into Trev's chest and slid her butt against his pelvis. Like a stretching cat, she tilted her head enough to elongate her neck, letting it linger exposed just beneath his waiting lips.

Trev released a disbelieving gasp and Imani responded with a whimper that sounded more like a soft, inviting moan. Trev reacted, but Imani could tell he still hedged his bets in case she cried foul. Instead of surrendering full on, he disengaged his right hand from hers and slid it back along her bare arm, slow and smooth.

Each hair on her arm stood on edge, shooting delightful tingles of anticipation through her core. She moaned again, this time even softer and more sensual than before.

Trev's left hand sprung around from his side and proceeded to travel up and down her left arm in sync with the right hand. Still slow and smooth, yet hungry and demanding.

Imani arched back into his broad but slender chest. She needn't worry she'd break his tall, lanky frame because his body felt quite hard beneath hers.

His lips brushed her neck and she groaned wanting him to devour her completely. He complied and left a trail of kisses from just under her earlobe down to her practically bare shoulder.

Against her wishes, Imani's butt acted like it had a mind of its own as it grinded against Trev's rock hard member.

Her inadvertent action provided the necessary catalyst, like the proverbial stick that broke the camel's back. Trevor whipped Imani around to face him and after the briefest, lustiest look, his hungry lips moved in to taste her anxious ones.

Surrendering never felt so good, she thought as her tongue parted his lips and explored his caramel-tasting mouth. Mmm, she'd never think of Werther's in the same way. She almost smiled, but the candy's sweet remnants made her long for more and she deepened their kiss.

Trevor ramped up as well and he gently pushed her back against the bookshelves. His hands roamed down her back and cupped her buttocks.

Wanting him to explore further, she captured his right hand and slid it up to her breasts.

Trevor pulled back from their kiss long enough to gasp in surprise, but then his lust-laden eyes zoomed in on her breasts as he kneaded them with both hands. He glanced up, his face filled with gratitude and feverish longing and he peeled his right hand off her breasts long enough to pull her thankful lips back to his.

Unable to tame the desire flowing through her loins, Imani kicked up one leg and hooked it around his waist.

Trev moaned and Imani guided his right hand down from her breast to her hot, yearning center. His hand took over and rubbed her in time with his left hand which continued kneading delightful circles around her breast and nipple.

Feeling bold and throwing caution to the wind, she reached between his legs and unzipped his jeans.

Trev tensed and hesitated and Imani knew she couldn't go too far, too fast out in public like this.

Easing her hand into the cramped confines of his jeans, she maneuvered her hand until she could comfortably rub it up and down along his immense hardness.

Trev shivered under her hands and continued his previous motions and kisses much to Imani's delight.

After five orgasm-inducing minutes of hot, heavy petting and feverish foreplay, Imani knew she wanted Trevor here and now. Her hands left his body long enough to steal his wallet from his back pocket like a skilled thief.

Trev managed to pull away from her lips and shoot her an inquisitive look as she opened his wallet and fished out one of his condoms. He frowned and shook his head. "We're in the middle of the library," he whispered, his voice sounded hoarse. "We can't do it in here."

Imani's mischievous smile made an appearance in its own sweet time as she slowly nodded. "Like you said earlier, it's ten o'clock on a Friday night. No one else is in here but us…" She peered over her shoulder and pushed a book aside enough to spy on the library's solitary other inhabitant located far away at the circulation desk. "And the poor student serving library duty tonight is snoring at the front desk."

She flicked the condom up in the air between them with her first and second fingers almost like a smoker gesturing with their cigarette. "I'll keep quiet if you can," she said with a seductive smirk.

Trev shook his head and smiled. "I can't believe this." He snatched the condom from her fingers and ripped it open. "You're a really bad influence."

Imani responded by slipping her hand inside his restrictive jeans again and releasing Trev's unbelievably long, thick penis from his black, boxer briefs. She smiled in approval of his smart underwear choice. No way in the world he'd want this beast flapping around free in boxers and currently she couldn't imagine a pair of briefs containing it.

With the massive monster free, she gasped at the heavy weight of it in her hand. Good Lord she didn't know if that thing was going to fit inside her, but her body seemed not to possess a care in the world. She felt her insides moisten and surge forward almost as if they licked their lips, unable to wait for the upcoming feast.

Trev smiled as though he'd eavesdropped on her entire internal conversation and he somehow rolled the condom over the entirety of his pulsating muscle.

Imani did lick her lips now and her hands grabbed Trev's butt as he prepared to drive his monster home into her waiting lair.

His lips reengaged with hers while his left hand cupped her bottom for support and his right hand slowly guided his condom-coated creature inside her.

The cool, condom tip sent sweet shivers through her body and she gasped in surprised submission as her body continued to expand until he filled her whole. By now the condom no longer felt cool; it burned like an oven from its overheated contents. Thankfully, Trev didn't ram in and out at a brisk clip. He seemed to know that they needed to take this nice and slow…at least until her body adjusted to its new inhabitant.

Between the beautiful music their bodies

orchestrated together and the underlying sense of danger stemming from the fact that they might get caught having sexual relations in this very public place, she knew they would conclude soon. They were both too sprung and in need of release to prolong the outcome more than these five, delicious minutes. As if on cue, she felt his pace quicken and his breathing intensify.

Imani couldn't believe how fast her body ramped up to meet Trev's impending explosions and she covered her mouth with her right hand and bit her lip to restrain her cries of ecstasy. Her left hand reached back and grabbed the bookshelf to brace her body as the spasms took over.

Hoping to extend and intensify the moment, she closed her eyes and relished in the most intense orgasm she'd ever experienced. Spent, she dropped her hand and let her panting body lurch forward—

—but instead of landing in Trevor's waiting arms, Imani felt herself falling. Immediately her left hand windmilled back as she tried to catch her balance and her eyes shot open. It was pitch black. She gasped in confusion and the orgasmic-staccato beating of her heart stuttered into a frantic, fearful rhythm.

Why was it so dark? She blinked and refocused her eyes on her surroundings. Her eyebrows knitted and she frowned trying to comprehend. What was going on? They weren't in the library, they were in her dorm room…and there was no they, she was quite alone.

Imani spun her head around and pieces of the puzzle fell into place. Her disheveled, twisted and tangled sheets lay half-untucked, wrapped tight around her legs. The fingers from her left hand were anchored to the black, enameled steel and faux oak headboard of her university-provided twin bed. Her hand was the only thing preventing Imani from falling face first onto the hard floor.

Bewildered, she used her tense left arm to pull her body back onto the sanctuary of the bed. Feeling somewhat safer her heartbeat settled and she dropped her arms in her lap. Vast sections of the sheets and bed were damp with sweat and...her female juices. She groaned aloud and then shook her head in disgusted disbelief. If she were a guy, she would have painted the room with cum from her powerful, vivid, and too damn realistic wet dream!

Careful to avoid the damp mess, she plopped onto her back and stared at the ceiling, trying to analyze the situation. She still couldn't believe that she dreamt the whole thing! Her right hand traveled up from her side and rested on her erratically racing yet normalizing heart. What were her dreams trying to tell her? Was it simply that all work and no play made Imani a very horny girl? Or was her normally trusty instinct stomping down its foot and stating in no uncertain terms that she should finally give Trev the chance he deserved?

"Argh!" She covered her eyes in confused frustration. Good thing Melody decided to spend the night at Kevin's. God knows she would follow the most obvious, romantic interpretation!

Imani sighed and got up. Maybe a clean bed, a long, hot shower, and time alone would help her think. She simply didn't know what would happen the next time she saw Trevor.

STUDYING AND MASSAGES

Lance arrived in their room right on time and scooped up Melody into his familiar bear hug.

Melody laughed as he twirled her around three times and planted a kiss on her cheek. His sandalwood soap smell tickled her nose as much as his fast movements tickled her stomach.

After Lance set her down, he went over and pecked Imani on the lips much to Melody's chagrin. She had hoped that the two of them would cut that nonsense out, but as of yet their inappropriate habit continued to strengthen and grow. She shuddered and watched as Lance plopped down on Imani's bed.

Imani shrugged and sat at her desk.

"Are you guys ready to go study?" Melody asked and then decided to make her question more specific. "In the dorm floor kitchen," she added, tempted to throw in a, 'like we usually do,' comment, too.

"Actually," Lance replied before he rubbed his hands over his face vigorously. "I'm kind of beat after football practice and I'd really just love to relax tonight." He sat up straight as he seemed to remember his manners. "That is if you two don't mind?"

Imani lifted her hands into a half-hearted shrug. "We have been burning the midnight oil a lot lately. I could use a break." Imani looked at her. "What about you, Melody?"

"Whatever!" Melody huffed and took a seat at her desk.

Imani looked like she wanted to come over and check on Melody, but Lance interrupted. "Hey, Imani, would you mind giving me one of your quick, mind-blowing massages?" he asked turning on his most charming smile.

"Boy, please!" Imani scoffed as she stood up and went over to her bed. "Flattery will get you nowhere with me." She slapped his back and gestured for him to lie down on his stomach so that she could straddle his back. "Mind you, I'm only agreeing to do this because I expect you to reciprocate in fifteen minutes when I'm done." Imani straddled Lance's back but refused to move a massage-giving muscle until he replied. "Do we have a deal?"

"But of course," Lance replied with a grin as he settled in for Imani to commence the massage.

Melody frowned. Neither of them asked her if she wanted a massage. Not that she wanted Lance to massage her. Again, that gesture, like a kiss on the lips, would have seemed way too personal unless he kept it strictly confined to her neck and shoulders. But Imani was a different story. Imani had given her a massage before and Melody couldn't lie, it felt heavenly.

Feeling left out, Melody tried to kick start a conversation. "So, Imani, I noticed you and Trevor have been spending a lot of time together lately..." She let her voice and the question trail off in her usual innocent manner.

This time though, she saw Imani visibly bristle. Like a viper, Imani whipped her head towards Melody in a flash and lashed out. "I don't know what you think you saw, but you're sorely mistaken," Imani said with such vehemence that Melody felt like Imani practically bit her head off.

Even Lance pulled himself out of his massage-induced moans long enough to peer over his shoulder and give Imani a curious look.

"Damn, Imani," Melody replied trying to bury her hurt feelings as she grabbed her backpack. "I was just trying to make polite conversation." She stood up and glared at Imani. "I didn't mean anything by it." As the hurt turned to anger, she stomped over to the coat closet and snatched her coat off its hanger.

Imani jumped off Lance's back and scrambled over to the door before Melody could leave. Despite her protests, Imani pulled Melody into a tight, apologetic hug. "Please don't go, Melody. I'm just tired and grumpy and you know our periods are about to start," Imani said trying to make a joke about their coinciding menstrual cycles. Evidently that was one of the odd tricks of Mother Nature that women realized when they lived together for too long.

Unable to stay mad at anyone for long, especially her best friends, Melody sighed. "It's fine."

"Are you sure?" Imani released her enough to pull back and study Melody's face.

Melody nodded. "Yeah, we're fine."

Imani frowned. "But?"

Melody didn't understand how Imani could almost read people's mind sometimes. In the past, she had joked on a couple of occasions about how she'd inherited a freaky sixth sense from her mother and her grandmother before her. Melody wrestled with her feelings. Although she wasn't mad anymore, she really didn't want to be here any longer. Inside she broke into a faint smile of hope.

Imani grinned full blast for her. "Go ahead and be with your man," she said nodding her head towards the door.

"Are you sure?" Melody asked wondering if maybe Imani and Kevin really were getting along.

"Yeah, sure," Imani replied. "I guess we should be glad that you still wanted to study with us at all."

"Thanks, Imani," she said as she leapt forward and hugged Imani. Halfway out the door, she yelled back over her shoulder, "see you later, Lance." Melody thought she heard him moan a response in his massage-induced coma-like state, but she had already descended the first of two flights of stairs to the exit.

When she erupted into the chilly, November night, she took a deep breath and let the beckoning lights of college activity lead her towards campus. Wondering if she should head towards the library were she knew Kevin was studying or to the Union, where she could grab a steaming cup of hot chocolate with whipped cream and a dash of cinnamon, Melody whipped out her phone.

Kevin answered on the first ring. "What's wrong?" he asked. "I thought you were studying with Lance and Imani?"

"We were supposed to but Lance didn't really feel like studying and I didn't really feel like hanging around with them any longer."

"Oh," Kevin replied, his voice sounded surprised and delighted all wrapped into one delicious, succulent candy. "Why don't you use your key and come on over to my room," he suggested all innocent and sweet. "I could wrap up with my study group in about another thirty minutes."

"Hmm, thanks for the offer," Melody replied her heart soaring. Thoughts of hot chocolate dissipated like a mirage as thoughts of her body wrapped up in Kevin's arms took precedent. "I can't wait to see you then."

"I'm looking forward to it, Beautiful," he replied before he disconnected.

Melody pocketed her cell phone and raced over to Kevin's dorm room, the big, cloud nine smile never once leaving her face.

FOOTBALL AND JEALOUSY - DECEMBER 2000

Lance raced out of his Managerial Economics class before the majority of the students poured out and crowded the halls. Free and clear, he surged down the hall towards the School of Business exit. Two doors ahead, he spotted Melody leaving her Behavioral Economics class and he sped up to purposefully bump into her. "Hey, Sunshine, where are you headed?"

Melody smiled and bumped him back. "I promised to meet Imani outside the library and then hook up with Kevin for lunch in the Union. You?"

"I hadn't decided on any particular plan of action, but that sounds like as good a choice as any." He surged ahead and held the door open for them to exit the building then he fell into step beside Melody.

Melody shuddered and zipped her coat all the way up as the bitter, northwestern, December wind felt like an express train barreling down from the Great Lakes. Lance adjusted his economics book to block the wind and just as suddenly, it howled to a stop. "Gotta love the weather here," he said with a smirk.

"Although we have a dome, I always wondered how you guys play football in the freezing cold without a coat and sometimes without wearing long sleeves. At least pull up your socks to protect you from the cold."

Lance chuckled and tossed his free arm around her shoulder. "Folks like Big Tony are the real freaks. I, at least, wear long sleeves, but when you're on the field, your adrenaline's pumping so hard you rarely notice anything else. The worst is when you're just waiting around on the sideline. Then if you're smart, you drape your coat over you."

"Well you may have to deal with the wintry weather a while longer. If you guys win this Saturday's game, it looks like we'll make it to a bowl game for the first time in over a decade!"

"Don't remind me. We're seven and four now, probably not strong enough to make it based on our strength of schedule. However, if we pull off a win against Syracuse for this last game of the season… Well, I'm not trying to jinx it by overthinking it."

"Please! I'm not sure what you guys did in training camp this summer, but whatever it was, it worked wonders. You've been kicking butt all year and I doubt that will change come Saturday afternoon."

"Let's hope so. Anyhow, thanks for the kind words."

"Well you need to get them when you can because I see Imani coming out of the library now," she said pointing towards their friend.

Lance spotted Imani immediately and laughed. "You know I could tell her what you said, just to get her going."

"Please don't," Melody replied rolling her eyes. "That would be all I need, Imani on another crazy rant."

Lance glanced back towards Imani then he

squinted. "Whoa, is that Kevin exiting behind Imani?" he asked in disbelief.

"Quit joking, they're not that friendly yet," Melody replied shooting him a skeptical look.

Lance redirected his attention back towards Imani and Kevin, just as Kevin glanced their direction. Kevin spied them and his face lit up in an instant. "I'm not kidding." He nodded his head in Kevin's direction as Kevin started sprinting over leaving Imani in the dust as she scowled and took her own sweet time.

Evidently Melody realized it, too, because she slipped out from under Lance's arm so fast that he almost fell over.

"Baaa-bieee," Melody squealed until Kevin scooped her up in his arms and planted a kiss on her waiting lips.

Unbelievably they continued the lustful kiss even after both he and Imani arrived. Channeling Big Tony, Lance averted his eyes and almost muttered, 'get a room!'

But Imani beat him to the punch as she cleared her throat much louder and ruder than necessary. "Alright, already."

Melody disengaged her lips from Kevin's slow as molasses, but she kept her body positioned snug under Kevin's arm. "We're sorry, sometimes we just can't help ourselves," she replied resting her head on Kevin's chest.

Kevin looked as content as Lance felt after sex. "When you find the perfect person, you never want to let them go." He glanced down at Melody and she smiled in response to some secret language they were utilizing. Kevin glanced back up to Lance. "In fact, since I don't want to let Melody go..."

"We gotta go," Melody replied and then giggled as she and Kevin turned and walked off in the direction of Kevin's dorm leaving him alone with Imani.

"Hmm, that was slightly awkward," he said chuckling at Imani's annoyed facial expression. "At least it appears like you and Kevin are getting along better."

"Shows what you know. Appearances can be deceiving." Imani snorted and put him in his place in an instant. "Please, when Kevin spotted me in the library, he assumed Melody would be with me. Much to his horror and shock, she was not." She let loose a half-evil laugh. "But he sure enough hightailed it and left me in the dust when he saw you two coming. I'm still not sure if he's possessive, jealous, or both."

"Who?" he asked not understanding her inference.

"Kevin, Silly! Who else were we talking about?" Imani frowned at him like he was dense. "I swore Kevin flew into a rage and took off like a bat out of hell when he saw you with your big beefy arm all draped over his woman like a cape."

"Please, I saw the whole incident unfold. Kevin's face lit up like a moonbeam when he saw Melody and he didn't give me a second glance. In fact, the boy acted fine when he came over and got her."

"Claimed his property or marked his territory is more like it!" Imani snorted. "It's not like you really paid them any attention. You're about as observant as a post. If you actually watch Kevin closely, his true, evil side shines through for a millisecond, just before he puts on a happy face mask for the rest of you nonobservant suckers."

"And now I see why Kevin dislikes you; he can't catch a break," he replied, purposefully yanking her chain. He positioned himself to make a speedy escape in case she gave chase.

Imani's mouth contorted and then she smirked and nodded, refusing to take the bait. "See that's why I don't talk to you, you're ignorant!"

CHRISTMAS SURPRISE

"You're so beautiful," Kevin said as he caught Melody's arm. With a flick of his wrist, he twirled her into his arms until her naked back nestled against his bare chest. He pointed her hand at their reflection in his bathroom mirror. "I want you to really look in the mirror and see what I see," he said, his soft yet insistent voice vibrated down her spine.

Without even looking at the mirror, his tone alone imparted so much confidence in Melody that she felt like she could storm into the Ford Modeling Agency and demand a go-see with *Vogue* or Calvin Klein. Not that she harbored the tiniest inclination to model, it's just that Kevin's approving gaze made her feel like the most desirable woman in the world.

Following his directions, Melody looked at their reflections. Due to her short height and their close proximity to the over the sink mirror, she could only see their bodies from her shoulders up. It was enough to bring a smile to her face. Her slightly damp, towel-dried blonde curls surrounded her face like a mane while his short blonde hair stood up in handsome spikes. Their faces still appeared flush from afterglow. In fact when you factored in her golden-tanned skin with his slightly lighter coloring, it looked like a complementary bowl of delicious peaches and cream.

Kevin leaned down and kissed her shoulder, sending electrical currents through her already rubbery legs. "You're perfect," he said before he kissed her neck and then her shoulder again.

Melody groaned and leaned against him for support as she wouldn't be able to stand on her own much longer. His wondrous fresh, Irish Spring scent reminded her of earlier when his soapy, clean smell mingled with her rose-scented cologne. The combination brought to mind visions of her favorite season, spring, with its Vincent van Gogh flurry of irises and colorful flowers in bloom. The thoughts of "flowers" blooming and his seductive scent made Melody want to indulge again.

With a knowing chuckle, Kevin stood up straight and redirected her attention to their reflections. "You know I always want to make you as happy as you make me, right?"

Melody gave him an enthusiastic nod.

"Well, I actually have a surprise for you."

"Really?" Melody asked perking up.

"If you hadn't been in such a rush to escape Lance and Imani an hour ago and jump my bones when we arrived, I would have told you then." His sky blue eyes sparkled in a mischievous dance.

Melody's mouth dropped open in feigned shock. "Me? If I recall correctly, you were the one doing all of the rushing, escaping, and jumping bones."

"Well, whoever's fault it was, I found a way to extend the fun...in New York City."

Melody frowned and turned around to face him.

"What are you saying?" she asked, holding her breath and hoping he meant what she thought he meant.

"I saved enough to get a hotel in the City--"

Melody squealed and jumped up and down.

Kevin tried to temper her response. "It's only for two days and it's the week before Christmas, that's all I could afford. I figured we could leave as soon as finals were over. Then afterwards you could continue home for Christmas break with your mom being none the wiser and I'll catch the bus back up here. But we could go to Rockefeller Center like you suggested last summer. Go ice skating, check out the tree. Maybe see the Rockettes. What do you think?"

"I think you are the most amazing man in the world," she said relishing in his loving arms.

CHRISTMAS PLANS

Elbowing her way through the busy Union, Imani grabbed the last seat at their table.

"You're late, half of us are done eating," Big Tony said while chewing a mouthful of lasagna. "We were just discussing our Christmas Break plans." Big Tony elbowed John who sat next to him drinking a milkshake. "We're saying that you guys need to wish us luck."

"Why?" Karen asked picking up a French fry. "We already know you're going to stomp Big East powerhouse, Syracuse, this Saturday. And then you're going to play in some bowl game somewhere and bring the first bowl trophy home since 1989."

"I wish we could all have her confidence," Joe said, slapping Lance on the back. "Maybe we should have her deliver coach's pre-game speech in the locker room."

"Humph, now that I wouldn't mind," Karen smiled as she ate another French fry. "All that beefcake and testosterone flying around."

"Oh, Lord, you're nasty," Krystal said shaking her head and setting down her burger.

"Well, one of us has to be," she replied giving both Krystal and Erycah a pointed look.

Imani wondered what that comment alluded to, but

she decided it best not to ask.

"Alrighty, then," Big Tony said, always one to steer conversations clear from anything remotely sexual or too intimate for group table conversations. "Where are you going, little Miss Melody?"

Melody gave them a secretive, coy grin. "Home," she replied blushing.

But Imani already knew that the heifer planned on spending the first two days of Christmas Break in a hotel with Kevin before she made it all the way home. Focusing on her spaghetti, she decided not to blow the girl's cover. Fortunately for Melody, no one else seemed to pick up on her lack of full disclosure.

"And what about you, Imani," Big Tony asked just as she was about to place a forkful of spaghetti into her drooling mouth. She frowned and rested her fork on her plate. "I'm going home, too. Spending time with the family," she said and then she picked up her fork and damn near devoured the bite to quiet her growling belly.

"Oh, so you're riding back with Trevor?" Big Tony asked, evidently all up in everyone's business today.

Luckily, Trev saved her from speaking with her mouth full. "Not exactly," he said. "I'm dropping her off at the Greyhound station because I'm flying to Jamaica to meet my father for Christmas."

Big Tony choked on his lasagna. "Damn, man, take me with you!"

For a quick second, Imani noticed Erycah whispering something into Trevor's ear before her attention diverted to Lance as he tilted and balanced his chair on its back two legs.

"You're not getting your big, scared butt on a plane," Lance said shaking his head. "I don't know why you even pretend."

"True," Big Tony replied with a huge grin.

"Wait, how's that work with your football games?" Krystal asked. "Not all of them are within driving distance."

"We have to knock him out," John replied, shaking his head while an unapologetic Big Tony grinned and chowed down on his lasagna.

"Now, that's a damn shame," Karen said shaking her head. She turned and gave her girlfriend, Erycah, a pointed look. "So, we already know that Krystal and I are going home. But I swear that you haven't shared where you're going."

Erycah blushed even through her walnut-colored skin tone.

Imani's eyebrow arched on its own. Damn, wherever Erycah was going must be good to generate such an intense reaction. While Erycah took her time replying, Imani stuffed another delicious, garlic and cheese-laden bite of spaghetti into her hungry mouth.

At first Imani didn't even recognize that Erycah was talking because she used the same sing-songy intonation that Melody typically employed. "I'm just flying home to Ohio. And Trev here is being kind enough to drop me off at the airport, too."

Not liking the schoolgirl crush sounds emanating from Erycah, Imani almost choked on her food. Making a quick recovery, Imani looked up to see what was *really* going on. But Erycah appeared to be her usual, bashful Bohemian self. Imani frowned, were her ears playing tricks on her? She hesitated. She doubted it, but when she glanced around no one else seemed to have picked up on anything untoward.

And to top it all off, Trev was speaking now and he was looking directly at Imani, giving her his full undivided attention. Definitely not the actions of someone that showed any interest in Erycah. "Her flight's an hour before mine, so it was an easy call," he replied seemingly wanting to explain his actions.

"Wait, why would you fly from Albany rather than New York?" Joe asked taking over Big Tony's nosy line of questioning. "I'm sure at least one of our three airports offered cheaper flights."

Imani refocused on her food, Trevor had already told her why when he reserved his flights.

"I thought so, too. But there's a charter flight of little, old, white, bridge and canasta-playing ladies, who have an unbelievable steal of a deal direct to and from Albany to Kingston. So, I'm taking one of their extra spaces."

"Now that's something you don't hear every day," Lance said as he chuckled and landed his chair back down on all four legs. "Reggae-bound, canasta players. Well, as much as I'd love to stay, I gotta go."

Half the table got up and cleared out with him, and Erycah stood up and whispered something in Trev's ear again. Her hand rested a little too comfortably on his shoulder and Imani swore the girl let it linger and slide off his shoulder as she smiled and departed.

Trev noticed Imani staring his way and he winked.

Imani rolled her eyes and fixated on her spaghetti. For whatever reason it didn't taste as delicious as before. She frowned and set down her fork while she struggled to swallow the starchy lump. Not one prone to jealousy, her apparent overreaction bothered her immensely. What the hell was going on?

Alpha Party, Part Two – January 2001

"Happy New Year," Lance said as he strolled in and pecked Imani on the lips.

"Happy New Year to you, Mr. You-Got-Dunn, You-Got-Lanced, Bowl Champion," she said as she shut her dorm room door behind him.

Lance actually played all modest and humble rather than his normal, boastful preening. He gave her a simple wink and then he went to greet Melody and Kevin.

Odd. Imani's eyebrow shot up and then she shrugged. Maybe Lance decided to turn over a new leaf for 2001. Just as Imani opened her mouth to ask him, someone knocked on their door. With a shake of her head, she waltzed over to answer it.

As she peered through the peephole, her mouth dropped open. No way! She frowned as she unlocked the door but managed a polite grin when she opened it.

"Hey Trev," she said welcoming him inside. As they hugged, she frowned again. Trevor wore the same exact clothing that he had on during her wet dream two months ago. The dream she refused to speak to anyone about, including Melody. The wet dream she'd almost managed to forget and erase from her memory banks.

She smiled as she glanced down at her cute but

warm, body-covering outfit. Luckily, the temperature tonight was much colder than in her dream, so already her dream veered drastically from reality. And last she checked they hadn't made any plans to stop by the library!

Trev squeezed her tight and she took the opportunity to really feel his body under the guise of a welcoming hug. Hmm, not quite as muscular as in her dream, still a beanpole but not bad. She got a whiff of his cologne and her nose crinkled in response to the odd smell. Definitely not in her dream and not the best choice, she thought as she pulled back and gestured him towards the waiting Lance, Melody, and Kevin.

As they exchanged greetings, she decided to get the show on the road. "So, are we all ready to finally go party?"

"Hold your horses, Woman," Lance fussed as he picked up Melody's coat off her bed. "Here you go, Melody," he said preparing to help her put it on, but Kevin snatched it away and beat Lance to the punch.

Imani frowned, but before she could comment an unfazed Lance grabbed Imani's coat and tossed it to her before donning his own coat.

Trev smiled and meandered over to stand by her side.

Imani couldn't help but sneak curious glances over at his private area trying to gauge how much was reality versus her wild and crazy fantasy. Knowing that steady state differed vastly from Action Jackson mode, she still didn't see how reality could measure up to her exaggerated dream. Although Trev looked like he was well-endowed, big feet, 6'2", half-Jamaican and all, it still seemed to come up short from her monster dream

"Oh, I miss all of us getting together," Melody said in her dreamy, romantic way. "We should hang out again tomorrow before we get busy with classes again."

Imani managed to hold her tongue although it burned her not to say, 'you're the only one who never hangs out with us anymore!' Instead she remained civil. "We could catch a movie tomorrow…if that works for you two," she added unable to completely behave.

"Ooo, we could see *Crouching Tiger, Hidden Dragon*," Trev said. "There's great action sequences and fight scenes for the guys and a love story and supposedly beautiful choreography for the girls."

"I'm down with that," Imani said wondering how Kevin would talk his way out of this one.

"Count me in, just pick an early time," Lance said moving towards Imani and the door.

"That sounds like fun," Melody almost cooed as she looked up to Kevin. "Do you want to hit the first show? It usually starts around noon."

Kevin beamed down at Melody. "Whatever you want, Baby."

Imani shrugged almost impressed. Maybe Kevin wasn't so bad after all. She opened the door, pushed Lance out, and gestured for the rest to follow.

Kevin reared back for a second. "Oh, I almost forgot. I'm supposed to meet my study group tomorrow at noon. Can we catch the second show instead?"

"I'd prefer noon, but two or three o'clock can work," Lance replied. "I'll just need to make a few phone calls and juggle things around."

"Either works for me," Trev said as he waited beside Imani.

"Fine, see you guys at the movies for the second showing. We can call each other tomorrow to finalize our plans," Imani said getting exasperated. "Now can we please go? I'm ready to kick loose for once and the Alpha party is calling my name!"

***

"Wow, and there he goes again," Melody said in amazement as Lance got escorted onto the dance floor by a familiar looking exotic beauty with hazel-colored, doe eyes and long black hair.

"And you're still surprised?" Imani shook her head and stood up. "Excuse me for a minute; I need to hit the Ladies room." She patted Melody's back and headed towards the bathroom.

Trevor looked slightly annoyed that Imani left, but he quickly recovered and turned to Melody. "You wanna dance?" he asked as he bopped about, the music clearly coursing through his body and controlling his movements.

Kevin jumped up and grabbed Melody's hand before she could respond. "I think not," he said as he led Melody onto the dance floor.

"That could have been misconstrued as rude," she teased, loving his chivalrous actions.

Kevin twirled her around, dipped her, and then slipped her back into his arms as she beamed with breathless delight. His lips hovered mere inches from hers. "I don't like you dancing with other guys."

Mm, was he jealous? "So, you want me all to yourself?" she said using her most flirtatious tone.

Kevin's breath hitched and his eyes widened as if her were surprised by her comment. Then he nodded and smiled, with those smoldering blue eyes. "Yes. Yes, I do," he replied in a husky voice as he pulled her tight. "You are mine and mine alone."

"I'm completely and unequivocally yours and yours alone," she replied feeling that sexy confidence that only Kevin invoked. His heated gaze turned her all googly inside and she melted into his strong arms. Oh, God, how could one guy love her this much? This beautiful, adoring gentleman loved and cared about *her*. She rested her head on his chest. No doubt about it, she really was the luckiest woman in the world.

***

"Ahh, poor baby's here all by his lonesome." Imani plopped down on the stool next to Trev.

Trevor smirked.

"I guess I'll have to keep you company," she said taking the opportunity to pat his shoulder and upper arm while really feeling for the muscle tone underneath again, just to make sure. Nope, not as good as in her dream but not bad either.

"Whew, I'm relieved to hear it. I don't know what I would have done here without you," he said pretending to wipe his forehead.

The motion brought her attention to his head. Another item that wasn't quite like in her dream. She reached out and touched one of Trev's newly forming dreadlocks. She loved ethnic hairstyles, but she didn't expect Trevor to embrace them with her own gusto. It was cool but not quite right or at least not what she expected. "So, you're really going to grow dreads, huh?"

He nodded with a sly smile.

"Even though your mom hates 'island men' and all their ways?" Funny how a baby could change things like that. Sometimes the very things you loved when you were young and naïve, weren't so fun and cute when responsibilities and maturity kick in. "You know she'll probably kill you when you go home for Spring Break?"

"Well that's the consequence of telling your son to connect with his Jamaican father over Christmas Break in Kingston."

"So you really had a nice time, huh?"

Trev nodded with a far-away smile on his face. "I did. We put a lot of hurt feelings out there in the open. Dealt with our issues. It was pretty cool." Trev half-chuckled then hesitated and Imani could tell that he toyed with what to say next.

She decided to break the ice first. "Hey, weird question. Do you ever keep in touch with any of your exes?"

Trev's eyes danced, but his mouth dropped open. "Talk about weird and completely random. Any particular reason you're asking?" His eyes twinkled as he tried to contain his toothy grin.

"No," she lied thinking of a way to play it off. "My high school ex called during Christmas break and I just wondered how you would have handled the same situation."

"Oh." Trev's face fell and Imani felt bad about lying. "Is your ex-boyfriend back in the picture now?"

"No, no, no," Imani replied and waved her hand, eager to clear up any confusion her stupid lie created. "He just wanted to check up on an old friend, let me know how he was doing at college. We've both moved on to bigger and better things."

"Oh," Trev replied with a shy smile. Looking more comfortable and relaxed, he leaned back and answered her question. "See, that's why my exes and I don't remain friends."

Imani tempered her reaction. "You never remain friends?" she asked finding that bold proclamation startling but rather unlikely. "So you're saying that if I were the type to go scrounging through your little, black book—which I'm not, but if I were—you're saying I wouldn't still see their numbers listed with big bold stars next to them?"

"Please, no way! Their names are either scratched out or erased. I'm telling you, once you cross the line between friends and lovers; it changes things and muddies the water. Causes confusion."

Now it was Imani's turn to mask her disappointment. "Mmm-hmm," she muttered as she grabbed her drink and pretended to sip it.

Looking happy and confident with his response, Trev followed suit and swiveled around to grab his drink.

Imani crunched on an ice cube while she processed his response. So if she did decide to follow her wild but increasingly inaccurate dream and God forbid they realize that a relationship just couldn't work out, she'd be minus a great study and lab partner. In addition to a great friend who she'd come to enjoy talking to and getting advice from. Was she really ready to risk all that on a dubious, romantic notion?

Trev tapped her arm, his toothy grin back in full effect. "You ready to hit the dance floor? You're starting to look a little serious, Labbie."

Imani plastered on a smile and nodded. "I'm fine, let's go," she said before he could put two and two together. As she followed Trev onto the floor, she spied Melody and Kevin looking happy as two peas in a pod. She already knew what Melody would say she should do. And seeing their ecstatic faces, Imani wondered if maybe, just maybe, her naïve, little optimistic friend had it right after all.

ALMOND EYES

Lance awakened when a hand slid across his chest, tickling his smattering of hairs. The hand came to rest on his left shoulder. Soon the head attached to the wayward hand nestled into the crook of his right arm.

He blinked to get his bearings. Hmm, definitely not my room. Same size and orientation but too pink and frilly. As he closed his eyes to remember, her peach-tinged smell hit him. Oh, yes, Miss Exotic Almond Eyes. A smile crept across his face. No way should he have forgotten her so soon. His smile widened as he replayed the evening's sexual highlights.

Tingles shot through his arm as it started to fall asleep from her heavy head. Time to leave.

He removed his left arm from under the covers to see the time. The glow-in-the-dark hands read: **2:35 a.m.** Oh yeah, time to go!

Slow and smooth, he eased his lower body out of bed while removing his right arm from under her head. Then he laid her wandering arm on the frilly, pink pillow. He gazed at her for a moment. She was definitely fine and knew how to work her body, his too for that matter.

Quiet as a whisper, he dressed fast and was almost done when she stirred. He stopped for fear of waking her with any noise.

Almond Eye's wandering arm slid across the pillow then down to the cooled sheets. When her hand encountered nothing but linen, she turned, awoke, and sat up.

"Sorry, I didn't mean to wake you."

"Mmm. I wouldn't mind if you were waking me for a little something, something." She grinned and stretched.

"Well, since you've already worked your way through my stash of jimmy hats, I need to be on my way."

"Like I told you before, I'm on the pill, Baby. No needs to worry." Throwing the covers back, she exposed her sumptuous, naked body and patted the bed for an express invitation.

"Now you know I'd hit that again in a second, but as they say, 'No glove, no love.'" He finished getting dressed.

Getting to her knees, she ran her sensuous hands across her chest. "You know you can't resist all this fine love, Baby."

Lance raised an eyebrow. "Ain't no love worth me becoming a Baby's Daddy or visiting the doctor with unexpected problems." He patted his pockets to make sure his wallet and keys were in place.

"You're kidding, right?" Almond Eyes started to catch an attitude. "As the crowds say when you're on the football field, I want to get *Dunn*! *Lance* me, Baby. Shit, Krystal bragged about all your good loving. Said you knew your way down South. I hope you planned on breaking me off some of that before you left?"

"Oh, so that's what this is about? Krystal?"

"Yeah! I know my chocolate pudding tastes way better than hers. So, you needs to come correct." She checked the attitude and poured on the love again. "They say third times the charm. Let's say we both experience a little ecstasy," she said spreading her legs open.

"Tempting as that is and as much as I appreciate Krystal's advertising, she failed to inform you that we only explored all peaks and valleys after she showed me her papers."

"Papers?"

"Yeah, papers, Baby. I waited in the Infirmary with Krystal when she got her HIV results. Not to mention a clean bill of health on all other nasty little STDs. Then and only then did we *celebrate* for a week."

"Oh, is that all, Honey? We can go get one of those when the Infirmary opens. Why don't you stay? I'll treat you to breakfast and we can talk about things. Get a box of condoms to pass away the night. I got what you need to be happy forever, no reason to leave."

Unhappy with her insinuations and banter, Lance grabbed his coat, moved to the door, and opened it ready to leave. "Maybe we'll get together again. But in case we don't, thank you for an enjoyable evening." With that he departed before she moved.

He sprinted to the end of the hall and down the four flights of stairs, not slowing until clear of her dormitory. He had a bad feeling about Almond Eyes. She was more persistent than the other women he slept with. They all seemed to understand it was just a one-time thing, but this one appeared to want more. And she had pursued him!

Krystal, huh? Nice to know she enjoyed the multiple rides enough to brag, but he needed to talk to her. Didn't want her advertising to just anybody. What the hell was that girl's real name anyway? He couldn't tell Krystal his concerns about some chick he dubbed Almond Eyes. Oh well, he would ring her tomorrow and see what nonsense she had gotten him into.

Lunch with Krystal

The alarm clock read 10:00 a.m. when Lance sat at his desk and picked up the telephone. All of a sudden Imani's past warning words worried him. What if Krystal did develop feelings and want more? He hesitated and then decided to go for broke. "Here goes nothing," he muttered as he dialed Krystal's number and waited for her to answer.

"Lance, Baby, what's up?" Krystal purred.

Not knowing how to take her tone, he forged ahead. "Hey, Krystal, would you like to get together for lunch today? I need to ask you something." He held his breath.

"That sounds exciting and mysterious. Are you trying to get back in my pants?"

Lance grimaced. Maybe Imani understood more than he gave her credit for. He kept his tone playful and friendly. "Actually, as wonderful as that sounds, I just wanted to catch up."

"Alright," she said laughing away his anxiety. "Wanna meet at the Union or Farley Dining Hall? I have to meet my study group in the library at one."

"The Union sounds good. I'll meet you by the Pizza Parlor at noon. Okay?"

"See you then, Lance."

He hung up relieved. With that done, he decided to

check on his girls.

Imani answered on the first ring. "Guess your latest conquest didn't pass the overnight test."

"No, I split around three. How about you? Should I dare ask if you finally gave Trevor some action?"

"How many different times and ways do I have to tell y'all that the boy's just a friend!"

"Oh-kay, Biz Markie."

"Skip you, Lance! Did you call for any particular reason besides to be your normal, annoying self?"

"Actually, I called for two reasons. One, are we still on for the movies at two because I'd like to know how to plan the rest of my day?"

"I haven't heard from Melody or Kevin, so I'm assuming we're still a go. What else?"

"Number two, I was wondering if we could talk over lunch at the Union. Does noon work for you? I need your opinion on a situation."

"A situation, huh? Problems with the hottie from last night?"

"You know me too well, Girl." He shook his head impressed by her reliable intuition. "So will I see you at noon?"

"Can't wait!"

SPONTANEOUS DECISION

"Let's go," Kevin whispered to Melody as he quit stroking her hair.

She checked her watch. It was only 10:15 am. To her dismay Kevin jumped out of bed and headed towards his bathroom. Reluctantly, she left the comforts of his cozy bed and followed him. "I thought we were going to sleep in, *play*, and then go to the movies now that we found out that your study group doesn't want to meet until 5:00.

"We'll retire to bed early tonight and play then," he said with a heart-stopping, suggestive smile. "I want to treat you now." He quickly turned on the shower and then he pulled her into his arms and her pace quickened with thoughts of scrumptious treats he could provide. "Since I know you would really prefer to see *What Women Want* instead of *Crouching Tiger, Hidden Dragon*, let's catch the early screening at noon and then get a hot fudge sundae at Friendly's."

Mm, that sounded fun and tasty just like him. She leaned up and he rewarded her with a delicious kiss. When her delightful fog of love dissipated a bit she remembered Imani. "We should call Imani and let her know our change in plans. They'll be happy to know we're hitting the early show."

"Mm-hmm." Kevin kissed her again, deeper this

time until her thoughts became as foggy and steamy as the bathroom mirror.

DISCUSSING SHANITA

Jogging downstairs into the Union basement, Lance found a sparse crowd, unusual for a Sunday afternoon. A boisterous group watched the basketball game on the big screen TV. Others played video games at the arcade. But the food court area was almost empty. Lance spied Krystal and Imani already eating together.

Imani somehow sensed him nearby and caught him staring at her and Krystal. She waved and he nodded in acknowledgement.

Krystal noticed Imani wave and then she waved, too.

Lance half returned her wave and hurried to place his order at the Chinese food counter. With his bottled water and beef and broccoli over brown rice in hand, he joined the girls.

"Right on time, Lance," Imani said.

"Afternoon, Ladies," he said getting settled. "Didn't think you'd beat me here and start without me."

Krystal shot Imani a sly look of intrigue. "So what happened with Shanita last night?"

Shanita—that was Almond Eyes name! "Okay, what have you vicious gossips been saying behind my back?"

With faux indignation, Imani answered after a bite

of fries. "Now is that any way to talk to your girls?" But she couldn't keep a straight face and both women giggled, almost spitting out their food.

It was Krystal's turn to start in on him. "Why in the world did you hook up with Shanita? I know she's cute, but that girl ain't right."

"What! You were the one that sicced her on me!"

"What you talking 'bout, Willis?"

"Almond—I mean, Shanita said that you were bragging on all the good loving I gave you. How I worked it out down South. Chickie started catching attitude when I left without giving her any."

Imani swiveled around in her chair and weaved her head and finger at Krystal, pretending to chew her out. "Oh, no you didn't spread all this man's business out there. Especially to scandalous types like Shanita. Girl, what's up with that?"

Krystal hung her head low and gave it a bewildered shake. "I swear I didn't tell that girl anything." Smiling, she shrugged, "I confess, I might have gotten a little carried away with what I said to Erycah and Karen after recollecting about a particularly good night with you. But Shanita wasn't...oh."

"Oh, what?" he asked.

"She was at the next table and I think Karen stopped by later with her big mouth."

"Whoops!" Imani made a face and left Krystal hanging.

"Mm-hmm." Lance stroked his moustache. "And how exactly do you plan on helping me out of this?"

"Hey, I didn't tell you to sleep with her. You need to control your penis better." Krystal rolled her eyes and bit into her pizza.

He cringed at her less than ladylike response. "Well you're forgetting she came onto me. In a big way. And almost jumped my bones at the party." Putting Krystal's response aside, he struck a pose that highlighted his guns. "Not my fault, you girls are so weak when it comes to this muscular, oh so handsome package."

"Puh-leeze!" Imani feigned disgust. "Control yourself why don't you."

"Come on, Girly Girl." Lance batted his eyelashes. "You know you want me, too."

"Like I want a hole in the head or a case of Herpes."

"Or as bad as she wants Trevor from what I hear," said Krystal.

"Oh, c'mon! Not you, too!" Imani took a sudden interest in examining her plate much to Lance's amusement.

"Hmm, looks like I hit a nerve, eh Lance?"

"Seems everyone's noticed how much Imani and Trev hang out except her. Boy's got it bad and she says he's just a friend."

"Well, Lance, you can't force things like who you love." Krystal elbowed Imani. "So, you're saying you wouldn't be mad if someone else say like Erycah, decided to put a move on your friend, right?"

"Damn, you's a schemer, Krystal!" Imani looked peeved and seemed one step away from erupting. "I can't restrict who Trev dates! If your girl wants to step to him, she can. I ain't the boy's Mama!"

"Well, since that little issue is settled," he said trying to break the tension, "you two mind telling me how to handle Shanita? I want to ensure I'm not stuck in some potentially volatile situation."

Krystal sucked her teeth. "Just stay away from her crazy ass. The more you talk to her, the more she'll think there's a chance with you. Leave her alone, she'll eventually get the hint."

"You concur?" he asked Imani.

"Yeah. It worked when she kept pushing up on me and Melody, acting all buddy, buddy. The fool only did it trying to use our names to get into Student Council."

That miffed him. "If you knew about her, why didn't you say something yesterday?"

"Boy, your ass disappeared before I looked up and then I never saw you again. Like Krystal said, control your penis, it ain't my job to screen your damn pussy!"

"Alright, no need to get vulgar." Backing down, he changed the subject. "Hear anything from Melody yet? We're going to need to leave soon to catch the two o'clock movies."

BUSTED

"I sure as hell know that better not be who I think it is," Imani whispered into Lance's ear as they walked through the mall towards the movie theaters.

Sure enough as they got closer, Imani saw Melody and Kevin exiting the theaters looking all lovey-dovey.

"It's not even worth it," Lance warned her as Kevin and Melody noticed them approaching.

Melody blanched and Kevin froze in his tracks. A guilty look plastered Melody's pathetic face while Kevin looked pissed enough to shoot bullets.

"Oh, it'll be worth every damn dime," she said as she quickened her pace to confront the lying assholes.

She overheard Lance warn Trevor about the impending fireworks and she could hear both guys speed up to make sure the situation didn't get out of hand.

"Before you get mad, Imani, I can explain," Melody said leaping in between her and Kevin as if her dainty behind could save them.

Kevin's eyes narrowed, but he refused to say a word.

"You can explain why your ass can't pick up a freaking phone—"

"Watch your language," Lance warned soft enough so that only Imani could overhear him.

It took extreme restraint on her part not to turn around and inform Lance that she didn't use the real "f" word for his sake, but she could change that in a hot second if he kept messing with her. Instead she continued her tirade to Melody and Kevin without seeming to skip a beat. "—for one minute to let us know that you're sneaking off to the movies. Especially considering you explicitly said you'd call if your plans changed." Imani stomped her foot and her hands flew to her hips. "Because I recall us wanting to go early so that we'd have our afternoon free to study or chill, but your ignorant ass boyfriend," she said glaring at Kevin, "insisted we wait for him and go later."

Kevin's jaw clenched and his eyes spewed fire, but the punk didn't dare open his mouth.

"It's my fault," Melody said and Imani knew the cow was lying through her teeth. Melody reached back and placed a comforting hand on Kevin's chest. "Kevin knew I really wanted to see *What Women Want*. So, when he suggested we see that instead of *Crouching Tiger, Hidden Dragon*, I got so excited I totally forgot to call. It slipped my mind and I'm so sorry. Can you please forgive me, Imani? I promise it won't happen again."

Imani was just about to tell her, 'hell, no,' when Lance stepped forward.

"We forgive you, Melody," he said and Imani had to restrain her right hand with her left hand not to lash out and sucker punch him in the kidneys. "But I'm not going to lie, that was extremely rude. You remember I had to move some things around to accommodate your schedule and then you bagged us."

"Mmm-hmm," she heard Trevor say as he waited in the background.

Melody looked like her heart was about to break into a million pieces and she ran over and hugged Lance. "I'm really, really sorry, guys."

Imani wanted to stay mad, but she just couldn't stay pissed off at Melody. She sucked her teeth which was as close to a, 'you're forgiven,' as she was going to give the cute, little cow. But she still exchanged warning glares with Kevin.

Melody caught Imani's eye before she released Lance from her hug and mouthed the words, 'I love you,' and winked.

Feeling somewhat appeased, but damned determined not to show it, she scowled at Melody. "Humph, we gotta go. Our movie's starting soon," she said glaring at Kevin one last time.

VALENTINE'S DAY BLUES - FEBRUARY 2001

"I know you better not even be thinking about talking to my man, you Bitch!" Shanita said chasing off the cute Spanish senorita that Lance had just struck up a conversation with.

Before he could reply, the sweet and spicy Mama salsa danced away and loud, annoying Shanita barreled up in his face.

A few people in the Union glanced their direction to check out the commotion.

Lance felt his nostrils flare. "What the hell is your problem?" he hissed through clenched teeth so that only she could hear him.

Shanita immediately threw on her syrupy sweet attitude. She even had the audacity to place her hand on his chest. "I hope you didn't forget it's Valentine's Day, Baby," she said batting her false eyelashes at him. "When I didn't hear from you, Sweetie, I figured you were planning me a big, old surprise."

Like that was ever a plan, Lance frowned. "No, my only plans were to go home and study. I have an Economics test coming up soon."

"Well, do you need any company? Because I could help you study," she said suggesting they study Anatomy instead.

Her hand started sliding down his chest and he caught it and tossed the offending appendage off his body. "No, I'm good, I'm meeting my study group soon," he lied, wondering if he could catch up to the saucy Spaniard.

Shanita caught an attitude again. "Look, I don't know how your other girlfriends let you treat them, but I am not the one!"

"Exactly!" Lance stood up straight and menacing. Although deep and threatening, his voice remained quiet enough that only Shanita could hear him. The last thing he wanted was to make a scene in public, but she was getting on his one, last nerve. "You're not the one, Shanita, and you never were *the one*. Please get it through your thick skull that we are not an item and you are not my girlfriend."

Shanita flipped her long, straight weave over her shoulder. "That's really hurtful, but I know you're just stressed about your test. So I'll forgive you. You can make it up to me with a Valentine's Day present tomorrow," she said as she sashayed away.

Lance stared after her in disbelief.

"I like flowers, chocolates, and jewelry," she said seductively over her shoulder. She blew him a kiss and disappeared up the Union steps as suddenly as she appeared.

With a long, slow exhale Lance relaxed and rubbed his hands over his tired face and head. Deflated, he took a seat at the nearest table and buried his head in his hands. What just happened and how in the world could he make the nightmare end?

"You okay?" a soft voice asked as the

accompanying hand touched his shoulder.

The smell of roses alerted Lance to the identity of his new visitor without him even having to recognize the sweet voice. "Hey, Melody," he said looking up into her worried eyes. "Just seeing you here makes me feel a lot better."

Melody's face erupted into her genuine, daffodils and sunshine smile at the compliment. She pulled up a chair beside him. "Do you want to talk about it? I thought I saw Shanita prancing up the stairs before you pretty much had a melt-down in this chair."

Lance sighed. "The girl is certifiably crazy and I don't know what to do." He shook his head and reflected on tonight's events. "She chased off someone I wanted to get to know and tried to stake her claim on me. That psycho keeps showing up at inappropriate times, scaring off every interested women by saying we're an item. Roaming the campus spreading lies about how we're getting checked out so that I can finish the job. When I informed her tonight of how delusional she really was she ignored every word I said and acted like she's expecting a Valentine's gift. Jewelry, no less!"

Melody stifled a giggle with her hand and then giggled some more until Lance joined in with a full on belly laugh.

"Maybe I can help you go jewelry shopping for her tomorrow after classes," Melody said with a straight face before she burst out laughing.

"I thought you had my back, little Melody," he said with a big smile.

"I do, I do, I'm sorry," she said before she came

over and gave him a big, comforting hug. "Seriously, Imani and I can talk to her if you'd like," she whispered near his ear.

"I might need to enlist your services," he replied as he hugged her back. "I wouldn't have this much exposure if I'd brought a Super Bowl commercial! I'm about to slap her into next week!"

Lance thought he felt Melody stiffen then he heard someone clear their throat nearby.

"Am I interrupting something?" Kevin asked.

Melody jumped up straight from hugging Lance and executed a perfect 180 degree turn to greet Kevin. "Hey, Baby," she squealed giving him a huge hug and a peck on the cheek.

"Hey, Kev," Lance said as he stood up. Might as well cut his losses for tonight and actually go home and study. He clapped Kevin on the back. "I'll catch you guys later. Melody, thanks again. I'm feeling much better," he said and then he raced up the stairs towards the exit.

VALENTINE'S DAY FIREWORKS

"Oww, you're hurting me," Melody wailed as Kevin quit yanking on her left arm long enough to painfully grab her wrist and shove her into his dorm room.

His eyes were ablaze when he locked his door and turned to face her. "You think *I hurt you*?" he sounded appalled and disbelieving. "You're the one who's hurting me, Melody! You're breaking my heart!"

Melody flinched and absentmindedly rubbed her throbbing arm and wrist. "How can you say that?" she pleaded, feeling hurt and offended. "Everything I do is with you in mind."

"Really?" Kevin sneered in her face. "So you were thinking of me when you were hanging all over Lance in the Union? You looked like a dog in heat! And you know what they call a female dog."

All the blood drained from her face at his cruel, suggestive words. She fought to blink back the tears; he'd never called her a Bitch before. "I, uh, we, umm," Melody stuttered in confusion. She exhaled a deep breath and fashioned her words into a coherent sentence. "What are you talking about?"

Kevin's eyes took on a threatening tone, so she attempted to clarify her question in a hurry.

"Please let me explain, Kevin. Shanita came over

earlier and upset Lance. I arrived soon thereafter and I just gave him an innocent hug to lift his spirits," she said praying that he would understand.

"I'm sure it lifted a lot more than his spirits. He seemed rather *thankful*," Kevin replied still fuming. Looking angry enough to spit, he stalked as far across the room as he could.

It felt like Kevin created a physical chasm between them to accompany the emotional distance. Unable to bear the separation and needing to explain, she chased after him and squeezed his arm. "One, that's gross! Lance and I are like brother and sister. It's called incest when you think that way about your siblings and that's what it would feel like between Lance and me."

Kevin stopped pacing long enough to listen although he still wouldn't look her in the face.

"Two, I could never have eyes for anyone but you, Kevin." Melody wormed her way into his arms and willed him to look at her. "I love you." She reached up and held his face in her hands. "No, one but you. Remember, I'm yours…all yours."

Kevin sighed and his shoulders drooped. "You tell me those words and I want to believe you." His eyes pierced hers, their blue coloring as sharp as steel.

"Believe me because it's true. I wouldn't lie to you, Kevin." She gave him her most earnest gaze as she stroked the light stubble on his cheeks.

He grabbed her non-sore right hand and held it flat against his heart. His eyes turned so sad that she wanted to cry. "Today's Valentine's Day, Melody. We're not supposed to fight. At least not today of all days."

Melody nodded. "I know. I'm sorry for any confusion I caused." She patted his heart with her hand that he still held. "You know I always want to make you as happy as you make me."

Kevin cracked a slight smile. "You're not supposed to steal my lines and use them against me." He paused and his smile withered. "It's just that I don't like seeing you with other men. I don't care who they are! When you tell me that you're mine, all mine…well, I take that seriously."

"I meant every word, Kevin," she said willing him to believe her. "Always remember whose arms I'm in now." She moved his hand from his heart to hers…and then she let it take a sensuous slide over to her breast. "Happy Valentine's Day."

COLLEGE CHILL-OUT

"Nice meeting you, Raj and Deepta. I'll call you Tuesday for lunch." Imani waved goodbye to the cute Indian couple that completed their College Chill-Out Meet 'n Greet forms.

"Done! Now let's turn these sheets in and hopefully win one of the prizes." Lance led her towards the proper booth. The President of Admissions, one of the many college administrators manning booths, took their forms and wished them luck.

"Since Melody's still a no-show as usual, what do you want to hit now?" Imani asked.

Lance checked his watch. "Well, it's a few minutes before seven. I'm supposed to meet Gary. He's hooking me up with some girl." They headed towards the concert stage.

"You mean Gary the Left Guard?"

"I love when you speak football terminology."

"I thought he was a nice, upstanding, Christian guy?"

"He is." Lance raised his eyebrow.

"So, why would he hook you up with what I'd assume is a sweet, Christian girl?"

"Gee, thanks!" Lance smirked. "I can't go out with a nice, sweet girl?"

Imani stopped dead in her tracks. "No offense Boy,

but you're not looking to settle down with a Wifey. Gary practices with you, hangs out with you, and I know he has to see how fast you run through women. So, why on earth would he subject his friend to you?"

"Wow, is that how you see me, Imani?" Lance looked almost hurt, almost.

Cocking her head to the side, Imani's hands flew to her hips. "You're not actually trying to tell me any different, are you?"

Lance held a straight face for a minute then broke into a big grin. "Nawww!" he said, recommencing their walk.

"So, then my question to Gary is what kind of friend is he, 'cuz with friends like that…" she quieted when they neared Gary, Joe, John, and a cute, bookish-looking female.

"Hey Man, right on time!" Gary greeted Lance with a big bear hug. Joe and John gave Lance pounds and Imani hugs while Gary maneuvered the bookish girl towards Lance. "Mr. You-Got-Dunn himself, Lance, this is Vanessa. Vanessa, Lance and our girl Imani."

Oozing charm, Lance kissed Vanessa's hand. "Pleased to make your acquaintance, Vanessa. Gary has told me so much about you."

"He raves about his Homie, You've Been Lanced, the star wide receiver, too."

Gary nudged Vanessa. "Aww, Girl, cut it out."

"Vanessa, don't be fooled into thinking that Lance lucked into a good football name," John said. "The name speaks more on his poor manners."

Vanessa blushed while Lance faux-punched John in the ribs and shoulder.

"Hey, y'all," came a silky drawl as Erycah rolled up with Trevor.

"Welcome to the party," Joe said as everyone greeted the couple.

When it was Trev's turn to acknowledge Imani he gave her an awkward hug and a sheepish grin. Next, Erycah clasped Imani's arm and gave her an are-you-sure-this-is-cool look. Imani returned a reassuring smile, but deep inside it bothered her to see them together.

"Look out at three o'clock," John warned Lance.

"Hey, Lance, Sweetie!" rang out a loud voice.

They all turned to see Shanita shimmy her way towards Lance.

"Oh, Lord! Here we go." Imani snickered under her breath.

Joe chortled in response and tapped Imani's leg. "Behave."

"Hi, everyone!" Shanita sidled up to Lance. "I've been looking everywhere for you, Darling," she said sliding a possessive, right hand up his arm and over his shoulder. Despite the cold, March weather, Shanita's jacket was halfway unzipped. Eyeing everyone, Shanita patted her left hand right above her ample, close-to-being-exposed cleavage. "What did I miss, Homies?"

Lance disengaged Shanita's arm with a quick, subtle shoulder shake. "You missed the introductions to Vanessa." He moved to Vanessa's side and positioned her in front of Shanita. "Vanessa is my date for tonight. Vanessa this is a chick we all know, Shanita."

The sweet as dripping honey act dropped like a bad habit. Attitude and a hand on the hip exposed the true Shanita. "Date! What in the hell do you mean a date?"

"Exactly what it sounds like, Ho," John said cold as ice.

Lance somewhat came to Shanita's defense. "Seriously, John, there's no need to disrespect the lady and call her names like that." Shanita puffed up at his reassurances and shot John an evil glare. Lance noticed her reaction and added, "no matter how disillusioned she may be."

"Maybe you'll change your tune when you hear how she was screaming out Donnell's name last night after she met him crying about you." John's eyes never left Shanita's face.

"Whaattt?" Lance's head swiveled to Shanita.

"Maybe we should go," Erycah whispered to Trevor taking his hand. Trevor didn't budge so a reluctant Erycah stayed put.

"Aww, sookie, sookie now!" Imani exclaimed, ready for some action.

Joe tapped her leg again while Gary and Vanessa appeared shocked as if watching the Jerry Springer Show for the first time, unable to believe all of the unfolding drama.

Shanita's tough façade cracked and everyone could see the cogs turning while she maneuvered to save face. "Don-who? I don't know anyone by that name…"

"Let me refresh your memory, then," Lance barked. "He's the star wide receiver for SUNY's team. One of my fiercest local competitors."

"What?" John flexed a pec as he steamed. "You think because he don't attend our college, we wouldn't know? Too bad you didn't know that not only are we frat brothers, but he's also my cousin." John sneered as Shanita's face fell. "Yeah, Ho, I've been knowing that boy since we was in diapers together. He called as soon as he bounced your ass out this morning. What, cat got 'ya tongue, now, 'ya skeeza?"

"Dammnnn!" Imani said as Shanita ran off before the tears burst through the dam.

Joe tapped her leg again and shook his head. "You people are just brutal! Remind me not to ever come incorrect to you people."

Lance turned to John. "Thanks, Man. What nonsense!"

"No problem, Dawg. I can't believe how scandalous that cow was. Telling Donnell how she was moving on because you wasn't working out and she wanted a real star. Then Bitch had the nerve to show up here all on top of you, like y'all was actually ever an item and shit."

Imani saw Lance flinch at John's excessive use of profanity, but he played it off before anyone else noticed. Shaking her head to stifle a laugh, Imani turned and patted Vanessa on the back. "Well, welcome to the family, Girl. You sure you still wanna hang with us?"

Gary answered first. "Hell, I'm not even sure I still want to associate with you crazies! Too much drama! We can't wait to see what's next, huh, Nessa?"

Vanessa beamed in response, looking thrilled to be part of the excitement.

CONVERSATIONS AFTER THE CHILL-OUT

Imani hung up with Melody, more annoyed than ever. Feeling exhausted, she reached for her nightgown.

The phone rang and she frowned before she answered it. ""Yeah."

"Hey, Imani, Baby," rumbled Lance's deepest, most sultry voice over the line.

She smirked. "Your date with Vanessa finished already?"

"You were right. She's way too innocent for me."

"Oh?" Imani couldn't resist a look of smug satisfaction as she rolled onto her back.

"Yeah, yeah, I know you're smiling." Lance chuckled. "Luckily Vanessa knew it too and she just wants to be friends. Muttered something about her heart's not able to handle all the excitement. Mind you she invited herself back for Greek Freak next month, though."

"Hope she brings her heart medication because that party gets quite freaky, literally."

"To say the least." Lance hesitated for a moment. "Hey, how are you doing?"

Imani knew what he meant, but she decided to play dumb. "My feet are killing me but otherwise I'm good. Nothing a few hours sleep won't cure."

"That's all well and good, Imani, but you know I was talking about Trevor showing up with Erycah. Looked like he still moped after you but… just barely."

"Trevor can go out with anyone he damn well pleases. You *were* at the same damn table when I let Krystal know that. Why you all up in my grill trying to start shit, Lance?"

"Ohh-kay," said Lance with a long groan. "Well, I guess I asked for it."

"Yes, you did!" She stretched and sighed, already ashamed of cursing at Lance even if he deserved it. "But I shouldn't have gone off on you. I'm sorry." She rolled on her side. "Look, I think I'm cool with Trevor and Erycah, but what if he really was meant for me and now I've pushed him away?"

"How exactly do you feel about him?"

"He's just a really good friend, like you. I don't get all hot and bothered when he's around." She conveniently left out saying, 'despite the intense dream.' "It's more a comfortable brotherly feeling. Hell, he's practically family. We grew up in the same neighborhood. His moms is like my moms." A load of bricks hit her. "Lance, what if the crap we tell Melody is true? What if romance and fireworks don't exist? Do you just settle for someone you like and respect?"

"Baby Girl, look at Melody. She seems to have found it all. You will, too." He paused for dramatic effect. "Keep hope alive!"

Imani cracked up. "See just when I started taking your dumb ass seriously. Serves me right." Yawning aloud, she suddenly felt dog tired and rubbed her heavy eyelids. "Yo, sorry about that. Guess I'm really beat. What's say I catch you tomorrow?"

"Sounds good."

"Great, see you tomorrow… and thanks for the talk." Imani hung up before Lance acknowledged her hurried admission.

Ready for bed, she undressed and threw on her nightgown. As she lay down, the phone rang. I know this Negro lost his mind calling again this late, she thought grabbing the phone in a huff. "What now, Man!"

"Sorry, I thought you'd still be up," Trevor replied. "I'll talk to you later."

"No, no, Trev," she soothed, "I thought it was Lance being an ass. I didn't check the Caller ID. I'm sorry for snapping at you. What's up, Boo? How'd you enjoy the Chill-Out?"

"It was crazy cool. How about you?"

"I couldn't get enough of Shanita squirming."

"Wasn't that wild?"

"John wouldn't let up at all, it was so nuts!"

"I know. Erycah wanted to bail because things were getting so tense."

Imani paused at the mention of Erycah's name.

"Are you really okay…with me going out with Erycah?"

Imani opened her mouth to explain, but Trevor spoke first.

"You know…" Trev paused and she could sense his discomfort through the phone lines. "I can kick her to the curb at any time. Everyone jokes about it and I'll probably regret telling you this, but…I would do anything for you, Imani.

"I know, Trev." Imani caressed the phone's mouthpiece. "You're the brother I never had."

Trevor cleared his throat. "Therein lies the problem, huh? I'm not exactly thinking of you as a sister here."

Jumping to her feet, she paced the room. "What am I supposed to tell you, Trev? I do love you but like a brother. We make the best study and lab partners." Her words hit home and compounded with his revelatory response from the Alpha party about not remaining friends with his ex-girlfriends. As the combined one, two punch sunk in, her head and heart aligned and she made her final decision.

"Realistically, I just don't want to ruin that chemistry speculating on a relationship that may or may not work." She quit pacing and ran her fingers over her knots. "Look, I am perturbed about Erycah, but she wants a boyfriend... not me. You know relationships come secondary to getting my education."

Trevor sounded more confused than upset. "So you're saying you're not looking for a man?"

Flustered, Imani threw up her free hand. "Look, Trev, I don't know what I want right now besides good grades, a diploma, and a slamming job. So, I can't hold you hostage while I sort out what we should be. You're a great catch, but for now, I can't risk ruining our friendship."

"I dig."

Exhausted, she plopped on her bed. "Lookie-here, enjoy things with Erycah. I may not be comfortable with it, but just know deep down, I'm happy if you're happy, even if it's due to her."

Trevor exhaled low and long. "Wow, that's pretty big of you, Imani. But I needed to hear it, so thanks."

"You're welcome, but please, let's drop it. I can't take anymore." She smiled, eager to switch topics. "What's say we grab lunch tomorrow at the Union?"

There was a short, uncomfortable silence. "Well, it's like this, I got plans now."

"Let me guess… with Erycah, huh?"

"Yep. Maybe we can hang out during the week after our study sessions?"

Striving to get used to this new reality, she made herself suck it up. "That would be nice, Trev. Catch ya later."

"Yeah. Have a nice night." He hesitated before disconnecting. "Thanks again, Imani." And he was gone.

Imani stared at the phone in her hand wondering if she'd just made a big mistake.

GREEK FREAK - MARCH 2001

"Oh, lookie at who just strolled through the door." Imani shouted in Lance's ear, in order to be heard over the thundering music that filled the auditorium. For some reason the volume of this particular song, *Atomic Dog*, seemed twice as loud as what played previously.

Swiveling in the direction that she pointed, Lance saw Melody and Kevin standing arm in arm by the coat check. His bellow sounded almost inaudible over the mass of other Greek Freak partygoers. "When was the last time you saw her?"

Imani's hands flew to her hips. "Girlfriend hasn't been home in over ten days! We damn near haven't spoken for three freaking weeks! What kinda shit is that?"

Lance waved to Kevin and Melody when they glanced around, and the couple started over. "Cut her some slack, Imani. As you can clearly see, the girl's got a man."

"Well, if she keeps this up all she'll have is a man, 'cuz her friends will be long gone from neglect," she replied before Kevin and Melody joined them. Managing to turn her indignation into a welcoming smile, she hugged Melody. Melody squealed with happiness, but Imani let loose again with Melody's ear nearby. "Damn near forgot what you looked like since

I don't see your ass anymore."

"Don't be mad," Melody said hugging her tighter. Then Melody stepped back, winked, and greeted Lance.

Kevin kissed Imani on the cheek and squeezed her shoulder while Lance entrapped Melody in a bearhug. Melody's head flew back with laughter as Lance swung her around and kissed both cheeks. Kevin's hand tightened on Imani's shoulder causing her to wince before he removed it.

Her head snapped up to check Kevin's reaction but his happiness to see Lance seemed genuine when he clapped Lance's back. Rubbing her shoulder, Imani watched Kevin stand beside Melody, a possessive arm draped over Melody's shoulders. Kevin had the audacity to smile at Imani and she swore he did it with a mocking smugness.

"Glad you guys could finally hook up with us," Lance shouted over the music.

Someone from the administration reached the DJ because the music decibels decreased to a more normal party level. Loud enough to feel the bass but low enough that folks could hear themselves think.

"Sorry it seems like we're always bailing, but things keep coming up," Kevin replied.

"Kevin agreed to help his friends setup for Greek Freak. So, we had to witness the results of his hard work." Melody beamed as Kevin hugged her closer.

Imani smirked. "Well we're so glad you decided to fit us in."

Lance threw her a sideways, cautioning look.

Kevin apparently missed her hurled barb because he

addressed Melody with the hospitality of a Southern gentleman. "Where are my manners? Would you like a drink, Honey?"

"Sure."

"Great. I'll be right back." Kevin lingered a moment with a loving gaze plastered on his face, his fingers slow to release Melody's shoulder before he left for the refreshment stands.

"I'd like one, too. Thanks for asking," Imani sniped at his retreating back.

Lance shook his head. "You really should try to behave yourself."

"That's impossible," Trevor said as he materialized from nowhere.

"Hey, Trev!" Imani batted her eyes.

"Oh, brother!" Lance laughed. "Let me save you from yourself." He grabbed Imani's hand and led her onto the dance floor.

***

Alone with Trevor, Melody was a little surprised when he took her hand and pulled her towards the dance floor.

"I really shouldn't," she protested to his back. "Kevin will be back with our drinks soon."

Stepping onto the dance floor, Trevor spun Melody around. "And he can have you right back after this song." As Shaggy's *It Wasn't Me* played, he danced circles around her.

Melody laughed, trying in vain to keep pace with Trevor.

Three minutes later, a non-amused Kevin tapped

Trevor's shoulder. "May I cut in," he stated rather than asked.

"Hey, Kevin, she's all yours." Trevor nudged her towards Kevin and bopped off in Imani and Lance's direction.

Once Trevor disappeared, Kevin leaned in close. His hot breath almost burned her face. "What was that shit, Melody? I leave you for a second to get drinks and you're dancing with other men?"

Attempting to look cool, Melody kept dancing although Kevin's sudden burst of jealous behavior shook her. "It's only Trevor," she replied nonchalantly. "I said you'd return soon, but he insisted." She shrugged. "I'm sorry. I didn't think it was that big a deal."

"Exactly the problem, you didn't think!" Kevin turned and left her scampering through the dancing crowd trying to catch him. Kevin stopped where his friend, Ty, waited with their drinks.

"Kevin, please talk to me." Melody felt close to tears and couldn't control the whininess of her tone. "I don't understand why you're so mad."

Kevin's leer scorched with its fire and vim. "You expect me to believe that?" The timbre of his voice tore off her head.

Shrinking back into her skin, Melody felt adrift. All this because of a dance with Trevor? Scrambling through options, she struggled to decide which one would best help her end the night peacefully with Kevin happy again.

"I'm going to take a whiz. Stay put, we'll talk later!" Kevin stormed away with Ty following on his heels.

Melody stood there, drained and ready to cry. It'll be okay, she thought.

"Hey there, Gorgeous."

Lance's appearance made her jump a foot.

"You okay?" he asked lifting her chin to study her face.

The last thing Melody wanted was for Lance to become involved. Remembering their nickname, she envisioned daffodils blooming in the sunshine and unleashed her biggest smile. "Perfectly fine. Where's Imani, I thought you two were dancing?"

Lance grinned and dropped her chin. "She dumped me for Trevor. Which is why I'm here," he replied engulfing her hand in his large one. "I need a dance partner, Darling."

Melody stood stock still. "No. Uh, no thanks."

"Are you going to leave me hanging?" Lance turned on his million-dollar charm.

"Sorry, Lance," she replied trying to retract her hand. "But Kevin just went to the restroom. He'll be back any moment."

"And?" Lance laughed and pulled her along.

Nearing the dreaded dance floor, she decided to stand her ground. However, Lance didn't discern her voluntary stop and he pulled her arm hard enough that she almost ran into him. Assuming that meant her readiness, Lance began bouncing to the music.

Against her better judgment, Melody swayed back and forth with him. "I really shouldn't be here, Kevin will get upset again."

"Why? He's cool with me." Lance bumped her hip.

"He knows you love his butt to pieces. You're acting like the boy is a jealous nut."

At this point, she didn't know what bothered Kevin, but Lance was right. Kevin had no reason to be mad now, he knew and trusted Lance. Melody felt silly for exaggerating Kevin's earlier behavior. Everything was fine; they'd dance together as soon as he returned, then cuddle, kiss, and have a wonderful night.

The song wound down and Lance prepared to escort Melody off the dance floor.

Kevin beat them to the punch. His face was unreadable, but Melody could sense the underlying fury, brimming to erupt.

"Hey Man, just keeping your girl safe during you absence." Lance moved aside to let Kevin cut in and then he returned Vanessa and Gary's wave. "Enjoy, alright?" Lance clapped Kevin's back and danced over to Vanessa and Gary.

Kevin's voice—cold as steel—sliced her to the core. "What the fuck's wrong with you?"

Melody froze in the middle of the floor, unable to move a muscle. Oh God, what now?

Antarctic glaciers couldn't have been more frigid than his glare. "Are you completely fucking stupid, Melody?" Kevin towered over her. Although he projected loud and clear, none of the neighboring couples overheard him or even suspected the berating he laid on thick as fresh poured cement. "I just went ballistic because you danced with one leech. Then I excuse myself to go piss after giving you explicit instructions to stay put. Imagine my surprise when first, I can't find you, and then secondly, I spot your idiotic ass dancing with yet another man…again! I repeat, what the fuck is wrong with you?"

Melody's legs went weak, her limbs felt like water. She wanted to collapse in a pile, but her body wouldn't respond to any commands. Anything she could think to say seemed inadequate. Feeling helpless, she stood before him ready to burst into tears.

Kevin seemed almost satisfied with her discomfort. "I can't be around you right now. Stay clear until I can get over your incompetent betrayal." He leaned in close so they stood nose to nose. His eyes, cold pools of the deepest blue waters, waited to drown all those who dared swim in their depths. "And I'd advise you to spend the time parked against the wall, not talking or dancing with anyone. You read me?" he spit out before he stalked off, leaving her trembling.

A minute passed before Melody's muscles obeyed and moved. Shuffling off the dance floor, she walked trance-like until she found a dark corner. Snagging an empty stool, she sat with her back to everyone, like a dunce relegated to the corner.

God, she was so stupid! Her head dropped in her hands. Kevin was furious. A hot tear slipped down her cheek, stinging her pores with its salt. She warned Lance to leave her alone; she hadn't even wanted to dance. What an idiot she was! And now Kevin didn't want her around. What could she do to placate him? Anything he asked, she decided, his happiness meant the world. Kevin was the man of her dreams, her one true love, and Melody swore she'd make things right.

***

Hot, thirsty, and tired, Imani left the auditorium for the relative peace and quiet of the concourse to grab a Sprite. While she guzzled the icy beverage straight down, she spotted Kevin talking to his buddy, Ty. Ty almost made the okay-looking lot, except his eyes sat too close together, lending him a goofy appearance. The guys appeared animated, like they were in the midst of a heated discussion as they drank their sodas.

Since she hadn't seen Melody in about twenty minutes, Imani figured she'd ask Kevin where the girl was hiding. Tossing her empty cup into a nearby trashcan, she approached them. The speakers surrounding the auditorium floor didn't permeate the concourse and she could overhear them chatting.

"What else can I do?" Kevin demanded rather than asked Ty. "I mean, if she can't follow simple fucking instructions then I have to assume she's just not the brightest light in the closet."

"It just means you need to teach her to do better. Hell, I, for one, prefer stupidity; it beats them smarting off all the damn time. Consider yourself lucky! My girl won't shut the hell up unless I put something in her mouth if you know what I mean?" Ty howled, pleased with his attempt at bedroom humor.

Kevin didn't laugh, but it looked like he contemplated Ty's suggestion. "Melody usually does what I tell her, but I might have to revamp my methods if she won't stay in line."

"I know you just didn't!" Imani felt her nostrils flare as her ire stoked. The way she saw it, Kevin had a few measly seconds to explain his comments before she went all the way off on his ignorant ass. She couldn't believe she'd heard him spouting this bullshit with Goofy here!

Kevin wheeled around in surprise then his face flushed with anger. "Mind your business, Imani."

"How dare you 'dis my girl like that you asshole!" Imani stood firm, her head and finger weaved back and forth like a snake charmer. "Keep her sex life private and furthermore, if Melody's supposedly not so bright, how does she maintain a 3.8 GPA?"

"Book smarts and common sense are two different things," Kevin replied coolly. "If she had any sense, she wouldn't hang with you because your mouth is going to get your ass into trouble you can't get out of, Bitch."

"I know you just didn't, Motherfucker."

Ty lunged in front of Kevin and caught Imani by the waist as she flew through the air to attack. Her long, manicured fingernails just missed grazing Kevin's face.

"Let me go!" Imani shrieked at Ty as she lunged again. But Ty tightened his grip and Kevin stepped back.

"I got her, Kev," Ty yelled over his shoulder. "Get the hell out of here."

"Crazy Bitch!" Kevin turned to leave, but then he decided to take one last shot while Ty held Imani captive. "That's why your ass can't get a man!"

"You call yourself a man?" Imani laughed, still struggling to escape from Ty.

Kevin tried to stare her down, but Imani looked straight into his soul and found the coward within. Smirking, she sensed Kevin retreat inwardly. His weak, little weaselly ass seemed terrified that she'd exposed the obvious truth for all to see. This controlling, pathetic prick could never be man enough for any woman!

Then, unexpectedly, the tides shifted as Kevin tapped into an empowering rage.

Imani flinched at his sudden change in demeanor.

"Watch your step, Imani!" Kevin spat. Back iron rod straight, he glared at her then he walked away confident.

***

A hand landed on Melody's shoulder and she jumped a foot. "I'm waiting for my boyfriend, I don't want to dance," she exhaled in one long breath before realizing it was Kevin.

Kevin scrutinized her, but then he gave her the sweetest smile. Leaning down he kissed her lips and she wanted to cry with relief. "Ready to go, Sweetheart?"

Unsure what had happened but ecstatic that everything appeared fine again; she threw her arms around his neck. "Oh yes, Kevin, let's go!"

They retrieved their coats and walked back to his dorm room arm in arm. The smell of wood-burning fireplaces tickled her nose and warmed her inside as she snuggled into Kevin. As they entered his dormitory he hugged her tight and kissed the top of her head.

However, once Kevin shut and locked his dorm room door, the smile faded. A dark cloud passed over his entire persona.

Melody noticed the immediate change. Confused and scared as a cornered mouse, she backed up until she ran into his bed. Her words tumbled out, each cascading over the other. "Kevin, please talk to me, I thought we were fine, oh God, please tell me what's wrong?"

"You never answered my question at the party, did you?" he asked ever so cool.

What in the world was he talking about? Her mind reeled, what question?

Kevin's smile looked eerie. "I asked if you were stupid because if you're not, then that means you think I'm stupid. So which one is it, Darling?" He eased about elbow-length away.

"Neither, Kevin," she stuttered and teetered. "Is this because I danced with Trevor and Lance, because if it is I'm so, so sorry. I didn't think you'd mind." Her hands wrung together. Melody wanted to touch Kevin, ease his anger, but she refrained for fear of his reaction. "You know I love you and would never purposefully upset you." Tears brimmed in her eyes.

"Exactly my point, Melody, you didn't think." Reaching out he stroked her cheek ever so soft. "Why would I want anyone else to touch you and hold you?"

"I'm so sorry, Baby." Anxious for him to forgive her, she rubbed her cheek into his hand. "I won't ever do it again, okay?" she said, her eyes pleading.

The slap stung swift and unexpected. The force knocked her to the bed. "No, it's not okay," he screamed in a scorching whisper. "You must think I'm stupid."

"No, Baby, I don't think you're stupid," she replied,

cowering on the bed.

"So, then you're stupid! You'd have to be to have friends like that, huh?" She didn't answer, so he continued ranting. "Do you think it's normal for Lance to paw all over you like that? Hugging and kissing you while I stand right there? Shows you must be a tramp to like that sort of treatment, right?" Kevin punched her cheek so hard that her head rocked backwards. "And that Bitch of a girlfriend. She went off on me for no reason at the party. You got a foul mouth on you like she does?"

"No, what are you talking about?" she asked confused and terrified. What did Imani have to do with this, what had she done to make Kevin so mad?

"You are the company you keep; therefore you must be a trash-talking, smart-mouth whore like your friends!" Kevin punched her again, but this time he clipped her jaw just so.

Her chin crashed closed and she couldn't focus. The room spun in chaotic circles while stars flashed. Melody never saw the next punch connect hard across her left temple. Crumpling to the floor, she landed in an awkward heap, splayed at his feet. Cries wracked her body. "Kevin, please," she pleaded.

The answer was a kick to the gut that forced the air from her lungs. She choked trying to gulp for breaths. Her only coherent thought was to protect her head. Kevin kicked her again and a piercing pain shot through her ribcage. "Kevin, I love you. Please," she cried bracing for the next kick. Instead arms pulled her up rough and swift, causing her side to scream with pain.

"Why?" he yelled at her. He cried now, too. "Why would you make me do this to you, Melody? You know not to make me mad! Why would you intentionally make me so crazy, I'd hit you?" He shook her.

Her head bounced around like a bobble-head doll. She couldn't answer.

Kevin pulled her to him and sobbed. "Why did you do this, Melody? I love you so much." Gently he laid her on the bed. Brushing her hair from her face, he stroked her sore cheek. "Oh, Baby, I'm so sorry. Please forgive me." He kissed her limp hands repeatedly. "I'll fix this. I promise." He disappeared and reappeared with blue ice packs from his freezer.

Praying it was over; she could do nothing more than lie there and cry. Her body had gone numb to protect her from the agonizing pain. Now coldness spiked her senses as Kevin applied an ice pack to her temple and cheek.

"It'll be okay now," he said soothingly. "It's all over now, everything will be fine. You know I love you, right?" Kevin's eyes were so sincere, sweet blue pools of calming elixir.

Melody managed to nod, but her mind had trouble reconciling that this same sweet man had just beat her senseless mere seconds ago. She knew Kevin loved her; he had to. The blissful moments they shared, the way he touched her and fulfilled her needs, the way they talked for hours, and could finish each other's sentences.

Dancing with those two must have devastated him. Otherwise he would never have hurt her. Next time she vowed to do better, even if it meant staying away from her friends. Kevin was probably right. Melody didn't want people to think she was a sexpot like Lance or as judgmental and crass as Imani. Yes, in the future she'd be more careful.

Kevin's light, feathery strokes caressed as his remorseful, loving coos soothed her to sleep.

Painful Homecoming

"Lance, I've been talking to you for an hour and I'm still pissed!" Imani fumed into the telephone before she plopped onto her desk chair.

"Although the cutie from Greek Freak rocked my world as promised, I feel energized. So I could beat up Kevin, if you want?"

Imani was about to reply affirmatively when she felt a draft coming from the doorway. "Hold up," she whispered as she tiptoed towards the door. Keeping the phone close to her ear, she approached the door as it cracked open, prepared to yell for help. Instead, she was startled to see Melody at the door trying to escape detection. "What the fuck?"

"Want to run that by me again?" Lance asked perplexed.

Recognizing that Lance overheard her exclamation, she clarified. "Not you, Lance. I just found a rat scuttling in unannounced." Imani directed her snarl towards Melody. "Right, Girlfriend? Finally creeping in to apologize for your asshole boyfriend?"

Trapped, Melody attempted to flee, but she hit her side on the doorknob and collapsed to the floor with a whimper.

"Melody!" Imani dropped the phone and rushed to her friend's side. "What's wrong, Sweetie?" Her attempts to hold Melody failed as Melody struggled to regain her footing. Frustrated, Imani stepped over Melody and positioned her body in the hallway, forcing Melody to remain in the room. With the advantage, Imani helped Melody stand…and noticed the black, blue, purple, and red lumps parading across her friend's once-pretty face. "Oh, my God!"

Melody fled across the room to her bed scrambling as fast as her pained body could manage.

A scratchy, warbling sound emanated from the floor. Imani realized Lance was shouting for someone to pick up the phone. She obliged. "Come over now. It looks like Kevin beat the shit out of Melody."

"No!" It wasn't quite a scream; Melody gulped trying to inhale enough air. "Tell him I'm fine," she croaked.

Imani stared at Melody in complete disbelief. "You're kidding, right?"

"I'm on my way now," Lance said before he hung up.

"You wanna tell me what happened?" Imani replaced the cordless phone in the charger. Sitting beside Melody, she swept her roommate's tussled, blonde hair back.

In the light she could see the full extent of the damage. A glossy, purplish-blue three-inch wide lump traversed from Melody's left temple down to her chin, enveloping her eye in a puffy mass of mottled skin. Tears could barely escape from the prison of flesh. "Oh, my God!" Imani blinked back searing tears of anger. "What did he do to you, Honey?"

"It wasn't him." Melody couldn't hold Imani's

incredulous stare. "I mean… he didn't mean it. I drove him to it."

Wanting to drive her fists through Kevin, it took every ounce of Imani's calm to gently raise Melody's chin so that she could look into her one good eye. "No matter what you did, Baby, it doesn't justify this. Real men do NOT hit women. Especially ones they proclaim to love."

"It's your fault!" Melody squeaked.

'Oh, hell no,' she wanted to scream since at this point it didn't take much to peak her ire. With her hands flying straight to her hips, Imani managed not to snap at Melody. "Excuse me, Honey?"

Melody sat up straight although she looked to be in considerable pain. "Yes, Imani, you heard me! Kevin said you cursed him out at the party! Between your big mouth and Lance always fondling me, Kevin couldn't take it anymore!"

Exhaling audibly, Imani extinguished her sudden flare-up. "Is that what he told you, Girl?" Her voice sounded tender even to her own ears.

Confusion burst Melody's irate bubble. "What do you mean?"

Imani stroked Melody's right cheek, the non-bruised, non-puffy side. "Baby Girl, I overheard Kevin telling Ty how stupid you were. They joked about shutting women up by sticking cocks in their mouths. You know I couldn't let that slide. Damn right I went off on him but only after he called me a Bitch."

"What?"

"Guess he didn't tell you all that before he slammed

his fists into your pretty little face?" Easing beside Melody, she held her as the tears slid down Melody's face.

A rapid-fire knock came from the door followed by Lance's forced whisper. "It's me."

Melody gripped Imani's arm, her good eye wild and terror-filled. "Oh, please, no!"

"That's not Kevin, Girl," she said trying to extract her arm. "Let go so I can open the door."

"No!" Melody pleaded holding tighter. "I don't want Lance to see me like this."

"You're kidding, right?" Imani broke free and let Lance inside. "Tell her she shouldn't be as worried about you seeing her as the cops when we report this."

Lance looked from one to the other than hurried over to Melody who lay curled up in a fetal position on the bed crying uncontrollably.

Melody tried to move away from Lance, but they all saw a bolt of pain shoot through her body. Melody gasped a soft scream that ended all her struggling.

Free to assess the damage, Lance jerked back stunned then exploded to his feet. Wild eyes searched her face. "Tell me this isn't what I think it is, Imani."

"Kevin told her it was our fault he used her for Tae-Bo practice. Apparently I went off on him with my big-ass mouth and evidently you don't know how to keep your horny mitts off his woman." Imani explained crystal cool, only arching her eyebrow to emphasize certain points.

"My car's downstairs. I'll drop you two off at the infirmary. Make sure she files charges with the campus police. Meanwhile, some of the boys and I will pay Kevin a visit."

Melody shot up in visible pain. "No, Lance, please. He didn't mean it. I'm not going to file charges against him. He promised it wouldn't happen again, this was the last time."

"Real men don't hit women, Melody," Lance said. "You're not going to be another battered woman statistic on my watch."

"What? You told me you were going to slap Shanita silly. So that's a little hypocritical, don't you think?"

Amazement flooded Lance's face and Imani shook her head.

"Are you serious, Melody?" Lance's knuckles rapped on Melody's desk like a spastic woodpecker while he exhaled a long, rhythmic breath. When he stepped toward Melody, his voice came out low and calm. "I don't even recall joking like that."

Lance squatted down to be at Melody's eye level. "However, you know me, Melody. You've seen me in action since we met during orientation last year." He placed his hands on Melody's legs. "Have I ever once hit any female or even talked seriously about it? Come on!"

"Maybe if either one of you had a real relationship, you'd understand. Kevin loves me and I love him. This is simply one of those bad times we need to work through. I'm standing by him and that's final!"

"Wait a damn minute!" A light bulb came on in Imani's head.

Melody glanced at her and deflated like a leaking balloon.

Imani shook her head at Lance and glared at Melody. "Melody, you said Kevin promised he wouldn't do this *again*, this was the *last time*. That means he did it before, didn't he?"

Melody blinked rapidly.

"That time last year when you were supposedly walking across the Quad and got nailed by the football, it never happened, did it?" she asked piecing the puzzle together.

Melody tightened herself into a ball.

"Oh, hell, no!" Imani turned to Lance. "Grab her now and put her in the car. I'll get the door and make sure we have everything."

They leaped into action. Melody was too defeated to resist.

INFIRMARY INFORMATION

Melody sat on the examination table waiting in silence.

"Nurse, could you please call Dr. Mary and ask her if she could come over here? We have another battered girl," the attending physician, Dr. Mike, stated matter-of-fact as he prepared to examine Melody.

"What do you mean another?" Imani stood by Melody's side holding her hand tightly.

Dr. Mike snapped on a second glove. "On a campus this big, we get at least two girls each weekend. That's only the ones with injuries severe enough to seek treatment."

"I dare not ask how many press charges, then?"

"Um, maybe one out of every seven." Dr. Mike paused and examined Melody's face. "No disrespect but just from watching you Melody, I believe you're one of the other six."

"No way," Imani replied.

Melody didn't make a sound.

"Well, we'll see. I hope you're right." Dr. Mike continued his thorough examination.

Forty-five minutes later Melody felt somewhat better once the pain medication soothed her nerves and various aches. Unused to the tight bandages encircling her torso and holding together her cracked lower rib, she sat up slowly. She touched the left side of her face. The swelling had receded a bit and she could see a tad more from her eye.

Imani withdrew her purse compact and passed it to Melody. Despite their vivid descriptions, she was not prepared for the shock of seeing her reflection in the mirror. Deep down, she knew the image would plague her like a splinter she couldn't quite remove.

Dr. Mike came back in and introduced Dr. Mary, a counselor from the nearby abused women's shelter, who immediately pressured her to get help. Dr. Mary had a response ready, like a bad script, for every excuse Melody mentioned to explain Kevin's behavior.

"But he doesn't mean it, I made him mad," she explained for the umpteenth time.

"Yet he controls his anger with others and doesn't hit anyone else?" Dr. Mary asked.

"Exactly, I push his buttons somehow. I'll be more careful in the future."

"How exactly?" Dr. Mary pulled up a chair and sat in front of them. "No matter what you do, something innocuous will trigger him. Last time it was his bad grades, friends dancing with you, your best friend defending your honor. What will it be next time, Melody?"

"I won't go out and expose myself to those types of situations," she replied indignantly.

"So you'll isolate yourself and allow him to further undermine your self-confidence?" Dr. Mary asked in a friendly yet no nonsense manner. "First, it starts with calling you stupid, ugly, or fat. Then you're never good enough, everything you do is wrong."

"He says he's sorry. I can change him." God she wished this woman would leave her alone.

"You can't change anyone except yourself." Dr. Mary replied.

"What then?" She threw her hands up until her cracked rib caused her to wince. "Am I just supposed to give up on him and love? What happened to 'no pain, no gain' or 'relationships are hard work?'"

"Love doesn't hurt, not like this." Dr. Mary pointed to Melody's bandages and her swollen face. "If he kills you, there will be no relationship, Melody." Dr. Mary crossed her arms. "Kevin needs professional help that you can't provide."

Imani clasped her hand reassuringly. Surprisingly, Imani held her tongue and stood like a strong buttress beside Melody while the good doctor pummeled her into silent reflection. Deep down, Melody knew Dr. Mary spoke the truth, but it was so very difficult not to run into Kevin's arms and have him kiss the situation away.

So This is Football

Kevin flew backwards and landed on his ass when the door flung open. Before he could protest, two muscular Black guys grabbed him by the arms and threw him into the wall, knocking his breath out in a huge gust. Another even larger, redwood tree trunk of an Italian guy clamped a meaty hand over his mouth, blocking any chance to shout for help. Kevin tried to bite the garlic-smelling hand, but it was positioned so he couldn't make contact.

Something about the three guys seemed familiar, but his racing mind couldn't place them. Surveying his tiny, darkened room, he scrambled to find an exit or a makeshift weapon that he could utilize to defend himself from these intruders. All the while he tried to break free from their iron-like chokeholds to tell them that they had the wrong guy, but he couldn't budge the big bastards.

A shadowy movement by his dorm room door caught his attention and he stopped breathing. His eyes locked in on the person entering from the hallway. Kevin went limp with fear as Lance closed and locked the door.

Oh shit, Melody must have betrayed him! Snuck out in the middle of the night while he slept and told this buffoon lies. He renewed his struggles to explain, but the goons held him tight.

Meanwhile Lance took his ominous time strolling over and Kevin's heart pounded against his chest. Anxiety wracked his body. He'd always considered himself fit and muscular, however it felt like Lance loomed in his face. Although Lance only stood two to three inches taller than Kevin and weighed maybe twenty to thirty pounds more, right now he towered over him.

"So, you like to beat up on innocent little girls half your size, huh?" Lance's deep voice brimmed with unimagined threats.

Apprehension dripped off Kevin like sweat. Eyes wide, he shook his head vigorously.

"If I have my boy remove his hand, are you going to scream like a little punk?"

He shook his head.

Lance nodded for the Italian tree trunk to uncover his mouth and Kevin remembered where he knew them from. He'd actually eaten lunch with these goons once when Melody insisted he eat with her stupid friends at the Union! As if it weren't bad enough that he had to deal with Lance and Imani, she'd subjected him to these additional fools!

His mind battled to remember their names. Joe and Jack or Jim and John, he couldn't quite remember and he could never tell them apart. Tweedledee and Tweedledum for all he knew and cared. He did however recall that the massive giant beside him was nicknamed Big Tony. His heart felt like it was about ready to explode. Back when they were all sitting around the Union table jawing he'd never realized how big they were until now.

Melody joked once and only once that Lance's muscles had muscles. Her comment pissed him off, but he couldn't blame her for noticing Lance. The arrogant, narcissistic idiot insisted on wearing skin-tight shirts and sweaters if he bothered to don one at all. Kevin's legs turned to water as he realized that unbelievably, Lance was the smallest of the bunch!

Lance cracked his knuckles. "Now you need to explain to me and my boys why we shouldn't beat you to within an inch of your life."

Anything Kevin said, he knew wouldn't matter. "Please, it won't happen again, Lance. I thought she was flirting with you and Trevor. My mistake."

"You're right about that." Lance punched Kevin's gut so hard that he would have collapsed if Tweedledee and Tweedledum hadn't supported his full weight. "We want you to recall this night if you ever contemplate touching Melody again. Hell, I'm thinking you best lose her number completely."

"Watch out, Lance." Big Tony, the tree trunk, moved Lance aside.

Kevin figured the meat locker stood about six foot five inches and at least three hundred twenty-five pounds. His insides grew queasy contemplating what horrid torture this goon had in store.

"We don't want the star receiver breaking his hands. Let me show you some of the tricks I learned growing up in Little Italy." Big Tony sneered in his face and his garlic breath burned Kevin's nostrils. "I know ways of hurting you that don't leave marks. Not that you would be dumb enough to report this, right?"

Terrified, his eyes widened as the Italian goon went to work.

It was the longest seven minutes of his life.

REUNIONS - APRIL 2001

Melody sighed not knowing how much more of this nonsense she could stand. Glancing over her shoulder, she easily picked out the jock that indiscreetly tailed her to the Union. After the "incident," as she now dubbed the events following Greek Freak three weeks ago, either Lance or Imani personally escorted her everywhere she went. And if they were busy, Lance ordered one of his football or basketball buddies to provide a constant vigil. Before the incident she had no clue that every single one of her classes contained a jock that was more than happy to assist Lance.

Sighing, she entered the Union and went downstairs to the food court. To make matters worse, she hadn't caught a glimpse of Kevin anywhere. Maybe Kevin really didn't want to see her again just like Lance proclaimed.

Looking around, she decided to join the long deli line. God, she felt so confused. At times she ached for Kevin, missed him so much that her soul hurt. But she also attended the local battered women's therapy group three times a week. With Dr. Mary's counsel, she understood now that their relationship wasn't healthy or normal. Kevin needed to deal with his anger issues that stemmed from his difficult and troubled upbringing. Although Dr. Mary disapproved, Melody still felt like she could help Kevin, if only she could just speak to him.

Melody tapped her foot impatiently, the deli line wasn't moving. Maybe she should have picked pizza or Chinese. As she checked the other two lines, she noticed the two guys switching off their tailing responsibilities were deep in conversation and not paying her any attention.

Her foot stopped tapping. Could she make a break for it and sneak out the back exit? Nervousness tossed her stomach. Should she even bother? The aching returned. Yes! It was essential that she see Kevin to gauge his reactions and hear him tell her the words firsthand. Ducking down, she blended in with other students and disappeared out the nearest exit.

Seeing a group of football players approaching the Union, Melody steered clear and remained inconspicuous as she fled to Kevin's dorm. Inside his dormitory at last, she raced up the stairs as fast as her painful ribs allowed, until she stood before his door. She glanced at her watch. Usually Kevin used this free time to relax in his room before his study group meeting. Melody knocked and waited, hoping Kevin still kept to his old timetable.

***

Kevin used caution when opening his door now, especially since he wasn't expecting anyone. He peered through the peephole. His breath caught in his throat…Melody. Even the peephole couldn't distort her loveliness. He threw open the door.

Melody stood motionless, staring at him with a

faint, hopeful smile.

Vacillating between anger and love, his hands balled into fists then reopened. Kevin wanted to hold Melody, cover her with kisses, and feel her sweet softness against his skin. At the same time, he wanted to slam the door in her face, kill her for causing him such pain.

After Lance and the other goons' *visit*, it took Kevin two days to recuperate before he could leave his room. True to Big Tony, the monstrous Italian's word—he never found a single bruise or scratch to prove his horrible ordeal ever occurred. Begrudgingly, Kevin took Lance's advice and kept a low profile on campus, maintaining his distance the few times he spotted Melody and her contingent of bodyguards.

Now Melody waited for his response.

Unexpectedly, he pulled her inside and locked the door without a moment's delay. Somehow she appeared in his arms with glistening eyes, her floral scent filling his head. When she kissed him tentatively, his dam of emotions burst. Love, anger, desire, then love again as his hungry kisses devoured her.

***

Before Melody knew it, Kevin worked her backwards but not to the bed. She felt the cold, hard cement wall against her back. Kevin tore open his jeans while he kissed her. His hands dove under her shirt and her bra disappeared like magic. Tongue, mouth, lips, she couldn't tell what he did to her body. All was a blur. Now, he slipped his hot hands under her skirt. How convenient that she wore one today she thought as he ripped off her panties.

Then he entered her. She didn't recall if he used a condom from his wallet, but his mouth covered hers and she couldn't utter a protest. His thrusts were hard, pounding her over and over into the unyielding wall, making her ribs groan. The pure visceral nature scared and excited her. He seemed oblivious, raw emotions taking over. She felt him swell up as he exploded with rapid thrusts, animalistic sounds escaped. Sated, he slowed and then stopped. Melody didn't know what to think.

DINNER WITH TREVOR

Imani finished chewing her mouthful of salad before answering Trevor's question. "Melody's recovering physically, but I'm really worried about that girl. She mopes around half the time although, to her credit, she did ace her midterms."

Trevor snickered and ate a French fry while Imani surveyed the half-full Union basement; she sighed, still no Melody. "It's just so weird, Trev. I know a lot of women, but I've never known anyone that's given themselves so completely to a man."

"That's because you surround yourself with strong women," Trevor replied. As he chomped another fry, Imani forked her salad. "My aunt's boyfriends always beat her. Moms says it's because Auntie doesn't believe she's good enough. Always needs a man around, no matter what kind."

"See, I never thought Melody was that far gone." Imani stabbed the last vestiges of her salad. "I wouldn't classify her as desperate. A little insecure, definitely eager to please, but she's never had a steady stream of men. Kevin's basically the first guy she's dated on the regular since we started college." Sadly, she shook her head. "I just don't get what makes a woman settle for that."

"And you never will. Making her attend the abuse

group was a good start. They might be able to get through to her where you can't." Trevor pushed away his empty food wrappers.

"I hope so."

Fiddling uncomfortably, Trevor gathered all his trash and put it in his fast food bag.

"What's up, Trev?" Imani could feel his uneasiness, but she sipped her water not wanting to push him.

Trevor shuffled the trash bag until she placed her hand on his, hoping he felt comfortable enough to share.

Trevor groaned. "I don't know what I should tell you anymore."

"What's up with you and Erycah?" Imani fought to hold back a knowing smile.

"Are you sure?" Trevor studied her face closely.

"It's cool," she said, squeezing his hand before she released it.

"I'm thinking about inviting Erycah home to meet Moms this summer." Imani could sense he waited with baited breath for any negative reaction.

"Oh, wow!" Although his news surprised her, there weren't any twinges of jealousy or discomfort, so a genuine smile emerged. "You know, Trev, I've watched you two. You have a really nice vibe together. I think your Moms will dig her, a lot."

Her ringing phone interrupted his Cheshire cat grin. "Excuse me, Trev," she said digging her phone out of her backpack.

"No problemo," he replied and leaned back more relaxed.

"It's Melody," she told Trev before she answered. "Yo, Girl, what's up?"

"Don't get mad, Imani."

"What do you mean, don't get mad," she replied already getting worked up.

"I'm at Kevin's."

"What! I know you don't mean beat-your-ass-silly Kevin?"

"I said don't get mad."

"Are you insane?"

"Look, if you're going to insult me, I'll just hang up now.

"Melody!" she pleaded.

"Please, Imani, I'm fine," Melody replied. "But I desperately needed some sense of closure. It was imperative that Kevin and I talked."

"So, you're finished talking and you're coming home, correct?"

"Not exactly."

"Meaning?"

"We've talked and he's agreed to get counseling."

"Good for him, Melody, he desperately needs it. What's that got to do with you?"

Melody hesitated, a beat too long. "We're going to work things out."

"Melody," Imani wailed. "This is not a good idea."

"We knew you'd think that, but it's different this time."

"*We?* Don't you recall that's what all abusers say, Melody? Give it some time to be sure."

"I'll be careful. Trust me, this time I recognize what to look for. Anyhow, it's not up for discussion. I just thought I should let you know. I gotta go—"

"Melody, please just come home! What about our study session with Lance in an hour?" Imani pleaded, scared for her roommate. Trevor reached across the table and held her free hand, his eyes worried.

"Later, okay. Thanks for understanding." And with that Melody hung up.

Imani stared at the dead phone in disbelief.

Trevor sighed. "I guess you had reason to be concerned."

PLEASE EXPLAIN - MAY 2001

Lance shut his business ethics book. "I miss studying in the kitchen."

"C'mon Lance, even you said that big, old kitchen table for ten, seemed excessive with just the two of us there," Imani replied from her desk.

After he tossed his book into his backpack, Lance laid back across Imani's bed. "I still don't get it. It's been three weeks since Melody slunk back to Kevin again—"

Imani pushed her chair away from her desk. "Look, I can't explain it, so let's just drop it, alright? My Physics IV homework's kicking my tail and I'm not in the mood to talk about Melody's weak ass."

"Hey, hey, come here," he said. As he sat up, he motioned for Imani to sit beside him. After she plopped down, he began massaging her shoulders.

Imani adjusted to a more comfortable position between his legs. "Ummm," she moaned as he felt her muscles loosen beneath his grip. "That feels so, so good."

"Well," he said as he formulated a plan to get her talking, "I'm finished with my homework. Do you want a full-body massage or do you need to remain focused for physics?"

"Oh, screw physics, I need the massage!"

Smiling, he got off the bed so that Imani could lie on her stomach. Once she got comfortable, he straddled her back and continued the massage with more intensity.

For five minutes, an almost constant stream of moans elicited from Imani.

"Not to intrude on your pleasure principles," he said, pleased to see his plan working.

"But let me guess, you're not going to drop this whole Melody issue, huh?"

"Look, you should be happy I'm stretching my egotistical, sexist mind," he replied garnering a snort from her. "I'll never want to breach a serious relationship until I truly understand this."

"Well, I don't know how much help I'll be. I don't get it either!"

"She's beautiful, intelligent—"

"And totally devoted to someone that beats the shit out of her." Imani flinched under his hands. "Oooh, right there! Could you work on that area some more, please, Lance Baby Baby?"

Chuckling, he obliged. "At least she's been coming home every night, though, right?"

"Mmm. Yeah, she says she's pacing it out and taking it slow."

"Well, we should be thankful for small miracles." He focused on another spot on her back. "Has he attended any counseling sessions?"

"Nope!"

"Any signs of abuse?" his voice deepened.

"Not, yet. But it's only a matter of time before he slips up and goes upside her head again."

"Let's hope not. I don't think I'd be able to stop Big Tony this time. John and Joe almost had to pull him off Kevin towards the end."

"It's hard to believe that sweet, docile teddy bear, Big Tony whooped Kevin's stupid ass. Man, I wish I could've been there that night." Imani's moaning decreased as he worked his way down her legs. Although she still seemed relaxed, this area didn't evoke as many "oo, ah" moments. "So, didn't I see you with Jodi the other night?"

Lance smirked in amusement. "You tailing me now?"

"Negro, please! It's not like your ass is subtle or discreet."

He laughed, no argument there. "Jodi was a sweet, sweet diversion."

"Damn! When's your ass gonna settle down with a nice little woman?"

"Are you serious, Imani? Why would I want to get tied down when so many fine, young Honeys insist on sharing the love? It'd be different if I had to actually work at getting girls, but they're pursuing me. Why shouldn't I reward them for their splendid efforts?"

"You are so sad!" She quit talking and he finished the quick foot massage.

His massaging fingers embarked back up her legs until they reached the point where her thighs and buttocks met. Although tonight was no different than the many times they had both massaged each other in the past, the sensuousness of what he was doing struck him now.

Imani's moaning picked up again and between it,

heavenly thoughts of Jodi, and the heat emanating from Imani's inner thighs, Lance found himself aroused. The light aroma of Imani's vanilla perfume beckoned and he fought to keep his hands from sliding over to her sweet spot.

What in the hell are you thinking, he scolded himself. Snap out of it, Lance! This is the exact moment when great friendships turn ugly. Forcing his hands to relocate to her back, he decided to wrap up the massage. As he kneaded her muscles, Imani moaned again. Before she could feel his throbbing dick, Lance sprung onto his knees and hovered a few inches above Imani's back. God, he didn't even want to imagine how bad she would cuss him out if she saw him now.

The jingling of Melody's keys in the door lock saved him. Swift yet casual, he jumped off Imani, grabbed his backpack, and sat on Melody's bed with the backpack covering his lap.

Imani didn't rouse and damn near snored when Melody entered.

Melody glanced at Imani as she crossed over to her bed. "Hey, there," she said then kissed his cheek.

Lance smiled as he zipped his backpack, making sure it still concealed his rock hard bulge. "Don't mind Sleepahontas over there. I just gave her a massage. How are you doing?"

"Good." Melody exhaled as she sat beside him.

"Are you sure?" He studied her.

"Yes," Melody said, sounding exasperated. "I promise, Lance. Kevin's great. It's been three weeks since we got back together and he's shown absolutely no sign of any problems whatsoever."

"And you would definitely tell me if there were?"

Melody returned his direct stare. "Yes, of course."

Imani snored and they both looked at her in awe.

Sensing that his traitorous dick had gone down, Lance decided it was safe to go. "On that note," he said, shouldering his backpack, "I bid you a very good night."

"Yeah, like I can sleep with all that racket." Melody shook her head as he left laughing.

TUTOR TIME

Melody hugged Big Tony and watched him leave the library exuberant. Much to her relief, he was getting the hang of computers, the World Wide Web, and HTML. After a moment, she gathered her books, turned, and bumped straight into Kevin.

"Hi, Sugar," she sang out, pleasantly surprised to see him.

"You look nice." His eyes lingered on her form-fitting dress. "The yellow color compliments your skin tone."

"Yeah?" Melody modeled for him, delighting in the way the outfit showcased her limber legs and accentuated her cleavage. This morning Imani had called her a sexy daffodil. "You mentioned before that you liked this dress. So, I thought of you when I picked it out."

"Funny thing is you weren't planning on seeing me today, though, right?"

The hairs on the back of Melody's neck stood up. She searched Kevin's eyes for any trace of humor, but they gave nothing away. "Baby, you remember I said I'd call you after tutoring Anthony at 3:30?" She still couldn't read his eyes; the blue glinted crystal clear. Sucking in her nervousness, she patted his arm. "I was just about to grab a bite and call you to see if you'd finished with your study group."

Kevin allowed the faintest trace of a smile. "Guess we can go eat together as I'm all free."

"Great!" She stood on her tiptoes and planted a kiss on his cheek.

As they departed for the Union, she hooked her arm through Kevin's. May was a gorgeous month on campus, she thought regaling in her favorite season. All the cherry and dogwood trees paraded their full blooms, tulips peaked out over fading daffodils and crocuses, and the wind relinquished its sharp, wintry bite. Melody inhaled a deep breath of fragrant air and relaxed.

They were almost at the Union when Kevin stopped. "I feel like eating in my room. Let's order something instead."

"Oh, but I really need to go to the Union," she said hesitating. "I have to give Imani a message from Trevor."

Kevin hooked her arm. "You can give it to her later. Let's go."

"But I already called her and said I was coming," she said resisting him. "If you're worried about seeing her, things are cool between you again."

"I'm not concerned about Imani. I want to spend some time alone with you." His eyes darkened now. "Since when do I have to beg my girl to spend time with me?"

Melody began to worry. One, she could give in and leave with Kevin, thereby preventing any arguments or flare-ups. Or two, she could go to the Union to give Imani Trevor's message and risk triggering a relapse.

At this point, she liked the idea of a public area, just in case.

His impatience grew as she stalled.

"Fine," she relented, sounding as cheerful as she could muster.

It looked like Kevin was about to smile, but then he became fixated on something over her shoulder and his face went blank. Melody turned to see what captured his attention.

"Howdy," boomed Lance as he approached.

Melody tried to contain her beaming smile upon seeing Lance. "Howdy, to you, too."

"Hey, Kevin. How's it going?" Lance half hugged Melody and left his arm hanging over her shoulder. Melody could see the mischievous twinkle in Lance's eyes challenge Kevin.

Kevin stiffened, but his features remained calm. Melody knew he didn't want to leave without her, but he didn't dare force it with Lance there either. "I gotta go," Kevin mumbled as he departed.

"Don't leave on my account," Lance yelled after him. "Why don't you join us?"

Kevin never turned around.

"Guess he had somewhere important to go." Lance smiled down at Melody. "Hope I didn't interrupt anything."

"No," she replied, feeling her tensions drain away. "Everything was fine, just fine." Hooking Lance's arm, they headed into the Union.

Who's Your Tutor?

In between bites of taco, Imani noticed how worried her friend looked, so she tapped Melody's arm. "You okay?"

That sunshine and daffodil smile returned, "I'm fine, Imani." Melody took another bite of her taco and swallowed before speaking again. "May I ask what was in Trevor's oh-so-important message to you?"

"No, you may not ask." Imani winked and took a sip of her Sprite. "Eh, Trev was just asking for advice regarding Erycah."

"Isn't that a little awkward for you?"

"It used to be but, honestly," she replied with a shrug, "not anymore. They've been going out almost all semester and I'm accustomed to them as a couple." Almost afraid to broach the subject, she paused and then took a stab at it anyway. "How are you and Kevin?"

Melody stopped eating and studied her for a moment. When Melody concluded that Imani's question was asked out of friendly concern rather than to start a lecture, she answered. "Really good. I mean… he seemed strange when he saw me tutoring Anthony today. But then he split so quickly after Lance arrived outside the Union, that I didn't get a chance to talk to him."

"By Anthony, you don't mean Big Tony, do you?" Imani tried hard to keep her eyes from bugging outta her head.

"Yeah, why?" Melody asked finishing her taco.

"Fool, don't you know he's the one that beat Kevin to a pulp?"

Melody's face registered her alarm. "Oh, shit!"

"Oh, shit is right! Did you tell Kevin you were tutoring him?"

"Yes, well, no. I mean, I said I was tutoring Anthony. But I figured Kevin didn't know him anyway, so what did it matter which Anthony I tutored."

"Didn't Lance ever tell you?"

"No, damn it! I just knew he took a couple of football players over there. I never wanted to know and Kevin sure as hell didn't mention it." Frantic, Melody gathered her belongings and prepared to leave.

"Where do you think you're going?"

"I have to explain everything to Kevin."

"No, no, no!" She stood and stopped Melody. "Girl, I *do not* think that's a good idea."

"I understand your apprehension, Imani..." Melody's voice trailed off.

Imani's expression didn't change an iota.

"Look, Imani, I promise to meet him someplace public, okay? I won't go over to his dorm room. But he'd be crazy to hit me anymore." Melody hugged her tight. "Don't worry so much. All of your lecturing has made me stronger and wiser."

Imani watched with butterflies, hell they were more like sparrows, doing somersaults in her stomach as

Melody left the Union. She tried to concentrate on her Advanced Chemistry textbook, but that deep gnawing in the pit of her gut grew and wouldn't stop. "Ah, hell," she muttered getting up to follow Melody.

MEET ME AT THE UNION!

Melody stood outside the Union and called Kevin's dorm number on her cell phone. Funny, he's not there, she thought leaving a message. "Guess I'll try his cell," she murmured to no one in particular.

A phone rang about thirty feet away, near the evergreens bordering the path that lead from the Union to the Chapel. She swore it sounded like Kevin's phone, but she couldn't be sure as he answered on the first ring. "Hi, Baby. Where are you?"

"I wasn't very hungry after all. So, I decided to study some more back at the Library.

"You hate studying at the Library unless your study group insists on it."

"Yeah, well, I didn't want to be alone in my room either. Library's as good a place as any."

"That's true. Well, I just found out something from Imani and I wondered if we could talk?"

"Want to meet in my room?"

Melody paced a bit at the suggestion. "Uh, since you're at the Library and I'm still at the Union, why don't you meet me over here so you can eat something? We'll grab one of the more private tables upstairs like the night we first met."

"I told you I'm not hungry." His voice sounded flat. "I know, let's go up to The Pointe."

The Pointe *was* a public place. Plus, other people would be there enjoying the warm, May weather. "The Pointe sounds great. Maybe we'll catch another falling star?"

"Maybe." He became silent.

"Kevin?"

"I'm almost there. Are you inside or outside the Union?"

"I'm outside near the path to the Chapel and the Library. So, I'll see you soon?"

On cue, Kevin's head appeared bobbing along the pathway. "You should see me now."

Disconnecting, she ran to him. "Hey, Baby!" She smiled and leapt into his arms, almost knocking him over.

"Whoa, there." Kevin grinned and set her down. "I guess someone's happy to see me?"

"You know it," she replied, giving him a quick peck on the cheek.

Kevin enveloped her in a huge hug. "Is that all the loving I get?"

"I've got more where that came from," she said before she kissed him. At first Kevin's kiss felt hesitant, but then he warmed up until they stood with their lips locked for a full minute. "Oh my! Ready to go up to The Pointe?"

"Yes, indeedy," he replied and they walked off holding hands.

A Long Walk

"Where in the hell are they going?" Imani watched Melody and Kevin damn near skip away. *I told her ass to stay someplace public and there she goes heading away from campus. Well, at least they're heading away from his dorm, too.* Imani continued to watch from the large, tinted windows on the main floor of the Union. Kevin and Melody appeared so damn happy that Imani wasn't sure why she'd been so alarmed when Melody first left.

She turned to go back downstairs and finish her chapter on chemical compounds. But that damn nagging feeling fired up in her gut again. "What?" she asked her stomach annoyed. "You saw them for yourself, they're fine." Her stomach tossed more. "Alright, already," she gave in to her trusty instincts and flew out the door, running to see where they had disappeared. *Good thing I decided to slum it and wear sweats and tracks today,* she thought as she spotted them ahead in the distance. Whew, she could slow down and catch her breath. They were moving fast, but where to?

Imani followed them making sure to keep out of sight. It wasn't like they were looking around though. They seemed entranced with each other. Was this what her crazy, overactive gut wanted her to see? Two people who were head over heels in love? A momentary pang of jealousy crept over her. Why couldn't she find a brother who looked at her like that? 'What about Trevor?' the Devil's Advocate side of her asked. 'He mooned after you.' Okay, let me rephrase that, why not someone who I'm equally loopy about? The Devil's Advocate side remained quiet. Yeah, I thought so. She checked her watch. Damn, it had been twenty-five minutes, where in heaven's name were they going?

As they headed up a steep winding pathway that branched off the sidewalk it dawned on her, The Pointe! Come on, Melody! This ain't exactly the public place she meant. Hell, hadn't the girl seen any scary movies at all? Lover's Lanes were some of the first places psychopathic murderers scrounged for victims. None of the other couples up there would be real attentive to anyone besides their own date. Unless of course they were voyeurs but that's not the type of person that would step in and help when you needed it.

Man, she didn't want to call Lance for fear he would think she was overreacting, but someone should know where they were, just in case. Not wanting to get spotted or overheard while on the phone, she held back until Kevin and Melody disappeared around the bend one hundred feet away.

"What's up?" Lance answered the phone.

"You're not going to believe this," she whispered.

"One, I probably won't believe it. Two, why are you whispering?"

"Melody told me at the Union that Kevin caught her tutoring Big Tony."

"Big Tony? That dummy!"

"You didn't know either?"

"Of course not! No wonder Kevin looked so pissed when I rolled up on them in front of the Union. First seeing Tony and then me."

"Exactly."

"So, then you're staying with her, right?"

"Well… kinda." Imani figured the coast was clear and headed up the winding pathway.

"Meaning?"

"Look, it's not my fault."

"Oh, God, what's not your fault, Imani?" Concern mounted in his voice.

"She insisted on calling Kevin and explaining things."

"Where is she, Imani? Time's wasting if I need to gather John, Joe, and Big Tony again."

"I'm following her up to The Pointe."

"The Pointe?"

"Yes, I know how crazy it sounds and I feel like an idiot," she said with a chuckle. "They're acting all lovey-dovey and I swear if they start making out, I'm going home. I can't take much more of this!"

Lance laughed. "Alright, so I won't round up the boys just yet. Maybe our last meeting has Kevin thinking twice about hurting her again."

"Yep, I think so, too. Just don't rub this crap in later, okay?"

"Alrighty Inspector Clouseau!"

"Yeah, screw you, too." Imani chuckled, hung up, and set her phone to vibrate. That shit always proved embarrassing or downright fatal in the movies. Here you are trying to hide and your phone rings giving the killer your position. Not happening to the kid!

Nearing the summit, she inched forward trying to locate Kevin and Melody without them seeing her first. Excellent, she was in luck; they stood at the far end of The Pointe that overlooked the city versus back towards campus. Like a ninja, she cut behind them and took refuge in some nearby evergreens.

Much to her surprise only a few couples milled around relishing the warm evening. Then again, it would get nice and dark in a half-hour and more folks would arrive to stargaze. Hopefully she wouldn't be around then, not with that chapter of Advanced Chemistry waiting.

Imani stole another glance from between pine branches. Good, it looked like Melody and Kevin were chatting. She settled down in the grass behind the evergreens where she could spy on them yet remain safe from observation. With any luck, they'd start kissing soon and she'd book it home.

A hummingbird darted by, attracting her attention. The bird flitted to and fro between some flowering bushes ten feet away. Imani remained motionless, in awe of the minute, redheaded bird. Its wings were a complete blur of black and white. The hummingbird ate or sucked its fill and it zipped away.

Restless and bored, she glanced over at Kevin and Melody—still talking. Sighing, she laid back and examined the few purple and pink clouds as the sun set. A peaceful tranquility enveloped her; this really was the life. This felt better than a yoga class and God provided the scenery for free. Boyfriend or not, she resolved to spend more time up here, getting away from it all, reconnecting with her spiritual side through nature. Yeah, nature, something she never quite experienced living in New York City, not unless you counted Central Park, and still that wasn't the same as tonight.

The skies darkened as the sun lowered beneath the horizon and the old-time lampposts that lined the pathways flickered on. Oh well, time to go! This spy shit was getting old and her Chem book beckoned. Staying hidden, Imani sat up and spied on Melody and Kevin.

Incredible! They were still talking! Melody was right; they *did* talk for hours. Imani smirked. Well, Homegirl's on her own because the making out would start soon enough and she sure as hell didn't want to see that shit. Getting up slowly, she stretched her legs. Damn, they hurt! Each leg felt cramped due to all that jogging and power walking without preparation.

Hearing a funny sound, she glanced at Melody and Kevin. Hold up, wait a minute. Were they still talking or did it look like they were arguing? Squatting down, she peered at them. Oh shit, they were arguing or more like Kevin yelled while Melody looked scared as hell.

Damn, Sherlock, what the hell should she do now? Imani groaned to herself. If she interrupted them, Kevin might explode. No biggie, she wasn't scared of his punk ass, but they were a little out of the way for any quick rescues if he happened to get in a good swing. And Melody's petite ass would positively be no damn help in an all-out brawl. Hmm, what to do? Eh, the hell with it, she decided, I'll take my chances with Kevin. She rose again then she saw him pull the gun out of his backpack.

"Oh, fuck!" she hissed under her breath popping back down again unseen. This was *not* a scenario she considered at all! *Oh God, think Imani think!* Her phone, she'd call 911. Oh, hell! You couldn't get here by car. Nothing she could do about that now. Wait, she would call Lance first, then 911. At least she knew that the football team ran the bleachers, so they could haul ass up here.

After getting off the phone in record time with Lance, she dialed 911 and prayed that the responding officers were the kind she saw biking around campus rather than the fat fucks she spotted at Dunkin Donuts. As Imani spoke with the 911 operator, she dared to peek out at Kevin and Melody to ensure she didn't need to change her request from assistance to the coroner. Kevin fussed and waved the gun around, but he didn't point it at Melody...yet. The 911 operator wanted to stay on the line, so Imani locked her keypad and pocketed the phone. Oh God, give me strength, she prayed as earnestly as she'd ever prayed before.

That was when Kevin put the gun to Melody's forehead.

CONFRONTATIONS

Kevin watched Melody tremble beneath the gun that he lodged against her head. Not daring to move or speak, she used her eyes to plead with him.

Things started out so perfect, he thought. They had held hands, laughed, and talked about their beautiful future together. Then she mentioned Big Tony.

At that moment he realized he couldn't control her every step anymore. Not how she flirted or how sexy she dressed nor how she allowed numerous men to touch, hug, grope, and kiss her.

How could she not understand that when she said she was his, all his, that meant totally his—mind, body, and soul? But she wasn't his, not like he needed. That realization killed him; it cut to the core.

That's when he had drawn the gun.

"Why, Melody?" he screamed, waving the gun, "Big Tony of all people?" The maniac whose demented face was eternally seared in his memory. He could still feel each and every punch and now she inflicted more pain, added salt to the open wounds.

Thoughts of Big Tony's beating and the possibility of losing Melody killed him. He loved her more than life, but he refused to share her and he would guarantee he didn't have to, not ever again. He explained this very eloquently, making certain she understood why he had to kill her.

Tired of talking and even more tired of listening to her fervent pleads and pledges of undying love, he put the gun to her head.

"I refuse to share you any longer, Melody."

She stood stone still, which pleased him. Never even attempted to move as their eyes locked. It would be nice to remember her like this, loving eyes fixated only on him. But then they weren't. The movement was almost imperceptible, but her eyes darted to the side... Shit! The bitch was communicating with someone else! He swung around, gun still up, ready to fire...and found...Imani!

"What the fuck?" he demanded as Imani screeched to a halt. His shock turned to delight at the opportunity to rid the world of one, big ass nuisance. Imani had meddled in his affairs for the last time!

While he watched her like a hawk, she shuffled towards Melody. Perfect, this would make it easier to shoot them both. "You just couldn't stay away, huh? Had to jump in between us one last time?" he snarled, aiming the gun at Imani's chest.

"I'll stay away, Kevin. Leave the two of you alone." Imani kept her arms raised in surrender. "You don't want to do this. Melody loves you to death." Imani blanched at her unfortunate choice of words and she shifted the conversation in an instant. "What about all the things you want to do together? Vacations on the beach, marriage, kids, and the white picket fence?"

God, did she really think all of her unrealistic ramblings would save them? "Enough! Would you please shut your big-ass mouth? You talk too damn much and I'm truly sick of it." He cocked the gun enjoying the way they trembled. Melody pleaded with her pathetic eyes while Imani seethed with hate and fury.

"You understand this is mostly your fault, right?" It took immense willpower not to shoot Imani right now; his index finger stroked the trigger. "You fill her beautiful head with doubts; make her question my undying love. Do you realize if it weren't for your interfering, she'd happily be in my room right this very fucking instance? But no, you and that damn Lance are forever butting in."

His tone became high-pitched as he mimicked Melody's voice, "I just have to deliver this message from Trevor to Imani. It's oh-so-fucking important." His voice dropped back to normal, "I almost had her convinced to come home with me, too, when that arrogant bastard sneaked up threatening me with his cocky-ass smile." He shook his head, lips curled back from his teeth, "but it all ends tonight."

A Blast at The Pointe

A cop car, lights blazing through the night, sat empty at the bottom of the pathway to The Pointe when Lance parked behind it. God, please don't let me be too late, he prayed.

When Imani called in a quiet panic five minutes ago, he flew into action. Calling his crew on the go, he drove like a bat out of hell, not daring to wait until he could pull them all together. His girls needed him now. And he'd never forgive himself if something happened to them.

Jumping out in a flash, he started sprinting up the pathway. The incline wasn't that bad, he could be at the top in no time flat. His mind raced. Why did he feel the need to provoke Kevin when he saw him earlier? If that's what ultimately set him off, Lance would be directly responsible for endangering his girls' safety.

A noise up ahead made him look up. In two steps he blew past a fat officer lumbering and out of breath only a quarter of the way up the pathway.

The officer's reflexes were as slow as his pace because he only managed to huff out a weak, "wait a minute, Son," at Lance's back after Lance had already rounded the next bend.

Lance shook his head and his thoughts took

precedent again. Maybe if he, John, Joe, and Big Tony had really put the fear of God in Kevin and beat him a little more when they had a chance, this wouldn't be happening now. Hell, this all could have been averted if they would have forced Melody to report the abuse, then Kevin would have been expelled from college and locked behind bars right now. Lance grunted. Regardless of what could have been, he needed to focus on the present. Melody and Imani meant everything in the world to him; he would have to find a way to save them.

Almost to the top Lance caught up with a second officer, much more in shape and moving fast. However, Lance was ten years his junior and they crested the hill simultaneously.

Both assessed the situation in an instant. Kevin had Melody *and* Imani cornered. It looked like a normal discussion—that is if you factored out the gun Kevin had trained on Imani.

The cop drew his gun and crept forward while Lance stayed glued to his left side. To Lance's surprise, none of the three noticed them, even when they drew within twenty feet. The cop halted Lance with a hand gesture before he addressed Kevin.

"Son, put down the gun," his voice thundered through the still night. "You don't want to do this. We can work this out without anyone getting hurt. Alright, Son?" The officer targeted Kevin's shoulder.

Lance stood as still as a statue, not wanting to distract the officer. He figured the cop was a good shot, though; from his confident stance and his no-nonsense demeanor, he didn't look like he missed much at target practice.

***

Kevin didn't swivel the gun towards the booming voice when he looked to see who addressed him, but rather kept it fixed on Imani. Ignoring the officer, he faced Melody and Imani again. "For God's sake, I should have known Lance would show up. Now, we're all one big happy family, huh?" He focused on Melody. "Do you finally see how they are always there? Between us? But not anymore."

Melody realized she wasn't the target of his rage now and she ran to him screaming his name.

In the background, the cop yelled something, but he didn't fire.

Kevin held the gun at his side as Melody approached. But it didn't matter; they were out of time. Everyone would make sure that he and Melody could never be together again. Imani would spew enough venomous lies to Melody to erode whatever little trust remained. Lance and his crew of brawny thugs would probably want to finish the damage they started after Greek Freak. Somehow, the cop or the university would twist his actions today into bogus charges and possibly imprison or expel him. Regardless, it was over. Their love would die here tonight. Melody's loving, deceitful eyes locked together eternally with his.

"I will haunt you forever," he said bringing the gun to his right temple with the speed of Clint Eastwood in *The Good, the Bad, and the Ugly*. There was a millisecond of remorse, but it was too late; his finger had pulled the trigger.

***

The nightmare would replay itself over and over in Melody's head like a broken record she couldn't stop. Only two measly feet away, his expression transfixed her to the spot. His smile wistful; eyes a mix of love, despair, and… hate? "I will haunt you forever," Kevin said and then the gun materialized at his head, and he was sorry, she saw it on his face for a fleeting moment—but the bullet erased it.

The BANG deafened her, and his body…it just balanced there with his head half gone, before teetering and falling somehow into her open arms. The weight of him, what was once her precious love, crumpled Melody to her knees, but she didn't let him fall to the ground, she couldn't. They belonged together.

"No! Kevin! No, no, no!" her anguished cries transformed into an inconsolable, interminable, heart-wrenching scream.

###

BOOK CLUB QUESTIONS

1. What do you believe is the metaphor between Melody and the daffodil?

2. What is the source of Lance's devotion to his girls?

3. Why does Imani struggle with her feelings towards Trevor?

4. Do you believe that Imani made the right decision to not date Trevor? Why or why not?

5. What warning signs should Melody have seen with Kevin and how should she have reacted?

6. In what ways could Imani or Lance have prevented what happened?

7. How do you think this experience will change Imani, Lance and Melody individually?

8. What scene did you find most memorable?

9. Which character did you relate to most and why?

10. Will their friendship survive and why or why not?

J-pad Publishing
proudly presents

THE COLORS OF LOVE

BY

K. R. RAYE

Coming November 19, 2013.

Continue reading for an excerpt from book two of the
Colors Trilogy, *The Colors of Love…*

PROLOGUE - MAY 2001

A cop car, lights blazing through the night, sat empty at the bottom of the pathway to The Pointe when Lance Dunn parked behind it. God, please don't let me be too late to help my girls.

Erupting from his car in a flash, he sprinted up the pathway to the private garden lookout. The incline wasn't that bad, nowhere near as taxing as running the bleachers during training camp, he could crest the top in no time flat.

A quarter of the way up, he blew past a fat officer lumbering and out of breath. The officer's reflexes were as slow as his pace because he only managed to huff out a weak, "wait a minute, Son," at Lance's back after Lance rounded the next bend.

Almost to the top Lance caught up with a second officer, much more in shape and moving fast. However, Lance was ten years his junior and they crested the hill simultaneously.

Both assessed the situation in an instant. About sixty feet away, Melody Wilkins *and* Imani Jordan stood side by side facing Melody's boyfriend, Kevin, who was about six feet from the girls. It appeared they were standing around having a normal discussion—except for the gun Kevin trained on Imani.

The cop drew his gun and crept forward and Lance stayed glued to his left side. He could see the trio better. Kevin's normally handsome face held a look of pure hatred. Poor Melody seemed even more petite and fragile than ever as she shivered in fear, her blonde curls shaking. And in contrast Imani looked ready to kick Kevin's ass if she could. Her round, brown face glared at Kevin, fists balled, and even each of her hair twists seemed to bristle with indignant fury.

To Lance's surprise, none of the three noticed him or the officer, even when they drew within twenty feet.

The cop halted Lance with a hand gesture before he addressed Kevin.

"Son, put down the gun," his voice thundered through the still night. "You don't want to do this. We can work this out without anyone getting hurt. Alright, Son?" The officer targeted Kevin's shoulder.

Lance stood as still as a statue, not wanting to distract the officer. He figured the cop was a good shot, though; from his confident stance and his no-nonsense demeanor, he didn't look like he missed much at target practice.

Kevin glanced their direction, but he kept the gun honed on Imani. Ignoring the officer, Kevin refocused on Melody and Imani and uttered something that Lance couldn't quite overhear.

Whatever he said, it made Melody run to Kevin screaming his name.

"Stop!" The cop yelled although he didn't fire.

Kevin dropped the gun to his side as Melody approached. Then Lance swore Kevin mouthed the words, "I will haunt you forever," and in a flash, Kevin put the gun to his right temple and pulled the trigger.

The unexpected movement and subsequent loud BOOM pummeled Lance like a bomb's shock wave. He recoiled and covered his head and ears. As he attempted to rationalize the situation, the sight of Melody trying to catch Kevin's half-headless corpse, chilled him to the bone. His limbs locked frozen solid.

Transfixed, he watched Kevin's dead weight force Melody down to her knees until she cradled his lifeless body screaming, "Nooooo!" for what seemed like hours. Her scream pierced straight through his soul. No amount of time could ever erase that sound from his memory

Unable to move and forever scarred, he vowed to protect Melody and Imani from further agony, even if it was the last thing he did. "Never again," he whispered.

SEPARATED

Although he swore a lifetime passed, in reality it only took ten seconds for Lance to react. Time slipped into slow motion and stalled for the first five seconds as Imani sprinted to Melody from her closer vantage point. Each movement exaggerated and drawn out similar to pulling salt water taffy.

For the next five seconds his mind repeated 'protect' like a scratched CD. As he prepared to rip off his shirt to cover Melody and cocoon her from all of the blood and gore, he glanced down and frowned. His tight, black T-shirt wouldn't provide near enough protection.

Imani seemed to read his mind and she removed her tracksuit jacket and draped it over Melody's shoulders.

Back in control, Lance took off to join them, but he became aware of a noise by his side.

The officer was yelling at him and Imani. "Stop, before you contaminate the scene!"

Please, he must be kidding! The only crime was letting Melody sit in a growing pool of blood as she screamed and held a headless corpse.

However, the cop's stance and tone left no room for argument. The cop blocked him just before he reached Melody. "Stand down, Son!"

Lance raised his hands in surrender while he tried to reason with the guy. "We need to get Melody out of there. Please, officer!"

"We'll take care of her, but we need to process the scene and get everyone's statements."

Annoyed but determined not to get into trouble with the law, Lance glanced over the cop's shoulder towards Melody and Imani. To his surprise about ten cops skittered around like cockroaches after you turned on the lights.

One officer sequestered Imani while the fat, lumbering officer disentangled Melody from the gory scene with minimal disturbance. Two cops interviewed a few couples who were using the landscaped garden as a vehicle-free Lover's Lane at the wrong time. The techs photographed the area and the fit cop secured the scene while another came over and questioned Lance.

As he answered the officer's pointless questions, two other cops cordoned off the pathway up to the Pointe. Too late, Lance heard his football teammates, John, Joe, and Big Tony at the top of the pathway answering his earlier call to help, but the officers ushered them away.

After Lance finished answering the cop's questions, he looked around to get his bearings. He spotted Melody and tried to go comfort her, wanting only to get her out of that bloodied yellow dress. But the fat cop and their university president kept him at bay. Lance frowned. When had the president arrived?

Turning in frustration, he saw one cop finishing

up with Imani. As soon as the officer left, he ran over. Imani practically leapt into his waiting arms, her body wracking from quakes and shudders. "It's okay," he repeated as he held Imani tight, trying to abate her trembles.

Minutes later the university president checked on them. Lance attempted to focus on the words coming out of the man's pasty, bald head, but he only processed snippets. "The university regrets such a horrible incident...promise to get you into mandatory counseling tomorrow...let's keep tonight's events private...treat this as an accidental discharge..."

When the president left, the fit cop came over with a grim look on his face. "You're free to go now. We'll be in touch if we need anything else."

"What about our friend?" Lance asked wanting to get both of his girls out of this hellhole.

"My partner already took her back to her dormitory room twenty minutes ago," the officer replied as he walked off to meet the coroner.

Shocked, Lance and Imani looked around, but Melody had vanished.

###

GET HELP

If you or someone you love is in an abusive relationship, please call the National Domestic Violence Hotline at 800-799-7233 for assistance.

OTHER WORKS BY K. R. RAYE

The Colors of Friendship
The Colors of Love
True Colors

CONNECT WITH K. R. RAYE:

If you enjoyed the book, please let others know and **post a review** on Amazon, Goodreads, Barnes & Noble, other retail sites, or your blog. Request your local library carry a copy.

Would you like to contact the author or schedule her to attend your event? Please email her at krraye@jpadpublishing.com. Keep tabs on specials and what's next by signing up for her monthly newsletter at https://www.krraye.com/.

Thank you for your support!

K. R. Raye

BookBub - https://www.bookbub.com/profile/k-r-raye
Facebook – https://www.facebook.com/KRRaye13
Goodreads – https://www.goodreads.com/author/show/7160771.K_R_Raye
Twitter – https://twitter.com/KRRaye
Website – https://krraye.com/

Made in the USA
Middletown, DE
23 March 2022